SADISTIC

Patrick Reuman

Patrick Reuman

Sadistic

No part of this publication may be reproduced, stored in a retrieval system or transmitted in any way by any means, electronic, mechanical, photocopy, recording or otherwise without the prior permission of the author except as provided by USA copyright law.

This novel is a work of fiction. Names, descriptions, entities, and incidents included in the story are products of the author's imagination. Any resemblance to actual persons, events, and entities is entirely coincidental.
Cover design by Johannus Steger

All rights reserved. Copyright © 2016 Patrick Reuman
All rights reserved.
ISBN-13: 978-1530571215

ISBN-10: 1530571219

DEDICATION

"To my wonderful son, Aidan, and all the readers that are prepared to delve into this dark abyss that is my mind"

Sadistic

CONTENTS

Acknowledgments   viii

Chapter   1---Pg. 1
Chapter   2---Pg. 18
Chapter   3---Pg. 30
Chapter   4---Pg. 43
Chapter   5---Pg. 55
Chapter   6---Pg. 69
Chapter   7---Pg. 73
Chapter   8---Pg. 88
Chapter   9---Pg. 101
Chapter   10---Pg. 114
Chapter   11---Pg. 129
Chapter   12---Pg. 138
Chapter   13---Pg. 150
Chapter   14---Pg. 165
Chapter   15---Pg. 177
Chapter   16---Pg. 187
Chapter   17---Pg. 196
Chapter   18---Pg. 210
Chapter   19---Pg. 220
Chapter   20---Pg. 232
Chapter   21---Pg. 244
Chapter   22---Pg. 261
Chapter   23---Pg. 268
Chapter   24---Pg. 276
Chapter   25---Pg. 284
Chapter   26---Pg. 293

Sadistic

ACKNOWLEDGMENTS

Thank you to my cover designer, Johannus Steger, and my editor Tony Keen for helping to make my novel something I can be proud of and to Polly Hanson, my high school English teacher, for always inspiring me with her kindness.

Sadistic

1

It takes only one step to slip into madness and be consumed by your own darkness

THE blade cut deep, piercing the outer layer and entering the soft layers hidden beneath. The outer shell bared no resistance to the sharp edge as it slit it open. A smile etched itself into Cyrus's face as he gazed down at the blade making its incisions.

"Cyrus," a voice cut in bringing him to attention. "You want a slice of cake?"

"No, thanks. Just a cup of soda, if that's all right," Cyrus replied.

"All right, but it's not often we have cake for someone's birthday," the voice continued.

Cyrus just nodded, picked up his cup, and started his way back to his desk.

The clock read 4.30 pm on Cyrus's computer as he leaned back in his chair and took a deep breath, allowing his body to slouch. The time slowly wound down as he clicked the small 'x' and watched each program disappear from the screen in preparation to head home. It had been a long day at work, as it was every first of the month. He glanced at the clock again, 4:31 pm. He groaned.

"Joe wants to see you before you head home," his friend Dave announced from behind him.

He turned around to see Dave at his own desk, packing up his things and sorting some papers into manila folders.

Dave and Cyrus had been stuck at the same job together for years now. Strangely, they had actually met at the supermarket a few days before they started working together in the Records Department at City Hall. They often joked about how they would eventually break out of their dead-end City Hall jobs, or as Dave claimed, he would become Mayor himself and make Cyrus his right-hand man.

"I wonder what Joe wants?" Cyrus asked as he tossed a piece of paper into the garbage. "I'm not in the mood for his crap today."

"Who knows? There always seems to be something we're doing wrong," Dave responded in an annoyed tone.

Joe, their boss, started only a week after Cyrus and Dave, and somehow had managed to get promoted, and ever since then he had been riding them about everything they did. Dave had a theory that he did it on purpose to rub his position in their face, and Cyrus didn't think that idea was very far-fetched.

Cyrus got up and began working his way to Joe's office. When he got there, the door was closed so he knocked.

"It's Cyrus, I was told I had to come see you," Cyrus said to the door.

There was no response, so he pressed his ear up against the door and knocked with the knuckle of his middle finger. After a short pause and no response, he leaned in again, but just as he did the door handle turned, almost causing Cyrus to fall forward. A man walked out, face red and eyebrows cocked, and tossed a fake smile at Cyrus as he walked past him.

"Come in," Joe said signaling Cyrus with his finger to enter his office.

"Nobody can follow rules around here," he said as he gestured out the door toward the man that had just left the room. "We are all supposed to be adults here, now sit down."

"I'm not really sure what I did to be brought in here, Joe," said Cyrus in an unenthused manner as he took a seat in front of Joe's desk.

As he tapped his pen on the palm of his hand, Joe let out an exaggerated sigh. Joe tossed the pen onto the desk, where it landed with a soft thump. He leaned back in his chair and looked at Cyrus.

"Were you late this morning?" Joe asked locking his hands together tightly.

"No," Cyrus countered shaking his head slightly.

"Yes, I think you were," Joe insisted.

"No, I wasn't late," Cyrus argued with more force this time as he clenched his fist in an attempt to keep his cool.

Joe turned his computer around and pointed at the monitor.

"Well, that's weird because the time clock says you were late by four minutes. Is the time clock lying, Cyrus?" Joe responded in a cocky manner.

"It's four minutes," Cyrus said holding back what he was really thinking. He was contemplating hitting Joe in the face, but that would just result in a one-way ticket to the unemployment line.

"Yeah, four minutes later than you were supposed to be here. Schedules were made for a reason, so let's start following them unless the schedule you want to follow involves looking for a new job," Joe rifled back while picking up a pen and writing something down. "Now, get out of my office and back to work. You still have ten minutes left," Joe added.

Cyrus didn't dignify Joe with a response. He just got up and walked out of the room, envisioning himself snatching the piece of paper away from Joe and throwing it in the garbage like he was sinking the game-winning free throw, and giving him the middle finger while he walked out. *He's lucky he doesn't get punched in the face.* With sweat dripping down his neck from frustration, Cyrus stormed back to his desk chair, sat down, and stared at his computer.

Cyrus was a tall man, almost 6'3 and in shape. He

had a medium length beard and medium length brown hair. Generally, people wouldn't challenge him head on, but Joe wasn't afraid because he had Cyrus's job in the palm of his hand.

That guy thinks he is the king of the damn world. Cyrus scrolled through some emails to make it look like he was doing work, but he couldn't think straight. DING…DING…DING. He could hear tapping from a desk to the side of him. A Newton's Cradle bounced back and forth like a pendulum of insanity. TAP…TAP…TAP. Someone was clicking a pencil somewhere in the room. DING… TAP…DING…TAP. Cyrus ground his finger nails on the table. DING…TAP…DING…TAP…DING…TAP. *Stop fucking tapping.* Just as he was about to reach his limit, his phone rang. He snatched it up and slammed it to his ear.

"Hey," said the voice on the phone.

It was his wife, Sara. After the long day at work, her voice was music to his ears. Sara was a small woman with long, light brown hair and a bright smile, but you couldn't let that fool you because she could go from quiet to crazy in the blink of an eye if she had to.

"Hey, what's up?" Cyrus asked a little lighter-hearted than he had been a moment ago.

"Just seeing if you're getting out of work soon. Chris's football game is in an hour or so," said Sara.

"Yeah, I just have to grab my stuff and I'll be heading home," Cyrus replied.

"Okay, I'll have some food ready, so we can eat and leave," Sara explained.

"All right, love you," Cyrus said finally showing signs of a better mood.

"Love you, too," she said before hanging up.

Talking to her seemed to have pulled him out of his state of anger at least for a moment; that's why he married her. He always said her best trait was that she could turn his bad day into a good one with a simple hello.

Cyrus grabbed his things, punched out, and headed out the door. He fiddled with his keys and got into his blue 2014 Nissan Altima that he could barely afford the payments for and switched on the ignition. The drive home seemed longer than usual. Cyrus usually hated the drive home because he was always forced to see classic examples of why he sometimes hated humanity. People not using their turn signals, speeding, cutting each other off. The behavior of others around him never ceased to amaze him. Driving was something most people did every day, but most were still terrible at it. Either that or they just chose to be reckless morons.

He pulled up his road and into the driveway. His family lived in a two-story purple house with white windows. Purple was one of Cyrus's least favorite colors, and he always told himself he was going to climb up there and paint the entire thing any other color, but he never got around to it. There was a better chance of them moving out than him painting the house, but they probably weren't going to do that any time soon because his wife enjoyed the size of the yard and the quiet side street location.

Cyrus immediately went in and flopped down onto

the couch, excited at the prospect of finally being able to relax. He didn't wait a moment to throw up the leg rest and get comfortable. The cold, soft fabric of his couch was a wonderful change from the office chair he had been sitting in all day.

"Cyrus is that you?" Sara shouted from the kitchen.

"Yes! It's just me!" He shouted back already wanting to lay back and fall asleep.

Knowing that he couldn't fall asleep right now, he sat up and switched on the TV, un-reclined the seat, and started scrolling through the channels.

"What are you doing?" Sara asked sternly as she entered the room with a plate of food.

"Oh, you even brought me the food! That's great, thanks!" He said in a happy, surprised, and sarcastic tone.

"Why are you turning the TV on when we have to go soon," she snapped at him ignoring his thanks.

"I just-," he started.

"We don't have time to get into anything right now!" She said cutting him off as she set the food down on the table in front of him.

Before Cyrus could get another word in, she grabbed the remote right out of his hand and turned off the TV.

"What the hell, we don't have to be at the game for another half hour!" He shouted angrily before getting to his feet. "I had plenty of time."

"Just eat your food and get ready," she said as she turned around and headed for the stairs. "Chris, it's almost time to go! Get ready and come downstairs!" She shouted upstairs to their son. Chris was 16 years old and kind of small for his age. He stood barely taller than his mother and had brown hair. As commanded, he came marching down the stairs carrying a big bag full of gear and pushed open the door with his foot, letting the door swing shut behind him.

"Someone unlock the car door!" Chris shouted back inside.

So much for relaxing. Cyrus sat down and swirled some spaghetti around his fork, and shoved it into his mouth.

They arrived just as the team was heading into the locker room to put on their football pads. It was Chris's first game of the season, and Cyrus was excited to watch his son play. They scaled the bleachers and found a spot to sit down. Moments later, the team came storming out of the locker room toward the field, shouting at the top of their lungs. They met up on the sideline for what Cyrus assumed was a pep talk, and a few of them headed to the center of the field for the coin toss.

Not able to contain his excitement, Cyrus stood up and shouted, "Go get 'em!"

"Cyrus!" His wife said in an embarrassed tone as she pulled him back down.

"Sorry," he said laughing.

The team went out for their first drive. They ran some runs and some passes. Cyrus looked around, but couldn't spot his son. A few plays in and Chris still hadn't been on the field. After some ill-fated plays, Chris's team had to punt the ball.

"What position does Chris play again?" Cyrus asked

Sara.

"Ummm, I'm not sure. I think he said he plays all the positions," Sara replied.

"All the positions?" Cyrus asked confused wondering why he even thought she'd know.

"Whatever position they need him to play I guess," she explained. "He's number 27 if that helps."

Accepting the explanation, Cyrus figured they were probably just planning on playing him in defense. The defensive line ran out on to the field, but there was still no sign of Chris.

"You said 27, right?" Cyrus asked out loud to reassure himself.

"Yes," Sara answered, but Cyrus wasn't paying attention. His eyes were firmly focused on the field.

Patience. Cyrus sat and waited eagerly, but a few plays later a number 27 still hadn't appeared on the field.

"Why aren't they playing him?" Cyrus asked Sara in a frustrated tone, as if she would somehow know.

"Well, how am I supposed to know?" She answered. "Let's just wait. I'm sure they will put him in," she continued as she put her hand on Cyrus's shoulder to reassure him.

The entire first quarter went by and there was no indication that they were going to put their son in the game anytime soon. Getting increasingly angry, Cyrus glanced over at Sara.

Noticing his glance, Sara turned her head and said, "Babe, relax. I'm sure they had it all figured out before the game who plays and when. He will get his turn."

This time, he didn't think that was an acceptable answer. He had seen Chris play before and knew he was good. Chris should be playing, not all these other kids. It wasn't like these kids were doing that well anyway, but despite his anger he waited and waited. Quarter after quarter went by, and before he knew it the game only had a few minutes left, and then it was over. Chris never stepped out onto the field.

Visibly pissed off, Cyrus stood up and shot down the bleachers in the direction of the sidelines.

"Cyrus, wait!" Sara exclaimed, but he didn't even look back.

Charging onto the sidelines, Cyrus shouted at the coach as he ran up to him. "What the hell is your problem? Why didn't my son play?!"

Before the coach could respond, Cyrus continued, his face turning red with anger as he stepped closer to the coach. "The rest of the team played and you still didn't win, so why didn't he play?!"

"Who's your son?" The coach asked feeling perplexed at the situation he found himself in.

"Dad!" Chris stood up and said in a quiet tone in an attempt to conceal what was happening, despite the fact that everyone was already staring at them.

The coach looked back at Chris, then back at Cyrus and explained, "Well, Chris isn't a starter-," but Cyrus quickly cut him off.

"But, all these other kids are. These are your starters? Clearly, you need to make a change," Cyrus suggested.

The coach stood there in shock and didn't respond.

Walking toward his son, Cyrus grabbed Chris's helmet and said, "Let's go."

Looking back at his friends, Chris shrugged and said, "Sorry guys," as he followed his dad away from the field.

Chris ran into the locker room to take off his gear and quickly returned just as Sara came running up to them angrily.

"What the hell was that?" Sara shouted at Cyrus flailing her hands about as they walked to the car. "No, it doesn't matter what that was because it was uncalled for."

"Just get in the car," Cyrus said as they approached the car.

They got in and buckled up. Quickly, Cyrus started the car and pulled out.

"Why did you have to do that? Do you realize how much you probably just embarrassed him?" Sara shouted.

"Mom, really, it's okay," Chris jumped in an attempt to defuse the situation.

"No! That was not okay!" She yelled back surprised at what her son had said. "That was embarrassing!"

"That was embarrassing? Defending our son was embarrassing?" Cyrus fired back.

"No! You know that's not what I meant at all!" She exclaimed defending herself. "It was totally uncalled for."

"What was uncalled for was them not playing Chris!" Cyrus responded.

"That's part of the game, Cyrus, not everyone gets to play every game!" Sara reasoned.

"Well, this is high school football, so yes he should get a chance to play, especially when I know he is better than most of the other kids on the field," Cyrus said.

After a momentary break in the back and forth bickering, Sara said, "It's the coach's choice on who gets to play, so there is no sense in yelling at the coach. That won't accomplish anything."

"Well, it's better than not doing anything at all," Cyrus responded calmly, but still clearly frustrated.

Silence returned to the car for a few minutes before Sara chimed in once more, "I don't know if he will be able to stay on the team anyway."

"What? Why not?" Cyrus snapped at her thinking she said what she did because of what had just occurred.

"Because after the first game they have to pay for the equipment they are using," she explained in a somber tone.

"So then we will pay it, what's the problem with that?" Cyrus asked sternly, as they got closer to their house.

"What's wrong with that is we are low on money, and it costs a few hundred dollars," Sara responded.

"Since when are we low on money?" Cyrus asked.

"Clearly, you haven't looked at our bank statements lately," she said, as she rested her head on her hand.

Sitting there in silence, Cyrus didn't have a response to his wife's news about their financial situation. He noticed that her eyes looked glassy, as if she was about to burst into tears. They pulled up to the house and got out of the car.

"I'm tired so we will have to figure this all out in the morning," she said as she approached the door, marching quickly ahead of them.

Neither of them were making a lot of money. He barely made a couple of dollars above minimum wage working his desk job at City Hall, and she made not much more than that teaching first grade at the local elementary school. She seemed to be at work every day, whether it was for class, a meeting, or something else, even on weekends. She sometimes called it her second home. Despite outward appearances, they were barely making enough to scrape by.

They went into the house and Chris immediately headed upstairs to his room. Cyrus headed into the kitchen, filled up a glass of water, and took a sip. Hugging Cyrus from behind as she rested her head on his back, Sara said, "We'll get through this," before going upstairs.

Cyrus stared at the wall in complete silence like he was trapped in a trance. He stood there like a stone pillar for what seemed like moments, but it was closer to half an hour. Finally, he snapped out of it and picked up his glass and took a drink. After putting the glass in the sink, he headed toward the stairs, dragging himself along in the dark until he reached his room, then quietly got under the blankets where his wife was already fast asleep.

At first, he laid there staring at the ceiling contemplating everything going on his life, before rolling onto his side and staring out the window. There seemed to be a million noises. Crickets outside, the house squeaking, the sound of a cat in the bathroom jumping off the counter. Tons of noises all put on the planet just to keep him awake.

Finally, he gave up trying to get to sleep and sat up. A drink sounded pretty good. He got out of bed, threw on some jeans and socks, and headed downstairs. The stairs creaked below his feet as he crept softly, trying not to wake anyone up. Cyrus opened a cupboard filled with a variety of alcoholic drinks, grabbed one before opening another cupboard and taking hold of a shot glass. He paused for a moment, then put the glass back in its rightful place before sitting down at the kitchen table. Popping the bottle open, he took a big gulp and started to gag. It went down hard. He wondered why people even liked it, but then he took another large gulp.

He stood up and opened a drawer near the sink, taking hold of a pile of papers and tossing them onto the table before sitting down. Cyrus began sorting through them and stopped on one. He placed the paper down in front of him and rested his chin on his hand. 358 dollars, that's what the paper said they had in their bank account. Cyrus flicked through another couple of papers and grabbed one out, and started skimming through it. It had a list of the bills they were paying.

Well, I could sell the car and get a cheaper one, or we could get rid of some of our TV channels or something. He took a big gulp and dropped the paper down onto the pile of other papers. He had been in worse situations before, and he could make it through this one just like he always had.

Sadistic

He took another big gulp from the bottle.

Almost half the bottle later, the effects started to hit hard. He began to mumble to himself, complaining about his wife's behavior earlier in the day. *Tell me it was uncalled for.* He started to get agitated.

Cyrus knew he couldn't go back to bed like this. If Sara woke up and saw him in a drunken state in the middle of the night, she would kill him. Plus, he wouldn't be able to fall asleep anyway. He stood up and looked out the window into the cold night. Stumbling in the direction of the door, he opened it, slid on his shoes, and walked out, barely able to keep his balance as he began up the sidewalk. A walk was what he needed. It took him three blocks of walking before he realized he had left his drink at home, but it was too late. He wasn't going to head back to the house just for that.

He made his way down the road illuminated by streetlights, and before he even realized how far he had walked, he was on the opposite side of town, stumbling around in a place he had not been before. The effects of the alcohol were beginning to fade away, but he was far from sober as he staggered down the road, putting his hand on anything within reach to help him keep his balance.

He came to a halt and scanned the unfamiliar territory he found himself in before deciding to turn around and head back home.

Shortly after, as he started walking back in the direction of his house, a door popped open in front of him and a man came stumbling out, shouting back at whomever was in his path. "I don't need your stupid ass bar anyway. Screw you," the man exclaimed before the door slammed shut.

Cyrus continued walking down the sidewalk, heading in the direction of the unknown man. As Cyrus closed in on the man, the man turned out of his way and shoulder bumped Cyrus as he walked past. Cyrus turned around and looked back at the guy who stared at Cyrus with pale brown, sagging eyes.

"And, what the fuck do you think you're looking at?" The drunk man snapped at Cyrus, cocking his shoulders up like he was ready to fight.

Cyrus just stood there, glaring into the man's eyes.

"If you don't quit staring at me, we're going to have a serious problem," the man stated as he threw up his hands and took a step toward Cyrus.

Cyrus looked down, then turned around. Turning back around, the man said, "That's what I thought, punk," before walking away.

Just then, Cyrus snapped his head back up and turned in the direction of the man. Hatred and anger coursed through his body. An overwhelming feeling he had never felt before nor had any control over. He took a step toward the man and stopped, but then he took another step and then another, and another as he began following him down the road. Walking faster and faster, he started to gain ground on him. Mindlessly and relentlessly, he pursued him all the while never breaking his adamant stare.

Finally, the man turned the corner of a darkened alleyway and quickly jerked around as Cyrus rounded the corner after him. "Why the f-," the man muttered, but he was cut off by a large piece of metal being thrust into his chest. Time seemed to come to a standstill. Looking down at the piece of metal pierced into his chest, the man placed his hands on in a desperate attempt to pull it out, but he couldn't. Blood started pouring out onto the cold metal blade and dripped down onto the ground. Blood filled his lungs. He tried talking, but no words came out as he gagged. His eyes filled with terror and then went blank as the last shred of life seeped out of him. Cyrus yanked the piece of metal out of the man's chest and watched him drop dead to the ground.

2

THE body laid lifeless in the shade of the alleyway, covered in blood. Cyrus stared intently at the body of the life he had just ended. As blood dripped from the tip of the shard of metal in his hand, Cyrus couldn't help but be mesmerized. He was frozen like a statue by the sight of the life he had put to an end.

A car drove by, jolting him out of his trance. Not knowing where he was, he took in his surroundings. Darkness surrounded him in the tight alleyway. He looked down at the body, then as he stepped back he bumped into the wall behind him, but there was no fear or anguish on his face. Instead, he stood there bleak and expressionless.

I need to get home. I need to get out of here. Turning around, he took a step out onto the sidewalk, but quickly jumped back under the cover of darkness. There was blood all over his shirt. What should he do? He tore off the shirt and ran to a nearby dumpster, and almost threw it in, but stopped himself. He couldn't leave the shirt there. He was sure they would search the dumpster. Luckily, there was only one small drop of blood on his jeans. Even though the blood was slowly seeping through to the other side, he decided to turn the shirt inside out and throw it back on. The shirt clung to his body from the sweat. After sliding the piece of metal under his shirt, he stepped back out onto the sidewalk and commenced his walk home, hoping no cops drove by and got suspicious.

As he walked down the sidewalk, his ears pricked at every noise he heard. Upon reaching a corner, he glanced around to make sure no cars were coming. With each step, he could feel his shirt swaying and the cold blood rubbing against his chest. The smell of blood rose up and seeped into his nose. Never in his life had he encountered such a stench; it overwhelmed him.

The light, gentle rumbling of water caught his attention as he moved through the night. Wanting to trace the source of the noise, he skipped between two houses and came to a river bank. He didn't even notice the river on his way through the first time. It was rare for him to pass by the river, and he almost forgot it was even there. After glancing around to ensure no one was watching him from a window, he pulled the metal shard out from under his shirt. He took one last glance at the shard of metal, then pulled his arm back and heaved it as far into the river as he could.

Although the blood had seeped through his shirt, he managed to get home without anyone stopping him, not even the police. Quietly, he slid the key into the lock and opened the door. It squeaked open as he inched his way into the house and looked around. Cyrus needed to find a place to abandon the blood covered shirt, but where? He began in the living room and then moved to the kitchen, before making his way to the dining room in search of somewhere to stash the shirt, but nowhere seemed to be a good place to hide it. He couldn't just lump it in with the dirty clothes.

But, then an idea struck him. Silently, he darted to the backdoor. He opened the door and looked around his yard. He could bury it. He went back inside and headed to the garage to grab a shovel. Once back outside, he headed to the corner of his fenced-in yard and started burying the shovel into the cold, hard ground before coming to a halt. *This will be too obvious.* There was no chance of his wife not noticing a dug up spot in the yard. How could he cover it up? He looked around the yard. *That's it.* Spotting his wife's flower garden, he hurried over and smoothly stuck the shovel deep enough into the dirt to get under the roots and pick the flowers up. He moved a small patch of flowers and started digging. About a foot in, he stopped and pulled at his shirt in an attempt to get it off. It slowly peeled across his back, fighting against the mixture of blood and sweat that had made itself at home on his shirt. Tugging hard, he finally got the shirt off and stuffed it into the ground, before filling the hole and pressing down on the soil with his bare hands to make sure it was packed tightly. He placed the flowers back on top and tried to rearrange them to how they looked before, undisturbed.

Upon reaching the stairs, a strange feeling struck him. He turned on a lamp and it flashed across his chest, revealing blood all over his hands, arms, and down his chest. Amidst the commotion in hiding his shirt, he didn't realize he had blood on himself.

Cyrus hurried toward the downstairs bathroom and switched on the light. He turned on the tap and placed his hands under the water, but upon looking up he not only noticed blood on his hands, arms, and body, but also in his hair. It must have got in his hair when he was taking off his shirt. Without giving it a second thought, he tore off his clothes and climbed into the shower. Upon disrobing, he saw blood splattered across almost his entire upper body.

The hot water coursed down him. The white of the soap had mixed with the blood, making a beautiful shade of red that engulfed his entire body. Looking down at himself, he watched the blood seep down the drain. He leaned his head back and let out a quiet but pleasure-filled moan.

Cyrus awoke the next morning feeling refreshed. He let out a loud yawn and flopped his arms to his side. He didn't even remember heading upstairs to go to bed. His wife was already at work. Upon rolling his head to the side, he saw that it was 8.30 am. Cyrus had slept in and was already an hour late for work. He started scrambling to get ready for work, but stopped. *Screw it*. Picking up the phone, he began to dial.

RING…RING…RING…CLICK.

"Hello, City Hall Records Department, this is Mark speaking."

"Hey, it's Cyrus," he said relieved that it wasn't Joe that had picked up the phone. "I'm feeling a little under the weather and won't be able to make it in today," Cyrus said in his best fake sick voice.

"All right, I'll let Joe know," Mark replied.

"Yeah, hopefully I'll feel well enough to come in tomorrow," Cyrus said enthusiastically.

"Well, get some rest and we'll see you tomorrow," Mark said.

Cyrus hung up the phone and stood there. It had been years since he last called in sick for work. He couldn't believe he'd called in and lied about being sick. He had done a pretty good job of it. *Maybe I should quit my job and become an actor.*

Cyrus walked over to the window and noticed that it was nice outside. Everything appeared normal. The day was fine, and there was a nice, cool breeze. Bikes rode by and cars slowly passed down the small side street. He had a strange feeling in the pit of his stomach. A man jogged by; jogging sounded like a great idea. There couldn't be a better day for it. Maybe just once or twice around the block.

After throwing on some shorts and a hoodie, he headed out the door. Once or twice around the block quickly turned into seven laps before he finally came to a stop in front of his house. He bent over panting for

Sadistic

air, realizing he had been around the block seven times without a break. He still had that gnawing feeling in the pit of his stomach.

He headed back inside the house. The garbage had to be taken out, so he took it out. The table needed to be wiped, so he wiped it down. There were dishes in the sink, so he did them. He did all of the house chores, then started pacing around.

Cyrus paced and paced. He paced for so long that the soles of his shoes started to wear thin. Upon looking at his watch, he noticed that it was almost 1:00 pm. He had gone for a jog, done some chores, and paced around the house, but he was still wired. He felt like he could run a marathon.

What else could I do? Glancing outside, he noticed that it was still nice outside, so he decided to venture outside again. This time, he chose to go for a walk instead of a run.

In the quietness of his surroundings, he couldn't help but think of the act he'd committed the previous night. He didn't feel scared or bad. As he thought about it some more, a grin slowly emerged on his face. He felt as if he had it in him to do it again. He didn't want to apologize or take it back. Having not felt this invigorated since he was a teenager, he wanted to repeat the act.

Just one more time. Just to see if it makes me feel the same way. Wait, what the hell am I thinking? He stopped walking and looked around. *I don't know what I'm thinking.* The scary part was that he knew if the opportunity presented itself again, he would hardly have to convince himself of going through with it.

After walking a little further, he heard a rattling noise and looked around. A man was dragging some garbage cans out back behind a rundown looking shop. Without hesitation, he jogged across the street toward the store. As he approached the corner of the small shop, the man came back around the corner and almost collided head on with Cyrus.

"Oh, I'm very sorry, sir," the man said.

"No, it's all right," Cyrus responded in a brusque tone in an attempt to bring the already uncomfortable conversation to an end.

"Ha, ha, you kind of startled me there. I almost walked right into you," the man continued.

"Yeah, you sure did," Cyrus said keeping it short.

"Well, sir, have a wonderful day," the man said bringing the conversation to an end, before grabbing the last garbage can and heading back behind the store.

Cyrus started walking down the road. *Why did he have to apologize? Why did he have to talk to me?* The anger was beginning to rise in him. As he continued down the road, he thought it might be a good idea to just head back home. He knew within himself that this was a bit crazy, but he made his way back across the street anyway and continued down a side road.

Just as he was about to start questioning what he was even doing out there, he spotted another man a couple of houses down across the street who was also taking out his garbage. He examined his surroundings to see if anyone was in the vicinity, but the coast was clear.

He looked back at the man who was fiddling around with a cell phone in his garage, before taking hold of the garbage can and heading toward the curb. Cyrus started walking down the sidewalk toward the man's house. The man plopped the garbage can down and began making his way to his garage. Just as Cyrus started to pick up speed to catch-up to the man, the garbage can fell over, prompting the man to turn around. In an attempt to avoid suspicion, Cyrus jerked back onto the sidewalk and dropped his phone as an excuse to stop walking.

The man glanced across the street and shouted, "Don't break your phone," then laughed and turned back around in the direction of his garage.

Silently, Cyrus darted across the street, and as soon as the man entered the garage, Cyrus bolted at him, pulled out his pocket knife, and stabbed him in the side before wrapping his arm around his mouth to keep him silent. As the man dropped to the ground, he bit at Cyrus's arm, but before he had a chance to pull away or scream, Cyrus stabbed him multiple times until the man's last breath escaped his lungs and his body fell limp.

Cyrus stood there gazing down at the body before finally hunching down to get closer. Slowly, he began to circle the body as a puddle of blood started to make its way out from under him. He couldn't help but admire the body. It was like a masterpiece, a beautiful work of art that was solely created for his pleasure.

What he'd done made him feel good inside. Actually, it felt even better than last time. Standing up, he looked at his watch and saw that it was 2.30 pm. His wife would be getting out of work right about now. Placing the knife in the pocket of his hoodie, he started to walk quickly down the road. He kept looking around for anyone that may have witnessed what he had done. As soon as reached the end of the road, he took off sprinting.

He got to his house and bolted inside. Reaching the kitchen, he pulled the knife out of his pocket. *Fuck*. He was in such a hurry that he had placed the bloody knife in his pocket. The inside of his pocket was now soaked in blood. Turning on the water, he began to rinse the knife.

He heard a squeal, and out the kitchen window he saw a car pull into the driveway. *Oh shit*. In a panicked state, he ran into the dining room and looked around, then hurried back into the kitchen. He heard the door open, so he opened the garbage can and tossed the hoodie in, and ran around the corner to make it look like he was coming out of a different room.

"Hey, babe, you're home," Cyrus said to Sara excitedly as she walked through the door and took off her shoes. "How was work? How was your day?" Cyrus continued.

"Oh, it was good. Are you okay?" Sara asked curiously.

"Yeah, I'm just happy to see you after the fight we had yesterday," Cyrus replied. He went over and hugged her.

"Well, I'm glad you're feeling better today," she responded happily and then curiously asked, "How was work for you? You shouldn't even be home yet."

"Oh, yeah, I took the day off. I woke up late plus my stomach was a little upset this morning. I figured it'd be best if I played it safe and stayed home," he explained.

"Well, I see you're feeling better," Sara noted.

"A lot better actually after having a day off to relax. Let's hope it stays that way," he responded.

"Did you stay home more because you were sick or because you were late?" Sara asked with a giggle.

Cyrus returned her cheeky question with a smile.

"Well, I'm going to start dinner," Sara continued as she walked into the kitchen. He started to walk away when all of a sudden Sara shouted at him, "Hey, is this the hoodie I got you that is in the garbage?"

Horror shot down his spine as he swung around and saw the end of the sleeve hanging out of the garbage. He darted toward the garbage can, grabbed the hoodie, and turned around with it in his possession. Thankfully, for Cyrus, she didn't have a chance to grab it.

"What was that doing in there?" She asked with a touch of sadness in her voice.

Not able to come up with a better excuse fast enough, Cyrus said, "I…I spilled some food on it earlier."

"So you threw it out?" Sara shot back sounding angrier than upset this time.

"I don't know what I was thinking. I'm sorry. I'll go toss it in the washer," he replied.

Without dignifying Cyrus with a response, she

turned around and reached into cupboards for ingredients for the night's meal. He darted upstairs to the bathroom to attempt to rinse some of the blood out of the hoodie pocket. Rigorously, he scraped at the blood with his fingers in a bid to clean it as best as he could before heading back downstairs to throw it in the wash with a bunch of other clothes. After adding a large amount of clothing bleach to the pile of clothes, he sat on the couch and hoped nothing else would come up.

"So how was school today, Chris?" Cyrus asked as he took a bite of pasta.

"It was fine," Chris replied in a manner which reflected his usual lack of interest in the topic.

"And football practice?" Cyrus continued.

"That was all right, too. You know, I don't even care if I play," Chris answered as he looked straight down at the table.

"Well, I'm going to see if I can pick up some more hours at work so you can keep playing if you want to play," Cyrus said in a vain attempt to console Chris.

"I promise we will figure something out, Chris," Sara chimed in.

"Yeah, don't worry about it," Cyrus added. "Like your mom said, we will figure something out," he continued reassuringly.

Once they were finished eating, Cyrus told Sara he would clean up the table and take care of the dishes, and then meet her in bed in a minute or two.

"Well, all right then, Mr. Helpful," she said as she giggled and made her way upstairs.

Once he had finished cleaning up, Cyrus headed to

their bedroom and laid down next to Sara. Rolling over, he gently massaged her waist and then leaned in for a hug.

"Thanks for dinner today, it was amazing," Cyrus said as he began kissing her on the neck.

"Well, you're welcome," Sara replied. "You're in an awfully good mood today." She leaned her head back, allowing Cyrus to move his lips up her neck "Much better than yesterday," Sara continued.

"I don't know, I guess I just had a good day," he said as he started to take off his shirt.

"A good day? More like a great day," Sara responded with a flirtatious giggle, as she lifted up her leg to let Cyrus slide off her pants.

"All right, maybe a great day. I just feel like a whole new person," he smiled as he got on top of her.

3

BACON sizzled in the skillet, filling the room with a delicious aroma as Cyrus flipped some eggs. His stomach was rumbling like a freight train careering down the tracks.

"What's that amazing smell?" Sara asked happily as she made her way down the stairs still just in her robe.

"Oh, just some delicious eggs and bacon. No big deal," he laughed.

"Since when do you get up early and make breakfast, Mr. Chef?" She asked in a playful manner as she hugged him from behind. "And, why aren't you at work?"

"Well, if I made breakfast for you too often you would get used to it and make me quit my job to serve you breakfast every morning, and we can't be having that now can we?" He replied in light-hearted tone as he turned and wrapped his arms around Sara. "And, work called me this morning and told me they would need me to come in later this afternoon after my normal shift and work the evening filing things after everyone goes home," he added.

"You don't have to do all that alone, do you?" Sara asked.

"No, Joe said there would be some others there, too," he replied before kissing her on the forehead.

"Well, that's good," she responded as she made her way to the living room.

He played around with the eggs until they were fried to perfection before placing them on a couple of plates. After pulling a couple of bagels out of the toaster, he put an egg and a slice of bacon on each, then grabbed both plates and proceeded into the living room with some egg already hanging out of his mouth.

"Babe!" Sara shouted from the living room just as Cyrus was making his way into the room.

"Yeah?" He answered as he seated himself on the couch and picked up his bagel.

"Did you see this?" She asked him as she grabbed the remote and turned up the volume.

"See what?" Cyrus asked as he looked up at the TV.

The food almost dropped out of his mouth and his stomach sunk as soon as he saw what was on the TV.

"Someone was stabbed!" Sara exclaimed hysterically. "That road isn't far away from us either," she added with a hint of fear in her voice.

With his gaze fixated on the TV as they showed the

house of the man he killed, Cyrus didn't dignify Sara with a response. He could picture himself standing right where one of the police officers was standing during the newscast, gazing down at his kill. There was a ringing in his ears.

"Cyrus? Cyrus!" She shouted at him.

"Yeah?" He finally replied.

"Are you hearing me?" She asked in an annoyed tone.

"Yeah, sorry, my... my mind was just wandering a bit," he said in his defense.

"That street is only like ten minutes away from us, babe," she stated with concern in her voice.

"Yeah it is," he replied. "Let's turn it up and see what they're saying about it," he said as he grabbed the remote off the table.

Just as he turned up the volume, the reporter ceased talking, allowing the Detective to get in front of the camera before being introduced.

This is Senior Detective Hughes on the scene.

Interviewer: What exactly do we have going on here?
Hughes: Well, we have a homicide victim with multiple stab wounds. At this stage, we cannot release the victim's name.
Interviewer: Is there anything you can tell us?
Hughes: As we believe the individual that committed this crime had access to the victim's garage, it's our belief that the victim knew the perpetrator.
Interviewer: Do you have any official leads? Anyone in

custody?

Hughes: At this stage, I am not at liberty to divulge any details, but I will encourage anyone that has any information or believes they may have seen or heard anything that may be of use to contact police immediately. Also, we have an anonymous tip-off line that we will provide in a few moments. We thank everyone for their help and hope to catch the criminal in a prompt manner.

Interviewer: All right, so there you have it.

As he turned down the TV, Sara looked at Cyrus with an even more terrified look on her face.

"I really hope they catch whoever did this," she said with a touch of fear still in her voice.

"Relax, babe, they will. It's no big deal," he responded in an attempt to try and calm her down.

"It's hard to relax when I've never lived this close to something like this, or at least it seems close," Sara continued.

"It's not that close. It's like fifteen minutes away from here," he explained.

"Yeah if you walk. If you drive, it's much closer," she snapped back.

"You're overreacting," he stated not knowing what else to say to calm her down as he stood up to take the dishes to the sink.

"Yeah, you're probably right," she conceded looking down at the floor.

Popping her head around the corner into the

kitchen, Sara told Cyrus she was going to their room to catch-up on a book since she had the day off work as a result of a superintendent's meeting being held that day.

A few hours later, Cyrus readied himself for work. Feeling tired, he was already counting down the minutes until he could head home. He pulled out of the driveway early so he would have time to stop at a store to grab a coffee and something to eat.

The wheels crumbled over the loose gravel as he turned into the parking lot of a store. He stepped out onto the pavement and gazed around at the half empty parking lot, his eyes squinting as they adjusted to the light after he removed his sunglasses.

Fearing he might be late for work if he took too long, he quickly walked through the store. A bottle of Gatorade sounded good, two sounded even better. As he stood in front of the deli counter, he couldn't decide if he was really hungry or the pizza just looked that good.

"I'll take one slice, please," he said giving into his craving.

The line was longer than he had hoped. He stood there bobbing his head back and forth, looking around people to see what was holding the line up. *Ugh, c'mon.* The line started moving faster. He glanced at his watch. *Still time.*

He tossed his items onto the belt and waited for the cashier to scan them. Beep. Beep. Beep.

"Hold on, this one isn't scanning," the woman said with a hint of a Southern accent. "I'm going to have to call a manager to undo the order."

"No, never mind. It's fine, I only need these ones," Cyrus said in an attempt to get out the store as quickly as possible.

"You sure?" The cashier asked.

"Yes, I'm sure," he said as he pulled out his card to swipe it.

He grabbed his bag and headed to the exit. As he passed through the automatic doors, he was once again blinded by the light. SCREEEECH. A truck came sliding to a stop next to Cyrus and came perilously close to hitting him. As Cyrus looked up, a window rolled down.

"How about you watch where you're going, jackass," a man shouted at Cyrus.

"Weren't you driving a little-," Cyrus was cut off mid-sentence by the man shouting.

"Cross the fuckin' street and get going," the man yelled at Cyrus.

Cyrus stood there for a moment, his eyes firmly fixed on the man.

"Well, fucking c'mon," the man said with anger in his voice.

"I'm sorry. Have a good day, sir," Cyrus said as he began walking the rest of the way across the parking lot to his vehicle. The truck floored it, squealing its tires.

As Cyrus pulled his keys up to the door to unlock his car, he fumbled and dropped them to the ground. Reaching down, he picked them up and forced them into the lock. Sitting in his car, he stared forward and slowly examined his surroundings. Silence filled the interior of his car as he placed his hands on the steering wheel.

"Rahhhhh!" He shouted in an animalistic manner as he started smashing his fists on the dashboard and flailing his arms about, smacking everything within reach. He proceeded to throw himself viciously into the back of his seat, then let his arms fall loosely onto his lap. After a brief pause, he looked at his watch once more before placing his keys in the ignition and starting his car.

He got to work and everyone else was already there. A few people he didn't really know were there, but Dave was present so at least there was a bright side. Everyone nodded and said hello to Cyrus as he walked in.

Sitting down, he logged onto his computer to kick-off the late work day.

"This is crap, man," Dave said to Cyrus.

"Yeah, but there's nothing we can do about it," Cyrus replied as he typed something into his computer.

Dave merely offered a nod and turned back to his work. Upon opening a few folders, Cyrus noticed why he had been called in. Loads of files had yet to be sorted, and other files needed to be placed in envelopes and prepared to be sent out.

"Did they just decide to leave all this work and call us in to finish it?" Cyrus pondered as he leaned back in his chair. "Do they not think we'd rather be home instead of cleaning up other people's unfinished work? Cyrus complained.

"Yeah, I know what you mean," Greg cut in.

Greg was the annoying guy at the office that always had something to say even if the conversation had nothing to do with him. He always managed to find a way to annoy someone without even knowing he was doing it, and his Newton's Cradle could drive the sanest man to the brink of insanity.

"My wife is at home freaking out after what happened the other night with that stabbing," Greg continued.

Upon hearing this statement, Cyrus's stomach dropped and his undivided attention turned to Greg.

"Stabbing?" Cyrus asked feigning confusion.

"Yeah, the one that happened yesterday," Greg answered. "It happened right down the road from my house. Just a few houses down actually."

"Oh wow, Greg. That sounds scary," Cyrus said sympathetically. He wondered if his act of ignorance sounded even remotely believable.

"I honestly cannot believe you didn't hear about it," Greg said as he rolled his chair closer to Cyrus and Dave. "It was all over the news this morning."

"Oh wait…was it the one that happened in the man's garage?" Cyrus said as if he just had an epiphany.

"Yeah, that's the one," Greg responded. "My wife is at home freaking out because from what I hear they have no idea who the killer is. She doesn't want to be home alone."

"None at all?" Cyrus replied. In the heat of committing the heinous act, Cyrus didn't even think about making sure he left no evidence at the scene, but he couldn't think of anything that he may have left behind.

"Nope. They think it may have been a family member, but I spoke to them quite a few times and his family seemed fine to me," Greg said in a befuddled tone.

"But, you never really know what's going on in someone else's house," Dave cut in. "There always ends up being something. Maybe he was cheating on his wife or something."

Everyone laughed in unison.

Cyrus leaned back relaxing a bit. He was just happy they had no leads. He didn't spend any time planning it out like he should.

Greg inched closer to Dave and Cyrus, and put his head down like he was about to share a secret. "I think it was someone else," Greg said catching everyone's attention.

"Like who?" Cyrus asked feeling a little nervous as a bead of sweat made its way onto the back of his neck, even though he knew there was no way anyone could possibly suspect him of having anything to do with the crime.

"I don't know," Greg said shrugging his shoulders. "I just don't think it was someone in his family, especially not his wife. They always seemed to get along just fine."

"Oh, so you knew him personally?" Cyrus responded.

"Well, I spoke to him from time to time, but my

little neighborhood is kind of nosey and you always heard about whatever drama was going on whether you cared or not, and Nathan and his wife were never really the topic of any discussion," Greg explained.

"I just hope they catch whoever did it," Cyrus said as he swung back in his chair to face his computer.

"Right," Dave said as he followed Cyrus' lead and swung his chair back around to his desk.

The engine roared to life as he pressed down on the gas and pulled out. He was excited to be on his way home. He pulled onto the main road and started down the dimly lit road. Turning up the radio, he started scrolling through channels before landing on the news network. He told himself he just wanted to listen to the news, but did he really just want to see if they mentioned the murder? Was he nervous or was it something else?

He was half-zoned out and half-listening to the weather on the radio when a car cut lanes right in front of him, forcing him to slam on the brakes and come to a screeching halt. *Motherfucker, I'll fucking kill you.* The car sped up and quickly drove away, leaving Cyrus in its wake.

Cars were passing around him as he gave himself a minute to regain his composure. He put his foot on the pedal and continued his journey. He was angry, but the driver of the car was no longer his overriding thought. At the forefront of his mind was killing the person in the car. It was far from a passing thought. He really wanted to inflict pain on the driver.

For a brief moment, the thought of how badly he wanted to kill scared him, but it was quickly replaced by fantasy. The rest of the drive seemingly flew by, as he fantasized about all the ways in which he could kill the driver.

As he pulled into his driveway, he felt flustered. Cyrus switched off the ignition and noticed that he was hard. He couldn't help but crack a smile. Upon entering the house, he realized that it was quiet and that only one light was on. It was likely that it was left on so he could see where he was going when he got home.

He removed his shoes and made his way upstairs. As he headed toward their bedroom, he noticed his erection was still present and tucked away in the band of his pants. He quietly slid the door open so as to not wake his potentially sleeping wife.

"Hey, babe," Sara said greeting him with a bright smile as she laid there reading a book.

"Hey, what are you still doing up this late?" He asked as he returned her smile.

"I just wanted to make sure you got home safe," Sara replied as she placed her book down on the bed. "You don't normally work this late, so I just wanted to make sure."

Placing his knee on the bed, Cyrus knelt down to give his wife a kiss. As she went to place her arm around him, she accidentally grazed his hard penis.

"Well, what do we have here?" Sara asked with a giant smile etched on her face.

"Oh, nothing," Cyrus replied as he moved in a little

closer. "Unless, maybe, you would like to find out for yourself," he continued as he started to kiss her neck.

"I wonder what you were thinking about on your way home," she said in a teasing manner.

He didn't respond and started to go a little limp, which his wife quickly noticed.

Surprised at her husband's current state, Sara sat up and asked, "Did I say something wrong?"

"No, you're fine," he replied as he gently pushed on her chest, laying her back down. "I....I just got a cramp in my leg. No big deal," he continued as a fake smile slowly emerged on his face.

As he laid back on top of her, she noticed his heart was pounding.

"No, there must be something wrong," she said as she placed her hand on him signaling for him to stop. "You aren't even hard anymore. What did I do?" She continued as she tried her best to hold back the tears.

"I'm fine," he reassured her as he removed his pants. "I just want to make love to you right here, right now."

Hearing him say it like that put the smile back on her face, prompting her to reach down and touch his penis.

"I'll just have to make you hard again," she whispered "Just imagine being deep inside me."

Slowly, he closed his eyes and as his mind drifted his erection returned, but he wasn't thinking about being inside her. He was thinking of something much different, much more sinister. A blade piercing the skin of the person that cut him off on his way home from work was at the front of his mind. As blood coursed through him, he started thrusting himself inside Sara. She clenched her arms tightly around him, pulling him in deeper as her moans filled the room.

4

THE light collapsed into Cyrus's room through the open curtains, forcing him to squint his eyes. Desperate to get back to sleep, he swatted at his eyes as if to shoo away the light. He pulled another pillow over his face but it was too late, he was already wide awake.

He sat straight up like Frankenstein coming to life and rubbed his eyes. Looking over at the clock, he saw that it read 12.30 pm. Although he'd overslept, he felt refreshed. A good night's sleep was hard to come by these days, but for the past two nights he'd slept better.

His feet pressed against the cold hardwood floor as he made his way downstairs. A hot shower and a freshly brewed cup of coffee were at the top of his agenda. After kicking the coffee maker into gear, he grabbed some clothes and jumped into the shower. Quickly, he scrubbed himself and hopped out of the shower. After drying himself off and getting dressed, he headed back downstairs. To his surprise and delight, he'd made it downstairs just as the coffee had finished brewing. He added some sugar and creamer to his coffee, and while stirring it he made his way over to the window and started dancing back and forth to some music that was playing on the TV. His wife had started leaving the TV on whenever she left the house in an attempt to deter any potential intruders.

What a wonderful start to the day.

Cyrus headed to the front door to grab his slippers, took a sip of coffee, and then checked the mail. Aside from the newspaper that was resting at his feet, there was nothing but junk mail. It must be that time of the week. He wondered why he still received the newspaper when he didn't even read it. Turning around, he headed toward the back door, tossing the paper on the kitchen table as he walked by.

Stopping at the screen door, he stared through the small squares in the door at a group of birds picking their beaks into small flowers that had grown as a result of his failure to mow the yard.

A sound captured his attention, causing him to turn in the direction of the other end of the yard. Tension shot down his spine. There was a man dressed in a dirty brown shirt, a ratty pair of jeans, and some faded brown work boots standing next to the garden staring down at the ground.

Cyrus turned and placed his cup of coffee down on the table. The door creaked as Cyrus slowly pushed it open and stepped outside. The thud of his shoes on the porch and the door swinging shut drew the man's attention to Cyrus.

"Who are you and what are you doing in my yard?" Cyrus asked the mysterious man as he inched closer toward the porch stairs.

"Do you have it?" The man sporadically shook. "Do you have the shit?"

Looking down at the man from atop the porch stairs, Cyrus noted that he was shaking and constantly rubbing his arms as if it was freezing outside.

"Is Tony here? The man continued as he turned to the side and attempted to peer into a window. "He said he'd be here."

"What are you looking for?" Cyrus coerced.

"The dope, man," the stranger responded.

Cyrus raised an eyebrow.

"The dope, the heroin, whatever," the man continued as he began to get more fidgety. "Stop fucking around and get Tony."

"All right, just wait here and relax, and I'll go get Tony," Cyrus responded.

Turning around, Cyrus headed back inside. The door swung shut behind him, and he peeked back out through the screen door to see the man nervously examining his surroundings.

Pulling open a closet door, he started pushing hanging coats to the side. *There it is*. He reached inside, wrapping his hand around the rubber handle of a long metal baseball bat. He pressed it up behind his back and proceeded back outside.

"Where's Tony? Is he coming out?" The man asked as Cyrus made his way down the porch steps.

Just as he was about to talk again, Cyrus pulled the bat out from behind his back and swung it as hard as he could at the man's head.

"Don't bring that shit to my house!" Cyrus shouted as the metal made contact with the man's skull.

He dropped to the ground like a falling tree, landing with a thud. *Fucking dirt bag.* Cyrus rose the bat up and held it there for a brief moment before swinging it down, hitting the man's chest with crushing force. With a smile beginning to stretch across his face, he tossed the baseball bat to the ground and nudged the body with the tip of his foot. With the body motionless, Cyrus headed back inside the house.

Quickly, he re-emerged from the house with a couple of black garbage bags in one hand and a pair of ropes in the other. He nudged the body again. Nothing. Cyrus took hold of the man by his feet, lifted them up, and slid them into the opening of a garbage bag. Sliding the bag up like a pair of pants, Cyrus managed to get the entire lower half of the man's body into the first bag.

Taking hold of the body, he wrapped the bronze colored rope around the garbage bag and pulled it tight, locking the bag in place. He tied the rope in a knot and let the legs fall back to the ground.

Just as he started to slide the second bag over the man's head, something caught Cyrus's eye. The man's chest was moving up and down ever so slightly.

"Are you breathing?" Cyrus asked with his ear just

inches away from the man's mouth. "It appears that you are."

Reaching down, Cyrus picked up the bat. Without hesitation, he forcefully swung another blow into the man's chest before throwing the bat back down.

Taking hold of the bag, he finished pulling it over the man's upper body and then wrapped the rope around him, pulling it tight until it was secure. Now, only the mid-point of the man's body wasn't covered by the garbage bag. Cyrus took in his surroundings and then bent down, straining as he lifted the man's body like it was a pile of lumber.

Trudging toward the tree line that sat at the end of his backyard, Cyrus tried with all his strength to maintain his balance as the limp body flopped from side-to-side with each step he made.

Upon reaching the woods, he made his way around tree after tree, all the while keeping his eyes firmly fixed on the ground to avoid tripping up. He continued deeper into the woods until he was able to look back and not sight his house. Relaxing his arms, Cyrus dropped the body to the ground. His shoulders cracked as he stretched his arms. *Heavy bastard.*

"Wait here," he cheekily uttered to the lifeless man before jogging back to his house.

Quickly, he returned with a shovel in hand and penetrated the ground. With a heavy heave, he dug up the first pile of dirt and tossed it to the side. This was going to take much longer than he thought. Glancing at his phone, he knew he had to work fast because it wouldn't be long until Sara arrived home.

He continued to dig deeper, the pile increasing in size at a rapid rate. Dragging his arm across his forehead, he wiped the sweat away. He was exhausted. Enough was enough.

He rolled the bag into the hole he had created and looked around for something to cover it with. It was deep enough, just barely, but it was deep enough. He started shoveling the dirt he dug up back into the hole to cover up the bag. Even with all the dirt back in the hole, things didn't look quite right to him. The area stuck out like a sore thumb. He dragged some small branches over and tossed them onto the sealed hole, then ran about 15 feet away and turned around to make sure it wasn't obvious from a distance.

Cyrus decided that it was good enough and hurried back to the house. Stepping onto the porch, he looked at the yard, taking note of the mess. There was a pool of blood painting the grass red, just waiting to tell its story to anyone prepared to listen.

Cyrus stepped back off the porch and fetched the garden hose. He cranked the switch and took aim at the blood, rinsing away the evidence and watching as it slowly seeped into the soil.

The blood was almost completely gone when he heard a noise coming from inside the house. Peering into the house through the back door window, he saw Sara making her way inside, rubbing her shoes off on the doormat.

Frantically, he started hosing the grass faster, swinging the hose from side-to-side to cover the whole area.

"Cyrus, is that you back there?!" Sara shouted as she approached the back door.

"Yeah, it's just me," he replied as he looked down and noticed a red blotch on his foot. *God dammit*.

He turned the hose to his feet, then pulled the hose away just before Sara opened the back door and poked her head outside.

"What are you doing?" She enquired squinting her eyes at the scene in front of her as she made her way out the door.

"A dog must have come back here," he answered quickly.

"A dog?" She asked sounding confused.

"Yeah, I came out here and there was dog poop in the yard, so I got the hose to clean it off," he responded. "One of the neighbor's dogs must have got loose or something. I don't know."

"Well, it looks like you missed a little," she said pointing down at his soaked feet.

"Oh, yeah, I stepped in it by accident when I first came out here," he replied. "Dumb dogs," he continued while lightly laughing.

She looked at the yard. "Looks like you did a little bit of overkill."

Cyrus couldn't help but laugh.

"Well, c'mon, get inside. I'm starting dinner in a few minutes," she said gesturing in the direction of the doorway.

"Already?" Cyrus asked. "You just got home from

work."

"I'm hungry," she answered as she disappeared into the house.

He took a deep breath and finally sat down for a moment on the bench, and picked up his cup of coffee. *That could have gone badly.* Pushing himself back up to his feet, he stepped out into the yard and began winding the hose back up. The yard resembled one big puddle from the amount of watering that had been done, but thankfully there was no sign of any blood. He walked back onto the porch and glanced out into the woods, tilting his head from side-to-side to see if he could spot anything from the porch. For a few minutes, he stared at the tree line before walking back into the house.

The smell of searing steaks filled the air, and the sizzling of the meat was music to his ears. Mindlessly, he flipped through the channels while his stomach rumbled. Since she had arrived home, Sara had pretty much stayed silent, tending to the food in the kitchen. He was beginning to wonder if something was on her mind.

"Dinner's ready," she shouted. They were the first words out of her mouth in what felt like hours, but they were the best words.

As Cyrus stood up, he heard the loud thumping of his son running down the stairs. He probably was as excited as him to sink his teeth into some hearty meat since the house had been filled with the smell of mouthwatering steaks for quite some time. Cyrus's yearning for food dragged him out into the kitchen.

By the time he made his way to the kitchen table,

Chris was already seated, ready to grab some food. Sara was laying plates and bowls of food across the center of the table. She always made the table and insisted the family had dinner together regularly; it was important to her.

He pulled up a chair and sat down as Chris went to grab some food. Cyrus reached out to stop him, leaned in, and whispered, "Wait until your mother sits down." Chris didn't look overly happy, but he obliged.

As soon as Sara was seated, Chris reached for some food, making it all the way without Cyrus stopping him. Cyrus and Sara followed his example and started filling their plates with food. There were steaks, mashed potatoes, creamed corn, gravy, and some mixed vegetables.

"Mmmm, chicken gravy, my favorite," Cyrus said to no response.

They sat there eating for a little while before Cyrus noticed that Sara was still silent. He had been so caught up with eating that he hadn't really noticed how quiet things were at the dinner table. Dinner was usually the time when they talked about different things, such as what they did that day or how work went.

"Wow, this food is really good," Cyrus said looking in Sara's direction. He then looked at Chris and nodded at him.

"Yeah, mom," Chris chimed in looking back at Cyrus. "It's great," Chris continued.

She nodded her head and uttered a quiet, "Thanks," then continued eating.

Looking at his father, Chris shrugged before proceeding to continue enjoying his food. Cyrus went back to filling his stomach as well. They sat in silence for a few more minutes before Cyrus piped up again.

"Is something wrong, Sara?" He asked placing his spoon down ready to investigate.

"I don't know," she answered quickly fending off his question.

Not ready to give up, Cyrus leaned in toward the table. "You have been quiet since you got home," he stated.

Chris sat there watching in silence, but was obviously curious as well as to what was troubling his mother as he had stopped shoveling food into his mouth.

"You aren't usually this quiet," Cyrus noted in a pleading tone. "Something must be bothering you. What's up?"

"I'm just worried," she looked at Cyrus finally providing him with an honest answer. "Some of the other teachers at work today were talking about that stabbing."

Chris's attention was now firmly focused on his mother. There was a brief silence before she continued. "It just happened so close and I'm not the only one that's worried," she said justifying her concern. "Another teacher lives in this area, too, and she said no one has any clue as to who killed the man. I'm scared."

"Don't be scared," he said in a quiet, soothing tone as he reached over and placed a hand on her shoulder.

"And what if he comes here, Cyrus? Huh? What

then?" Her tone quickly rising in intensity. "What if he comes here and hurts you? What if he hurts Chris? Then what?"

"That won't happen," he fired back, but not in an angry way.

"A lot of kids at school are talking about it, too," Chris chimed in. "I don't really understand why because much worse things have happened around here than some guy getting stabbed in his garage," he said almost jokingly "I don't even think it's that big of a deal."

"How isn't a big deal?" Sara shot back at Chris. "Did you know that the killer didn't even take anything from the man? All his money was still in his wallet, meaning whoever did this wasn't even trying to rob him. Whoever did it just wanted to kill him."

Just as Cyrus was about to speak, Sara piped up again, "That's why I'm scared."

Chris turned to his mom. "They also found another body a few days before or so I heard," Chris added. "My friend said it happened a couple blocks from his house the other night."

Sara's attention turned to Chris.

"They found a guy in an alleyway near a bar," Chris continued as if he was telling a ghost story. "He was also stabbed."

"Stop trying to scare your mother," Cyrus jumped in.

"I'm not!" He shouted at Cyrus.

"If it was near a bar, it's likely he just got into a fight with someone there and it didn't go well for him," Cyrus explained in an attempt to try and lessen the tension in the room.

"Cyrus-," Sara started before being cut off.

"There's no need to be scared. I will protect you...I will protect both of you," Cyrus said in a reassuring manner.

"What if you can't?" She asked.

"That's not an option," he responded.

"What if something happens? What if you're at work?" She shot back in frustration.

Sara and Chris were now both firmly focused on Cyrus.

"How can you say that when you can't be by both of our sides 24/7," she said as she looked Cyrus dead in the eyes.

He put his hand on hers. "You are my family," he said as he looked at Sara and then at Chris. "I love you both. I would never let anything happen to either of you. I promise."

She stood up, and as she hugged Cyrus tears started streaming down her face.

"I'm sorry. I didn't mean to attack you like that. I have just been on edge. I'm scared. This has just been a lot. I'm really sorry," she said as she squeezed Cyrus tightly.

"Hey, it's fine," he replied as he pulled his head back to look her in the eyes. "Everything is going to be fine."

5

"**NO**, no, no, no," Cyrus said as he flipped through the TV channels. "There's never anything good to watch." Full from dinner, he just wanted to lay there, maybe roll onto his stomach, and never get up.

He threw his legs up onto the couch and laid down.

"Feet off the couch," Sara said pushing his feet off the couch before making her way into the kitchen.

"I'm bored," Cyrus complained. "Maybe we should rent a movie or something?"

"Like what? Sara asked upon returning to the living room with a glass of water.

"I don't know. Anything I guess. You pick," he said before flipping through the channels again.

She flung her hand up toward Cyrus "Wait, stop!"

"What? You want to watch this?" He asked.

"Yeah, I love this movie," she said.

He clicked on the information button and it brought up the title, ***Nights in the City***. "Well, this sounds interesting," he said in a sarcastic manner. "What's it about?"

"A hooker," she answered.

Letting out a laugh, Cyrus replied, "A hooker?"

"Yeah, you know, a prostitute," she answered.

"Oh, well now this movie sounds even more interesting!" He laughed as he was about to change the channel.

She turned to him, "No! I'm serious! It's about a girl that ends up on the streets at a young age. It's sad. Leave it here, please."

A man smacked the prostitute in the movie. "Well, that guy is just plain rude," he said jokingly.

"Well, yeah, she's a prostitute. That's part of the movie. It shows how poorly they're treated and how society views them," she explained. "Nobody really cares enough to do anything about it. It motivates the girl to get away from it all."

Just then, Cyrus got an idea. He stood up and hurried into the kitchen.

"What are you doing?" Sara shouted after him.

Opening a drawer, he pulled out a pair of latex gloves and put them in his pocket. Just as his wife rounded the corner, he pulled out his phone and pretended to hang it up.

"Cyrus, what are you doing?" She asked again.

He pushed by her and headed toward the front

door, where he slid on his shoes. "I just got called in to work," he said as he swung the door open and walked out.

"What?" She shouted to him out the door, but he was already halfway to his car.

"I'll be right back!" He yelled as he got into the car and pulled out of the driveway.

Cyrus drove down the road, turning corner after corner until he ended up on a highway. His phone rang in his pocket, but he chose to ignore it. A short while later, he was back off the highway. He pulled up to a red light and stopped.

Water dripped from the roofs of houses and the street gutters were lined with garbage. The streets were silent, hanging back in the night as if the sounds of the city had been muted.

The light turned green and he pulled forward, driving slowly down the road. He was driving through an area of the city he'd only heard about from friends. Bars lined the sidewalks, and the only people outside were creeped back in alleys, only visible by the whites of their eyes.

He stopped at another red light. Aside from a few stray cars making their way through the darkness, the streets were barren. He heard a noise and shifted his glance to the side window. A ragged-looking man with a long, grease-filled beard emerged from an alley and was making his way toward his car. He looked back up at the light. Still red. As he looked down to make sure the doors were locked, the light turned green. He placed his foot on the gas and sped away, leaving the homeless-looking man on the side of the street in his wake.

He turned down a road that held a little more life. This road was lined with bars and what he believed to be small clubs. There were a few people standing outside of bars smoking cigarettes and talking. Slowing down, he took a thorough look around the sides of the street until someone caught his eye. He pulled up a little further down the road, passing a bar.

Coming to a stop, he cracked his window. "Hey, are you...," he stopped not sure how to ask what was on his mind.

"Yes, I am," the woman outside the window answered. She put her arm halfway into the window. "Are you looking for some company?" She asked with a big smile. Her long blonde hair flowed into the window.

Cyrus looked back and forth around his car to see if anyone was watching. "Yes, I am," he answered somewhat shakily.

He pushed the button on the door and unlocked it. Cyrus nudged the door open, and the woman climbed into the car and sat down.

"You look a little shaky," she noted as she placed her hand on his leg. "First time?"

"No, it's not my first time," he responded nervously.

"Oh, so you do this often then, huh?" She asked as a large grin formed from ear to ear.

"Wait, you mean this?" He asked. "I've never done this before, I'm married," he immediately got angry with himself. *She didn't need to know that I'm married.*

"That's fine, we get married guys a lot," she assured

him. "There seem to be a lot of unhappy men around looking for something new."

"No, that's not it at all," he replied as he put his foot on the gas and started driving, all the while looking too see if anyone had noticed her get into his car.

"Oh, why are you out here then?" She asked thinking she was clever.

As he glanced at her, a smile returned to his face. "To have some fun of course," he said.

"Well, then you came to the right place," she replied cheekily.

They pulled up and down a few roads before she broke the silence. "So, where are we going?"

"I'm not sure. A motel or something," he muttered. "Isn't that what we are supposed to do?"

"Well, I know a few," she responded. "If you turn right here," she pointed down the road.

"Well, it has to be one where no one will see us," Cyrus insisted.

"Oh... don't want anyone to see us. I get it," she responded. "Turn down this road and go all the way down to the end," she added pointing her finger at a small back road.

He turned down the road she pointed at and drove slowly, looking at each side of the road.

"I don't see anything," he said.

"Well, it's not on this road. Turn right at this road here," she said pointing at another side road. The road opened up into a normal-looking city area.

"Okay, right there," she said pointing at a small

hotel with a big neon sign that read, ***The Rest Inn**.*

"Here?" He asked in a confused tone since it clearly wasn't the backwater motel that he was expecting.

"Yeah, it's not so big that people will see us, but it's also not small enough that we are the only ones there. Plus, it's pretty cheap for a room. Good, huh?" She replied.

As he stepped out of the car, his phone started to ring. He looked at it, then put it back in his pocket.

"The wife?" She asked.

He just looked at her, then ducked back into the car. Cyrus had no interest in discussing his wife with a prostitute. He fished around in the back seat until he found a hat and put it on, before stepping back out onto the road.

"You really don't want anyone to recognize you, do you?" She laughed.

Once again, Cyrus didn't respond. They walked up onto the sidewalk toward the front door before coming to a halt. The inside of the inn was swarming with people. He also noticed a few cameras.

"I thought you said this place wasn't filled with people," he said with a hint of frustration in his voice.

"Well, there aren't that many," she responded.

"I don't feel comfortable with this," he said as he turned around and headed back to the car.

"What do you mean?" She rushed after him.

"I need privacy," he said. "I'm having sex with a prostitute for crying out loud." He opened his car door. "I don't want people to see me, and my wife knows a lot of people," he explained.

"All right, all right," she climbed back into the car and sat down with Cyrus. "I know another place we can go to," she said.

"You also knew this place," he fired back.

"Well, this one is different," she explained. "It's actually a friend's house, so no one will see us."

"A friend's house?" He asked showing his irritation.

"Well, fine, it's my house," she responded.

"Are you sure you want to go to your house?" He asked sounding concerned.

It seemed like a rather stupid idea, but how smart could he expect a prostitute to be.

"Well, you seem nice enough," she noted. "I suppose I can trust you. You don't look like the stealing type, not that I have anything worth stealing," she laughed.

After driving down the road for a while, passing building after building, they reached a part of town that looked even worse than the area in which he'd found her.

"There's my house," she said pointing at a large rundown apartment building.

Cyrus wasn't the least bit surprised at the state of the building in which she lived. He had thought she looked really bad, even for a hooker. The black dress she had on was all torn up and dirty, and he was surprised that he was able to tolerate the smells she filled the car with.

They made their way into the building and up a flight of stairs. The walls were cracked and tinted yellow from who knows what. There were marks on the ceiling from what appeared to be water trying to leak through. The place was just as he had imagined. His biggest concern now was what her apartment would smell like. He could only imagine it was even worse than her.

They reached the third floor and entered her apartment. It was just as much of a dump as the rest of the building. Cyrus wondered if she had ever contemplated giving the place a clean. For a second, he thought he saw a rat scurry across the floor, but it was just a cat.

"Well, this is it. Home sweet home," she muttered.

"Yeah, really sweet," he replied sarcastically.

After closing the door, she turned around, wrapped her arms around him, and began to kiss him. She moved her hands up and down, teasing him, and rubbing his body. Not wanting to kiss her, he pulled away in disgust. She looked a bit shocked.

"Where's the bed?" He asked.

She grabbed his hand. "In here," she said as she guided him into another room.

Slowly, she laid down on the bed and slid her pointer finger into her mouth in a feeble attempt to be sexy. Refusing to even acknowledge her attempt to seduce him, Cyrus began pacing back and forth.

What do you want to do to me?" She asked him with a big smile as she slowly rubbed her legs together.

Cyrus continued pacing around, whispering to himself. "What are you going to do? What are you going to do? What are you going to do?"

She looked at him with a blank stare, wondering

Sadistic

what he was doing. "So what do you want to do?" She asked as she sat back up.

Ignoring her again, he continued to pace around, repeatedly whispering to himself, "What are you going to do?"

"Hey!" She said a little bit louder, but still no success as he continued to pace back and forth.

She'd finally had enough and shouted, "C'mon! What the Fuck! What the hell is this?!"

"I'm thinking!" He shouted back at her as he threw up his hands in frustration. "Wait! I got it!" He exclaimed before she had a chance to say anything.

As she stared back at him with a half-smile, he climbed on top of her, leaned her back, and looked her up and down.

"You like what you see?" She caught him looking her up and down. "Then, why do we still have our clothes on?" She said in a sexy voice, but Cyrus refused to acknowledge her.

Reaching into his pocket, he pulled out the latex gloves and put them on.

"What the hell are those for?" She shouted at him in an alarmed tone.

Ignoring her, Cyrus started rubbing his hands up and down her body. Pressing on her chest, he ran his fingers across her breasts and down to her thighs.

She reached out slowly and said, "Listen, I don't know what this is."

It turns me on, okay," he quickly responded.

"What does?" She asked her gaze firmly fixated on

his hands.

He reached over and pulled a blanket over her body. Leaning in an upwards direction, she placed her hands on his sides to push him off and say something, but before she could he lunged forward and tightly wrapped his hands around her neck.

She flailed from side-to-side in an attempt to escape his grasp, but Cyrus held her down with a firm grip. Loudly, she gasped for air as she tried to push him off her, but she was held down by the blanket Cyrus had placed on her. She twisted back and forth, pulling and tugging at the bed. Desperate for air, she frantically shook her head. Her gasps grew ever quieter as his grip on her thin neck tightened. She stopped fighting back and stared at him with what little energy she had left. She gave one last half-hearted attempt to push him away before her arms fell limp onto the bed and life escaped her.

He still didn't release his grip as her face turned pale, squeezing even tighter now that there was nothing pushing back. He gave one final jerk of her neck before letting her go.

Leaning back, Cyrus admired the woman's cold, pale face as it stared up at the ceiling. He stood up and stepped back, his gaze never leaving her eyes.

He felt a strong vibration on his leg, and upon looking at his pocket he realized he had an incoming call. Pulling out the phone, he looked at it. His wife was calling again. Seven missed calls. He looked up from the phone to the dead body lying on the bed.

Backing up into the wall, he slid to the floor

trembling. *What am I doing here?* Placing his hands on his head, he clenched down hard. *Why am I here?* The conversation with his wife earlier about her being scared shot back into his mind as he clenched down harder on his head. *I'm doing this while my wife is at home scared....of me.* A tear dropped from his eye as he grasped with what he had become. *She's afraid of me.* He started smacking himself in the head, then wiped his arm across his eyes to clear away the tears.

Cyrus stood up and blinked a few times in an attempt to regain his composure before making his way over to the bed. The black and blue marks from his fingers went all the way around her neck, sticking out like a new diamond necklace. He lifted his hands up and examined them. They were sweaty, but he still had his latex gloves on. He walked over to the side of the bed to where her head was resting.

What have I become? Grabbing the blanket, he lifted it up to cover the remainder of the body. He dragged his arm across his face to wipe away the remaining tears.

Cyrus placed his hand on her chest almost as if to say goodbye before rushing out of the apartment. Turning back around, he opened the door and reached around to lock it before closing it again, figuring it would buy him some time before anyone went in and found the body.

He got into his car and froze. *What if I were to get caught? My family…everything would be gone.* He stepped on the gas and sped away from the dingy apartment. *I can't...I don't know.*

He drove as fast as he could, weaving in and out of the small amount of traffic that was out at this time of night. Cyrus knew he had to get back to his wife as soon as possible. He flew through red lights and didn't stop at stop signs, and hoped against hope that a police officer wouldn't happen to drive by until he reached his driveway.

Cyrus pulled into the driveway and got out, slowly and silently creeping his way toward the front door. Upon entering the house, he looked around the door to ensure Sara wasn't standing there waiting for him. For a moment, he thought he was in the clear until his wife came storming down the stairs.

"Where the hell did you go?!" She screamed at him. "And don't say work because we both damn well know that you wouldn't be at work this late. Also, you said you'd be right back. Why would you be right back if you were going to work?"

"I was at Dave's," he said. He wondered why he hadn't come up with a more believable story on his way home to cover his tracks.

"Then, what the hell is this?!" She shouted. Reaching into Cyrus's pocket, she pulled out the crinkled up latex gloves he had in his possession.

"If you were at Dave's, what the hell were these for?" She screamed. "You complain about being bored, then you leave, and now you return with latex gloves in your pocket. Didn't you think I'd notice? Next time, closing the drawer that the gloves are in might be a good idea."

As Cyrus began to talk, Sara cut him off. "Tell me you weren't with another woman. Tell me!"

"No! Of course not! Wait…that's what you thought I was doing? Why would I be doing that?" Cyrus said sounding almost relieved. "No, I swear I was really at Dave's. You thought I would leave in the middle of a movie to do that? There is no way I would be out seeing another woman. Never."

"Then, what were the gloves for?" Sara fired back.

"I had to bring them because his drain was clogged," he explained. "His dishwasher was overflowing, which is why I was in such a rush."

"His drain was clogged?" Sara enquired.

"Yes."

"You expect me to believe that?" She asked.

Cyrus wasn't sure what else to say. He just looked at her for what felt like an eternity before nodding his head.

"Fine, I believe you," she said much to his relief. "Only because this was the first time something like this has happened."

"Thank you," he said. He leaned in to give her a kiss, but she lifted her hand up blocking him.

"But, I'm still mad at you for lying," she said with a hint of a smile on her face.

He reached over and pulled her in for a hug. "I can live with that," he said.

Tightly, he squeezed her as she rested her head on his chest. "I'm sorry," he whispered while grazing his fingers across her back.

"You should be," she said in a light-hearted manner as she grabbed him by the arm and led him upstairs. She came to a sudden stop and gave him another hug. "You had me scared," she continued.

"Like I said earlier, babe, there's no need to be scared," he said as he held her firmly around the waist.

Taking hold of Cyrus by the hand, Sara yanked him in the direction of their bedroom. "Well, now you owe me," she said as she closed the bedroom door behind them.

6

HE laid there, staring into his eyelids, exploring the darkness that was his mind. Tossing and turning, he rolled over and then rolled over again, pressing his eyes shut, pushing thoughts away. Images of himself pressing a cold knife deep into someone's body, piercing the skin like butter, played over and over in his head like a broken projector. A smile cracked along his face.

Finally, he sprang to life and opened his eyes, only to experience a new darkness. Aside from a small ray of light pouring in from a street lamp outside the bedroom window, his bedroom was completely filled with darkness.

He rubbed his eyes to help him adjust and glanced to his side, where his wife laid soundly asleep. He dragged his hands across his face and into his hair, and took a deep breath. Slowly, his shirt peeled away from his sweat covered back.

I can't fucking sleep in here, it must be 100 degrees. Getting to his feet, he placed a box fan in the window and cranked it to full blast. *That should do it.* Outside the window, the normally bustling side road was hauntingly quiet. The bed sank under his weight as he sat back down for a moment to contemplate, peering into the darkness. A light flicker caught his attention as it illuminated the wall ever so slightly in the corner of the room.

The floor creaked with each step as he approached the light. He looked back at his wife after every creak until he reached a desk. The dim light flickered in the darkness in front of Cyrus. As he reached toward it, he felt the chill of the cold plastic top of his laptop that sat on the charger. He immediately pulled out the plug, putting out the light that had drawn him there, and made his way back to bed, where his wife was still fast asleep.

Laying the laptop on the bed ever so softly that he wouldn't have noticed it was there had he not been the one that placed it there, he pressed the switch and slowly opened the computer.

I can't sleep, I may as well check my email. As he pressed the power button, the room filled with immense light, forcing him to look away. It was like he was staring gun barrel straight into the headlights of an oncoming car. Quickly, he reached out and closed it, shutting out the blinding light. He looked at his wife to make sure she was still asleep, then tilted the laptop away from her and re-opened it.

His tapping of the keyboard seemed as loud as fireworks. Even the wheel of his mouse sounded louder than normal as he scrolled through his emails. *Spam, spam, spam.* There was nothing of interest. He opened up a search page and stared at it with a blank expression. *Hmmmm.* He began to type slowly. *Mental disorders.* A breath escaped his lungs as he briefly paused and looked back at his sleepy wife once more, before carefully clicking the enter key like he was signing his own death certificate with the simple click of a button.

Hundreds of results popped up on the screen. Mental disorders, eating disorders, and other mental health problems. He clicked on the first link that read, 'Mental disorders from A to Z'. As he scrolled through a long list of complicated scientific terms, he couldn't even pretend to understand all the complex scientific names and the details that came with the disorders, so he clicked the back button, returning to the previous page. Tap, tap, tap…he tapped his finger on the keyboard faster and faster. Cyrus felt drained. He cupped his hands against his face before sluggishly dragging them back down toward the keyboard.

Mental disorders that make you want to kill people, he typed quickly as if someone was about to burst through the door to try and stop him. Once again, the screen was lined with results from top to bottom. He tilted the screen a little bit further away from his wife's potential line of view.

He clicked on a link that read, *'Mental disorders that can cause behavioral issues: Bipolar disorder, Schizophrenia, Obsessive Compulsive Disorder'*. Hearing voices, walking through doors multiple times, and having drastic changes in mood. None of the symptoms associated with the disorders matched how he was feeling. Sure, he sometimes seemed a bit bipolar with his anger, but it wasn't consistent enough to be considered a full-on disorder or was it?

None of them said anything like, "Randomly start wanting to kill people or can't sleep because I want to kill people." The screech of his teeth grinding echoed in his head. His fists clenched as he fought the urge to throw his fist into the computer screen. *Then, what the fuck is wrong with me?*

7

AS he itched his toe with his other foot, he threw the blankets over his face to avoid the sunlight as it urged him to wake up. "Ugh, get out of here," he groaned as he rolled onto his back and flung his arm over his face.

"What time is it?" He asked as he pulled his arm away from his face.

Rolling over, he noticed that the other side of the bed was empty.

"Babe!" He shouted as he threw his arm back over his face.

"What!" He heard shouting back up to him.

"What are you doing? Come back to bed!" He pleaded.

"No, I'm making breakfast lazy! I have to head into

work soon!" She stated.

He rolled onto his stomach and pulled a pillow over his head.

The belt clanked as he wrapped it around his jeans. He threw on a shirt. The minty toothpaste spread evenly across his toothbrush as he prepared to scrape his teeth clean. Thud, Thud, Thud! He heard a knocking at the door all the way from upstairs.

He paused for a moment, trying to hear who it was at the door. "Babe, who is it?!!" There was no reply. "Babe!" He shouted.

"It's the police!" She shouted back.

He froze as his toothbrush plummeted into the sink. His heart dropped as if it had just been pushed down a well. Spitting out the toothpaste, he stumbled down the stairs as fast as he could, almost tripping himself up in the process.

"What can I help you with, officers?" He asked as he reached the door and saw that Sara had already let them in.

The Detective looked him up and down, then transferred his gaze back to Sara. "As I was telling you, I'm Detective Hughes and this here is Officer Lopez. A beak-in occurred next door last night and we were wondering if you heard or saw anything."

"Oh, no we didn't," Cyrus replied. "We weren't up that late."

"Is that right?" The Detective enquired. "Well, one of Mr. Roberts' kids was certain he heard you pull in late last night," Hughes added.

Just as his wife opened her mouth to say something,

Cyrus cut her off. "Sorry, he must have been mistaken," Cyrus insisted.

The Detective stared at Cyrus for a moment, then turned his attention toward Sara.

"You were about to say something, ma'am?" Detective Hughes asked in a curious tone.

"I was just going to say that, yes, we were sleeping," Sara said causing Cyrus to breathe a mental sigh of relief.

"Sorry for bothering you folks, there was a break in a few blocks down; turned out it was some guy looking for drugs." the Detective said. "If you see or hear anything, please give us a call."

They were about to make their way out the door when Cyrus shouted, "Wait! Weren't you the cop on the TV doing the thing about the murder a few blocks from here?" Detective Hughes didn't dignify Cyrus with a response.

"I saw the stuff on the TV about the murders." Hughes looked at Cyrus with a curious expression on his face. "It's just that it has my wife and her friends all worked up," Cyrus continued. "Any luck catching the person? Any clues as to who it may be?" Cyrus asked.

The Detective looked at Cyrus, then Sara before finally returning his focus back to Cyrus. "We aren't at liberty to discuss that case," the Detective said. "Have a nice day."

"You too," Cyrus muttered as he closed the door behind them.

"Well, that was weird," Sara said. "I hope they're

okay."

Cyrus nodded his head.

"Why did you cut me off?" She asked.

"Cut you off?" He answered.

"Yeah, you cut me off just as I was about to mention that you had to go to your friends and got home late, but you interrupted me. Why?" She demanded curiously.

"Because it didn't matter," Cyrus answered before walking into the kitchen and turning on the tap.

"It didn't matter? How didn't it matter?" She asked as Cyrus opened the cupboard and grabbed a cup.

Cyrus turned off the water and slammed the cupboard shut. "What difference would it have made if I'd told him I got home late?" Cyrus enquired. "All it would have resulted in was them treating us like we were suspects. Nothing positive would have come out of it!" He exclaimed.

She stomped her feet as she marched into the living room and hopped onto the couch. Cyrus took a big gulp of water before following her into the living room. He looked at Sara as if to ask for permission, then took a seat next to her on the couch.

"Maybe we should go and see if everything is okay," Sara said as she rested her head on Cyrus's shoulder.

Cyrus placed his arm around her and rubbed her arm. "Yeah, I'll go check it out in a little bit," he said. "They're probably still sorting things out with the police, so it's best that we not interrupt."

Finally, Sara stopped on a horror channel and

started to get into a movie that was playing. A man was trying to find a way to get out of a psychiatric ward, and was stuck at the end of a hallway as the guards slowly moved in on him.

"Hey, now this movie has got me thinking," Sara said. "What was that stuff on your computer this morning all about?" Her curiosity at an all-time high.

A big gulp made its way down his throat "What stuff?" He asked all the while hoping against hope that she wasn't talking about what he thought she was talking about.

"It was something about mental disorders," she explained.

He looked at her for a moment. "You know, I think it said something about bipolar disorder and I'm pretty sure there was also something about schizophrenia," she added.

Cyrus almost bit the inside of his mouth. He couldn't believe he'd fallen asleep before shutting down his computer; what a stupid move.

"Oh, yeah, my friend told me to look it up for him because he thought someone from work was acting like they had one of those disorders," he explained.

"Honestly, I think he was just joking," Cyrus added as a single drop of sweat trickled down the back of his neck. He was hoping like hell that his explanation would see the conversation come to an end.

"You and your friends are weird," she said as her head fell back down onto his shoulder.

Close call. Have to stop messing up like that. Messing up?

What exactly was he messing up?

He wasn't sure if she'd believed his story or she just wasn't in the mood for an argument, but either way he was glad she had let the issue slide.

"Ugh," Sara muttered.

Cyrus's nervousness came rushing back to his stomach.

"What's that?" He asked hesitatingly.

"I have to go in to work soon," she said as she rose to her feet.

"I was actually wondering why you were still home," he responded noticing the time on his watch.

She stood up and stretched her arms. "Yeah, the kids had an assembly this morning, so they said I could come in a little later today if I wanted. I couldn't pass it up," she said.

"I don't blame you," Cyrus replied.

"When do you have to be in today?" Cyrus asked. "I have to be in soon, too," he continued sounding unenthused. "Since I was in late last night, I didn't have to be in really early this morning, but I need to go in today to get my schedule back on track."

"Hey, it's better than doing another late shift, right?" Sara reminded him.

"Yeah, I guess you're right," he conceded. "It was actually kind of relaxing working the late shift. It was peaceful."

"Well, if you like it so much why don't you switch shifts?" She mockingly suggested.

"Nah, I'm good," he smiled.

"Well, I'm going to get ready for work," Sara said as

Sadistic

she made her way out the room.

There was a knock on the door as Sara walked by.

"Now what?" Cyrus groaned as he rose to his feet.

As Sara opened the door, Cyrus stepped in front of her.

"Hey," the man at the door said.

"Oh, hey, Adam," Cyrus responded as he simultaneously moved over to allow Adam inside.

"Hello, Adam," Sara said.

"Sorry," Adam said as he brushed by Cyrus.

"No, it's quite all right. Just glad you aren't the cops again," Cyrus laughed.

"Yeah, sorry about that," Adam said as Cyrus closed the door behind him.

"Not your fault," he said. "So, how is everything over there?" Cyrus enquired.

"Well, they didn't take anything," Adam responded.

"Really?"

"Yeah, that's the weird part," Adam continued.

"I hate to leave like this, but I need to go to work," Sara interrupted.

Quickly, Sara quickly headed up the stairs before returning with a bag of school-related items.

"Well, have fun today," Cyrus said before kissing her on the cheek.

"Oh, I will," she said as she stepped out the door.

"Have a nice day, Sara," Adam chimed in.

As she closed the door behind her, Cyrus signaled Adam into the living room. "Want to sit down?" Cyrus asked as he walked toward the couch.

"Sure," Adam said taking a seat.

"So, they didn't take anything?" Cyrus said returning to the initial topic of conversation.

"No, they didn't come into any of our rooms either," Adam explained.

Cyrus rubbed his mustache and looked at Adam. "I'm honestly not sure what to make of that," Cyrus added.

"Neither were the police," Adam responded. "They suspect that whatever he was looking for was in one of the bedrooms, and he didn't want to risk going in and waking one of us up so he just left."

"Well, that doesn't make much sense to me," Cyrus replied. "If whatever they were looking for was in one of your rooms they must have foreseen the possibility that you all would be home, so why not break in when you guys are at work?"

"To be honest, I have no idea what they may have been looking for," Adam added.

They both sat there for a moment trying to make sense of the situation.

"The only thing I can think of is that whoever broke into the house realized they had the wrong house," Adam said shrugging his shoulders.

"Wrong house?" Cyrus stared at him blankly.

"Yeah, I mean it would somewhat make sense and explain why they didn't take anything, but at the same time it doesn't seem feasible that you'd break into the wrong house in the first place. Like, wouldn't you plan these things out?" Adam reasoned.

"You would think so, wouldn't you?" Cyrus

responded nodding his head. "Well you're all safe, which is the most important thing," he added.

"Yeah, I guess you're right," Adam agreed.

"Things could've been worse," Cyrus continued.

"Yeah, it could have been whoever got that other guy," Adam said.

"What other guy?" Cyrus asked sounding confused, but deep down he knew what Adam was talking about.

"The one that got stabbed in his garage," Adam said like he was letting Cyrus in on a big secret. "The cops don't seem to think it was a family member that stabbed him."

Adam now had Cyrus's full attention. "What do you mean?" Cyrus asked.

"Well, they asked me a few questions about it, such as whether I'd ever met or spoken to the guy that was killed, which I hadn't," Adam responded.

Cyrus looked at Adam, waiting for him to continue.

"They said at this stage they weren't going to rule anything out and reminded me to keep my doors locked at all times," Adam explained. "And, they asked me if I had a weapon anywhere in the house that I could use as protection. I told them no and they suggested that I should get one. They said you can never be too careful, but they were clearly a bit worried," Adam said his tone growing graver by the second.

"Yeah, getting a weapon would probably be a good idea," Cyrus said not sure what else to say. Had they found something at the scene of the crime that made them think it was someone other than a family member?

Had he dropped something while he was there? Perhaps that explains why Detective Hughes was so quick to dismiss his questions about the incident. Maybe they had a lead or perhaps they didn't want to discuss the matter because they had no solid leads at all. Cyrus hated the situation he was in. He hated not knowing.

"I just hope they catch this bastard so we can have some peace," Adam said. "This is causing way too much drama for one simple murder, but I guess it isn't that simple which is why they're making a big deal out of it."

"Or maybe they aren't," Cyrus chimed in bringing Adam to attention. "Maybe we're the ones turning it into something it's not."

"Maybe," Adam muttered.

"I'm sure they will figure it out," Cyrus said in a meager attempt to reassure Adam. "I mean that is what they're paid to do."

"They said they're going to be keeping an eye out," Adam replied. "More police patrols and stuff like that."

"Well, I should probably get going," Adam said noticing the time on his watch.

"Yeah, I have to get ready and head to work soon," Cyrus said rising to his feet. "I'll stop by sometime and see how things are going, all right?" Cyrus added.

"Sounds good," Adam said as he opened the door. "Cya, man."

"Cya," Cyrus closed the door behind him, then just stood there.

Cyrus wished there was some way he could find out what the police knew, but he couldn't think of a way in which to get ahold of the information he needed. He didn't know any cops, and it wasn't like he could walk into a police station and ask them what they knew.

Looking at the time, Cyrus realized he had to be out of the house in less than 20 minutes. Hurrying upstairs, he climbed into the shower. As he scrubbed his hair, he couldn't get the police investigation out of his mind. What if he left a finger print on something or a piece of his hair fell out during the struggle?

As he looked down, he saw blood rinsing into the drain. He jumped back in shock and looked at his body, but he didn't see any blood on himself. Upon looking down at the drain, he noticed there was no blood in sight. The blood was in his head, just like his need to kill. Everything was in his head. He was seeing the blood because it was what he wanted to see.

Stepping out of the shower, he wiped the misty layer of water off the mirror and examined his reflection. It was his reflection, but was it even him anymore? His reflection stared back at him, making him sick to his stomach, but if he was so disgusted in himself why was he still smiling?

If the cops were going to start targeting him, then he had to start working harder. He had to be one step ahead of the police at all times. He needed to be careful. No mistakes could be made.

Cyrus pulled up to work and punched in with no time to spare. He walked to his desk and sat down in his chair.

"Hey, man," Dave said.

"Hey," Cyrus replied as he turned on his computer.

"Joe's on the rampage today," Dave said. "I've already seen him yell at two people today and I've only been here for 30 minutes."

Just what he needed, a cranky boss. "Hopefully he stays away from us," Cyrus replied.

Cyrus reached for a file and started glancing through some papers. Out the corner of his eye, he spotted Joe on the warpath doing his typical pissed off walk. He gathered himself in readiness to take on Joe, but Joe walked right past him and stopped at someone else's desk about 10 feet away. *Yes, thank you.*

Cyrus heard the beginning of what sounded like a heated argument, but he wasn't sure what it was about. He was just happy he wasn't smack bang in the middle of it. There was far too much on his mind today to deal with Joe.

A few minutes later, his phone started vibrating. It was Sara. He pulled out his phone and tilted his head down so it wouldn't be obvious to anyone that walked by that he was on the phone.

"Yeah, what's up?" He whispered.

"Nothing, how's work?" Sara asked.

"It's fine. Joe's on the rampage so I can't really talk," Cyrus said.

"Okay, well I was just wondering what Adam said after I left," Sara continued.

"He was just saying that whoever broke into his house didn't take anything and the police weren't sure what to make of it," Cyrus replied. He didn't want to tell her everything he knew because he was sure it would alarm her. "They just think that they were afraid to wake them up, so they left before they took anything," he added.

"That's it?" She asked.

"That's it," Cyrus answered.

"All right, well let me know if you hear anything else," Sara said. "I'll see you tonight, honey."

"All right, love you," Cyrus said peeking around to make sure Joe wasn't nearby.

"Love you, too," she said as they hung up simultaneously.

He didn't like lying to her. Well, he didn't really lie. He just didn't tell her everything, even though lying seemed like something he was getting good at.

"What was that?" Dave turned around.

"What was what?" Cyrus asked even though he knew deep down that Dave must have overheard the conversation with his wife.

"There were police at your house? Someone broke in?" Dave asked in a concerned tone.

"No, someone broke into my neighbor's house," Cyrus corrected him.

"Oh, all right," Dave responded.

"Yeah, it's no big deal," Cyrus said as he turned back around in his chair. He didn't really feel like discussing the matter further. To be honest, he didn't feel like talking at all.

Sliding his hand into his desk, he pulled out a blank sheet of paper. *No one around*. He glanced over his shoulder at Dave who was also typing away at his keyboard. *Coast looks clear*.

He looked down at the blank piece of paper. *Okay, hmm.* He placed the pen at the top line of the paper, then paused for a brief moment before looking around again. The coast was still clear. He wrote *latex gloves* on the first line. *Cleaner* went on the second line. Popping his head up, he looked around again. Still clear. He felt paranoid, but there was nowhere else to do this. What else would he need? Cyrus needed to start being more cautious. He had to prepare. He had to get gloves so his wife wouldn't notice that gloves were going missing. If she did, he would have to come up with a logical explanation as to why they were suddenly vanishing.

What else would he need? He had never had to think about this before, and didn't think it would be this difficult. Maybe a better knife; his old pocket knife was starting to get dull. *Chloroform*; he wasn't even sure where to get that. *Garbage bags, rags, towels, shirts, pants.* He didn't want to ruin his perfectly good clothes.

"Hey, man, what you doing?" Dave asked startling Cyrus.

"Nothing, I'm just making a shopping list for later," Cyrus answered as he tucked the list into his pocket.

"I don't do the shopping at my house," Dave laughed. "Anyways, do you want to grab something for lunch?" He asked. All I have are leftovers from last night and they don't exactly taste that good."

"No, I'm not really hungry today," he said much to the disappointment of Dave.

"All right, man. Next time then," he said as he headed back to his desk and sat down.

Turning back around, Cyrus grabbed the piece of

paper and un-crumpled it. *Duct tape. Rope. Scissors.* He wasn't sure if he'd need any of those things, but like Detective Hughes told Adam, better safe than sorry.

8

I suppose I should just start at the top of the list. He told Sara he would be stopping off at the store, so before he arrived home he would need to grab a few groceries.

Latex gloves were at the top of the list. The supermarket wasn't far from City Hall, so that's where he was heading. Cyrus felt like a child picking up supplies for his first day of school.

He parked in the back of the parking lot as though he felt guilty, even though nothing he was buying would be considered illegal. Still, no need to draw attention to himself.

Grabbing a cart, he made his way up an aisle all the while looking at his shopping list. Latex gloves and cleaner were at the top of the list followed by chloroform. Now that he was giving it more thought, where could he even get chloroform? He doubted he could get it at the supermarket. Maybe that was something that was best ordered online.

He headed up the aisles in search of the sign that said, *Cleaning Supplies*. Finally, he found it. *Latex gloves, latex gloves where are you?* He finally found them. There were more kinds to choose from than he expected. There were even latex gloves that weren't made from latex, and there were some with powder in them to prevent the latex from rubbing your hands or drying them out. *Hmmm.*

Cyrus grabbed the cheapest ones available and tossed them into his cart. He looked up the aisle to spot the cleaners. Floor cleaner, counter cleaner, wood cleaner, glass cleaner, but no blood cleaner. Things were never that easy.

An all-purpose cleaner caught his eye, but would it do the job? Cleans all surfaces, removing tough grease, and other hard to remove substances. It looked good enough, so he placed it in his cart. What's next?

As he walked down the aisle, he almost bumped into someone that was entering the aisle.

"Sorry, excuse me," the man said.

"Oh hey, Detective Hughes, right?" Cyrus asked with a lump forming in the back of his throat.

"Yes, and you're that guy that lived next door to where that robbery occurred, correct?" Hughes enquired.

"That's me," Cyrus said as he tried to make his way past Hughes.

"What have you got there?" Hughes asked stopping Cyrus in his tracks.

"Nothing really, just doing some shopping," Cyrus explained as Hughes examined the contents of his cart.

"You have some cleaning to do at home?" Hughes asked. "Gloves, that sounds like the type of cleaning I wouldn't want to do," he continued.

"Yeah, it's not going to be fun, the dog made a mess," Cyrus muttered. He didn't want to continue talking to Hughes. He just wanted to keep walking.

"Yeah, dogs can be messy," Hughes admitted. "Is this all you're getting?" Hughes asked continuing his interrogation.

"No, I'm going to grab some food," Cyrus answered quickly. "But, I really should get going. My wife is waiting for me at home. Don't want to make her mad."

"Yeah, the wife being mad is never a good thing," Hughes nodded.

Cyrus just nodded back in agreement and started walking. What could be worse than bumping into that guy, and what was with the million questions? He looked back over his shoulder at Hughes walking in the other direction.

He left the aisle and hurried away. Once he felt like he was a safe distance away from Hughes, he retrieved his list. *Okay, skipping chloroform for now. Garbage bags, rags, towels, shirts, pants, duct tape, rope, scissors.* He should probably purchase some of these things at different stores so as to not arouse suspicion.

As he passed the main aisle, he spotted a display of garbage bags, so he grabbed a box and placed them in the cart before heading down the aisle. All he needed to get now was some bread, sandwich meat, and mustard for his wife's work lunches.

Since this was the cheapest place he knew in town, he started looking around for some clothes. What clothes should he get?

As he made his way through the clothing aisle, he saw some black long sleeve shirts which seemed perfect. There were also some cheap black dress pants nearby. *Perfect.*

He headed to the register and got in line. The contents of his cart looked weird or did they just look weird to him? Cleaning supplies and sandwiches were a quirky combination. Looking around, he saw Hughes approaching. *Please don't stop. Don't get in my line.* Hughes got in his line.

"I see you've finished your shopping. Making some sandwiches?" Hughes asked in a light-hearted manner.

Stop laughing. "Yeah, for lunch," Cyrus said as he slowly inched his way forward in the line.

"Must be fun cleaning up a dog mess after work, where do you work anyways?" Hughes enquired.

"Yeah, it's not something I want to do, but sometimes life sucks," Cyrus replied ignoring Hughes's question about his occupation. He didn't need to know the ins and outs of his life.

The person in front of Cyrus finished, and he stepped forward to place his items on the register belt. Cyrus did his best to not continue the conversation with Hughes, avoiding eye contact as he waited for the cashier to ring up his items.

The cashier finished ringing up his items and Cyrus paid for them. He placed the bags in his cart and hurried away, completely ignoring Hughes's goodbyes.

As he placed the bags in the trunk of his car, he noticed Hughes exiting the store, so he hurried into his car and pulled out. Cyrus felt like Hughes was on his trail, but why would he be after him? He had to get such thoughts out of his head.

He still needed to purchase rags, towels, duct tape, rope, and scissors. To avoid suspicion, he decided to get the rope separate at a home improvement store. After purchasing the rope, he remembered there was another store on his way home where he could grab the remaining items on his list.

Cyrus got the items on his way home and hurried back to his house. He had been gone longer than he had planned and was concerned that his wife would bombard him with questions upon his arrival.

He pulled into the driveway and parked his car. After popping open the trunk and grabbing the groceries, he stared at the remainder of the items he'd purchased. He couldn't bring them in now. There was no way he could possibly explain the random bag of items to his wife.

Cyrus opened the door and walked into the house. "Babe! I'm home!" He shouted as he peeked into the kitchen and then the living room looking for Sara.

Cyrus placed the bag on the counter top and opened it up. "I got the bread and the sandwich meat!" He exclaimed.

After putting the meat away, Cyrus made his way upstairs. Upon nudging the bedroom door open, he noticed that his wife was sleeping soundly; this was not a usual occurrence. Never in their time together had he come home to her sleeping. She must have had a rough day at work. Since his wife was asleep, perhaps he should take his time and bring in the bag of items. He crept down the stairs, and just as he was about to open the door and go back outside, he heard the bedroom door creak open behind him.

"Sorry, babe, I was asleep," Sara said as she grabbed the railing and headed down the stairs.

"Yeah, I noticed. Hard day at work?" He asked stepping away from the door.

"No, I'm just more tired than usual I guess," she answered as she yawned and laid on the couch.

"I got the things you wanted," Cyrus said.

"Oh, great, thanks," Sara responded.

Cyrus jogged up the stairs and headed into his bedroom to get changed. He placed his pants on the dresser next to the bed and tossed his shirt on top. Opening the dresser, he pulled out some shorts and a t-shirt. After putting them on, he headed back downstairs.

"So, is everything good with Adam?" Sara enquired.

"Yeah, they think it was just a nervous burglar," Cyrus answered.

"Well, they're lucky," Sara replied. "Nervous burglars are why a lot of home invasions end up with someone getting killed. A nervous idiot gets trigger happy."

"Yeah, you're probably right," Cyrus agreed as he leaned back in his reclining chair and crossed his feet.

"Ooooh, this movie looks good," Cyrus said upon landing on a movie displaying a few people laughing around a fire.

"I can't get too comfortable, I have to go out to the garden soon," Sara said.

"Why?" He asked.

"I don't know why, but for some reason some of the plants by the porch are starting to die," she responded. "I might have to dig them up and move them somewhere else. I am not sure yet."

"Is it just those plants that are dying?" He asked hoping she would say no.

In the back of his mind, Cyrus knew why the plants were dying. What other plausible reason could there be? He dug them up. There was a blood soaked shirt right under them.

"I'm not sure, but I'm going to head out there and have a look as soon as I get the motivation to get up," she said as she leaned back.

Cyrus knew he had to get out there before she did and recover the shirt before it was found, then figure out how to permanently dispose of the evidence. He couldn't let this issue linger any longer.

How was he going to get outside without her knowing? Sitting there for a moment trying to conjure up a solution to his dilemma, his lips began to crack as nothing sprang to mind. He ground his teeth while thinking until he noticed Sara getting to her feet.

He jumped to his feet. "You know what?" He said

as he walked over to Sara. "Maybe you don't have to tear them up," he added.

"Why?" She asked.

"Well, I know there's a lot of things you can use to help save plants," he said. "I see commercials about them all the time." It was the best lie he could come up with on the spot.

"Yeah, maybe," she hesitatingly agreed.

"I'd head to the store and have a look, but you know more about plants than me," he said.

"Who's going to make dinner then?" She asked.

"Me, of course. By the way, where's Chris?" Cyrus replied.

"He'll be back later tonight from a friend's place," Sara answered. "Just make whatever."

"I'll just make spaghetti," Cyrus said smiling.

"All right, then, I will be back soon," Sara responded.

"Hurry back, babe," Cyrus said giving her a kiss as she headed toward the door. She put on her shoes and made her way out the door. He looked out the window as she headed to her car, hopped in, and started the engine. After he was sure she was out of view, he hurried to his car to grab a pair of latex gloves. He had only had them for a couple of hours and already had a need for them.

As soon as he reached the house, he made his way into the yard and headed straight to the garden. He had no time to waste. To him, the plants all looked fine but he wasn't the one that was responsible for them. Gently, he slid his hands into the soil at the point where he'd buried the shirt and lifted up the handful of plants, setting them aside.

Cyrus didn't see a shirt. He pushed dirt from side-to-side, but still nothing. *Fuck*. He must have forgotten exactly where in the garden he'd buried the shirt. Picking the flowers back up, he placed them back in the hole, patted them down, and then reached to the side of them and buried his hands once more. He lifted the plants up and once again didn't see anything. *What the hell*. He pushed the dirt around and didn't find anything. He wanted to puke.

After putting the flowers back and moving to the other side, Cyrus gently placed his hands into the soil and lifted up some plants. This time, he could see the end of a piece of cloth protruding from the dirt. As he buried his hands in deeper, he pulled out the shirt. It was still covered with dark red blood stains.

Cyrus took a deep sigh of relief as he placed the shirt next to him. He tossed the plant back in and rose to his feet, grabbing the shirt. Now, what was he going to do with the shirt?

The only way he could think of getting rid of the evidence once and for all was to burn the shirt. Heading inside, he grabbed a container of lighter fluid and a box of matches before making his way back outdoors. It was time to finally dispose of this headache.

Without giving it a moment's thought, he tossed the shirt on the ground and started dousing it in lighter fluid. After taking one last look around, he lit the match and dropped it onto the shirt, causing the shirt to burst into flames.

The flames reflected off of his gaze as he stared intently into the fire that was ending a small chapter of his sordid story. Once the flame had started to die down, he hosed it with even more lighter fluid so as to not run the risk of leaving behind any evidence of his deadly act.

Cyrus scraped up what little remained of the shirt and ash before placing it into a plastic bag. The door swung shut behind him just as he entered the house. He tossed the bag into the garbage and grabbed the newspaper off the kitchen table, tossing it on top to cover up what remained of the shirt. Exhausted but relieved, he flopped down into the chair. He felt as if he hadn't stopped for a breath in the last half hour.

He felt bad for hiding such things from his wife, but he couldn't exactly tell her what he'd been doing. He always had to be one step ahead of her and two ahead of the police. In a game like this, a single mistake could put his life in jeopardy.

Cyrus wasn't in the mood for making dinner, but he had to. He got up and headed into the kitchen. The water had come to a boil, so he placed the spaghetti in the pot. Sara should be home any minute and would wonder why the food wasn't ready.

Lights flashed into the windows as a car pulled into the driveway. There she was. He heard the car door close and footsteps approach.

"I'm back!" She shouted as she walked into the

house.

"Hey, I'm right here," Cyrus said in response.

"Food done?" She asked.

"Not yet," Cyrus answered.

"Sorry I took so long," she said. "The people at the store felt compelled to tell me about every possible item instead of just suggesting an item and giving it to me, and let's not forget trying to sell me a hundred other items that I don't really need," she laughed as she sorted through her bag.

"I got this fertilizer grower stuff," she added. "I'm not really sure what it is, but they said it should help." She placed a small container down on the table before heading upstairs.

"I'm going to run to the bathroom, then go outside and put this stuff in the garden," Sara said.

As he stood there stirring the noodles, lost in the cyclone that was made from the spinning water, Sara started back down the stairs and grabbed hold of the container.

"It has all sorts of weird ingredients in it," she said as she looked up at Cyrus who was still stirring the pot. "I hope it's good for all the plants, and not just the flowers."

Cyrus didn't give Sara a response. "Babe, is Chris home yet?" She asked.

He still didn't reply. "Cyrus, is Chris home yet?!?" Sara continued.

"No, sorry," he responded.

"You're in your own little world over there, aren't you?" She asked jokingly.

"I guess so," Cyrus laughed.

She grabbed the container and said, "I'll be right back," then made her way toward the back door.

Picking up the pot, he dumped the noodles into a strainer, then back into the pot. He opened up a cupboard and pulled out a jar of spaghetti sauce, and started pouring it into the pot. Just as he started to stir the sauce in with the noodles, a clearly agitated Sara made her way back into the room.

"What happened to my garden?" She shot a terrible stare in Cyrus's direction.

"What do you mean?" He asked.

"Come with me," she said signaling for him to follow her.

Quickly, they walked out the back door and headed into the yard.

"This!" She shouted pointing at the disaster that was once her lovely garden.

"I moved the flowers around," Cyrus said. "You said you were going to dig them up, so I thought I'd try to see what was wrong."

The condition of the garden wasn't even close to how he remembered leaving it. He put the plants back in their rightful places, and patted down the dirt before taking care of his shirt. He was certain the flowers looked a lot nicer than they did previously. Maybe he was just in too much of a hurry and figured they were all nicely put away, when in reality that wasn't the case.

Now, he couldn't precisely remember what he'd done as he looked back up at his wife's angry face.

"This is what you call helping?" She asked with a hint of anger in her voice.

He felt like a child being yelled at for misbehaving, but after one look at the garden he knew he was deserving of a verbal spray. Kneeling down, Cyrus placed his hand on the dirt in an attempt to rearrange the flowers and make them look nice again, but Sara reached down and stopped him.

"No, it's all right, I'll get it," she said not wanting him to mess it up even more.

Desperate not to get locked into another argument with his wife, he rose to his feet and made his way to the door.

"It smells like someone started a fire out here," Sara noted. "You smell that?" She asked.

"No, I don't smell anything," Cyrus answered quickly in a bid to put her thought to rest.

"Maybe not," she said as she got down on her knees and opened the container. "I'll see you inside in a little while. I'm going to try and fix these plants up a bit."

"All right, see you soon," Cyrus replied as he headed inside.

9

CYRUS punched in and made his way toward his desk. Another day at his meaningless job doing things that no one particularly cared about. He was beginning to wonder if anyone would even notice if he stopped working. If he just sat there daydreaming, would he be called into the office and forced to listen to one of Joe's rants about how we all should be working harder?

He could just kill Joe. What a relief it would be to finally shut him up. It would be so easy. All he would have to do is follow that stupid little green car of his home, and then wait for him to get out. He didn't look very strong; overpowering him would be easy enough. *Then he wouldn't be trying to tell me what to do with that smug little look on his face.*

Begging for his life wouldn't help either. Joe's voice

was worse than the sound of nails scraping a chalkboard. He would have to put an end to that quickly. One swift swing of a knife and his throat would be wide open. No more talking for Joe.

"Hey, Cyrus, are you okay?" Dave asked.

"Yeah, of course," Cyrus answered.

"Well, it's just that you've been sitting there staring at your computer," Dave said sounding concerned. Cyrus just looked at him like he was from another planet. "Figured I'd make sure," Dave continued as he rolled his chair back to his desk.

Cyrus clicked on the computer screen, opening a folder. He began to read through it. Upon reaching the end of the file, he realized he didn't remember any of it. He hadn't retained a single word of the document.

It had only been a couple of days since he had last killed, and it was already throwing his mind off. He couldn't focus on anything. Agitation and aggression coursed through his veins. Killing had passed through his head multiple times this morning and it was still early. Is this what addiction felt like?

He wasn't sure. The closest thing he had come to an addiction was when he couldn't stop drinking Mountain Dew as a teenager. If he told that to a real addict, they would just laugh at him. The hunger to kill coursed through his veins. He wasn't sure what to call it, but he knew he had to feed it.

Struggling to focus, he patted his foot on the floor. How was he going to make it through work? He could barely make it through the moments that were currently passing.

Desperate for some fresh air in his lungs, Cyrus got up and headed for the door. His car was in view of the front door. If he didn't have bills to pay, he would up and leave right now.

He took a final deep breath of the cold morning air, then pushed the door open and made his way back inside.

"Where did you go?" Dave asked as Cyrus sat back down.

"Just outside to grab some fresh air," Cyrus answered shaking his computer mouse to make the screen light up once more.

Dave didn't say anything in response, and Cyrus re-opened the file to give reading it another go. Looking up at the clock on the wall, he still had seven hours to go before he could even think about heading home. Six hours and fifty-nine minutes. Six hours and fifty-eight minutes. He had to stop staring at the clock, and so he transferred his gaze to the words on the screen:

The Mayor and Board have deemed it unnecessary to close down Route 142 for the construction of-

Looking up at the clock once more, he had six hours and fifty-seven minutes left. Some people do other things to satisfy their cravings. He wasn't sure what those things were. There was only one thing that could satisfy him. He had to kill again.

But, who could he kill? No matter how much he

wanted to, he couldn't really kill Joe. That would be like a red flag to the police. Detective Hughes already looked at him weird, and Joe's murder would give him every reason to come sniffing around.

He couldn't kill anyone he knew, and no one the police could link back to him. The other people had basically fallen into his lap.

Either way, he needed to figure something out pronto. He couldn't let this deep-seated desire to kill keep impacting his life. If this is what he had to do to maintain stability, then so be it.

Cyrus made it through the day and got out of work. He avoided Dave on the way out to his car because he didn't want to talk. He had things to do.

Cyrus had all day at work to conjure up a plan, but he had come up blank. He still had all the items in the trunk that he had purchased the previous day. Cyrus ordered the chloroform right before bed, so it shouldn't be too far away from arriving. This time, though, he not only closed out the page, but deleted the site he purchased it from off the computer's internet history. He was playing everything safe.

Driving through the city, Cyrus wasn't exactly sure where he was going. He couldn't head home until he'd completed what needed to be done. Given his current mental state, he couldn't be around his family.

It didn't matter what street he wound up on, so long as he wasn't too close to his house. He drove around until he was out of ideas. A park came into view, then a couple of benches with some houses across the street. He had an idea.

Cyrus pulled his car into a parking lot just a little way down the road. He shifted his focus to the backseat to see what junk there was. There was a book on the floor. *Perfect*. Picking up the book, he headed down the sidewalk until he reached the benches. There was no one there, so he sat down and pretended to read the book.

His phone vibrated. "Where are you?" The text message was from Sara.

He replied, telling her that he was going to hang out at Dave's for a bit and shoot some pool. She was fine with that since he had already done it a few times before.

Clouds started rolling in as he flipped through the pages of the book. He hoped it wouldn't start to rain. He was there for what seemed like an hour watching the houses across the street, waiting to see if anyone came in or out, or if there was any movement from inside.

As it was starting to get darker because of the cloud cover, he began to give serious thought to heading home. He scanned through a few more pages, but wasn't really taking any of it in. With nothing left to do, he flipped to the last page and looked at the picture of the author.

Just then, a car pulled into the driveway directly across from where Cyrus was seated and a man got out. As he had hoped, the man was alone. He waited until the man headed into his house before hurrying back to his car. Cyrus popped the trunk, grabbed one of the bags of items before closing the trunk. Before he walked away, he put on a pair of gloves, popped the trunk open again, and looked around. *Hmmmm*. He lifted up the carpet and grabbed the tire iron.

He walked back down the road and crossed the street. Without hesitation, Cyrus approached the door of the house the man had walked into.

Cyrus pressed his ear up against the door and listened intently. He then quietly wrapped his hand around the door handle and wiggled it. *Locked*. He placed the palm of his hand on the door before knocking. After standing there quietly for a moment, he heard footsteps coming toward the door from the other side.

The door handle wiggled a bit, then the door opened. At the first sign of a person, Cyrus swung the tire iron. It smacked the man dead in the face, knocking him to the ground. Quickly, Cyrus stepped into the house, closing the door behind him. The man laid there on the floor, blood dripping down his face from the side of his head. He wasn't dead, but he also didn't appear to be knocked out cold because he was still making groaning noises.

Cyrus stepped passed him and looked into the rooms that were around them. No one was there. Grabbing the man by his shoulders, he dragged him into a dining room and lifted him up onto a chair. The man's head slouched to the side as it bobbled around.

Cyrus examined the contents of his bag and pulled out the rope. He went behind the chair the man was seated on and wrapped the rope around his wrists, and then around the back of the chair.

Next, he pulled out the duct tape. *Can't have you screaming for help*. He placed the duct tape over the man's mouth. *Hmm, I wonder what your name is. We're gonna call you Steve. Yeah, Steve, I like that.*

He noticed that the man's feet were moving. *I don't want to deal with you kicking me*. Taking hold of some more rope, he wrapped it around the man's feet and tied them to the chair.

Cyrus pulled up a chair and sat across from the man, watching him bob his head as he slowly came to. His eyes opened, then closed again. It was like his body was fighting a losing battle against death. Cyrus laughed as he lifted the man's head up and then watched it drop to the other side.

Reaching into his bag, Cyrus grabbed some more rope. He wrapped it around the man's neck, then held it on both sides and pulled, causing it to tighten.

As the man gagged, his eyes opened. "Sorry about that," Cyrus said smiling and releasing his grip of the rope. "You were sleeping. I had to wake you up."

Just as Cyrus leaned in to remove the rope from the man's neck, he caught movement out the corner of his eye. Looking out the window, he saw another person, a woman, staring at him from a window next door. They both were frozen as they glared into each other's eyes for what seemed like an eternity, but in reality it was barely a second.

The person in the other house bolted away from the window. Cyrus ran into the dining room, where the man still hadn't fully regained consciousness. After making sure everything was in his bag, he retrieved a knife out of his pocket and sank it into the man's chest. Even though the man was basically knocked out the entire time, there was the possibility that he could've got a glimpse of him. He couldn't afford to take any risks.

Cyrus waited until the man stopped moving before pulling the knife out, releasing the blood out of the wound. Sadly, for him, he couldn't give a moment's thought to the kill. He had to get out of there as quick as possible. The woman next door would surely call the police, and he had to be long gone before they got there.

He opened the door and immediately began scanning the area, but didn't sight anyone. It had started to pour with rain, which he was thankful for because it might help him cover his tracks. Maybe no one would see him get into his car.

The woman mustn't have been watching for very long because the police still hadn't arrived. The water splashed under his feet as he ran as fast as he could to his car. He pulled out his keys and tried to find the correct key. A bright light flashed around the corner as a police car turned onto the road.

Shit. Cyrus dropped down to the ground behind his car. The police car quickly flew by him and pulled up in front of the house. Two men got out of the car with their guns at the ready, and rushed toward the front door with their heads ducked.

Cyrus cracked open his car door and slid in, closing the door quietly behind him. One of the cops knocked on the door, but there was no answer. Upon noticing the door was unlocked, the officers rushed in.

As soon as they were both inside, Cyrus started his car under the cover of the roaring thunderstorm and pulled out. He didn't turn on his headlights until the front of the car was facing away from the house.

Cyrus drove to the end of the road and turned the corner. Not even a minute later, two more cops came flying down the road and passed him, sirens blaring. He saw them disappear around the corner in his rearview mirror.

His entire body was shaking uncontrollably. He couldn't keep his arms still as they shook the steering wheel. The windshield wipers pushed the rain off his window, giving him a small glimpse of the road as he fought for visibility.

Cyrus kept looking into the rearview mirror, waiting for a cop to be trailing behind him, trying to pull him over. He wasn't going to go down without a fight.

Just then, a car pulled out from a side road and Cyrus almost smashed into it. Slamming on the brakes, he came to a screeching halt on the water covered road.

A loud honk filled the air from the other car as it completed its turn onto the road Cyrus was on. The headlights of the cars behind him stuck in his rearview mirror, blinding him. Cyrus put his foot on the gas and pulled onto the side road. He couldn't drive like this. He was too on edge.

Cyrus put his hands over his face. *Fuck. Fuck. Fuck.* For the first time, he had no idea what to do. He just needed to make it home, and then he could figure it out from there.

Cyrus managed to get back onto the main road and commenced the journey back home. He didn't see any more police cars drive by. He was in the clear for the time being. But, how long would it take for them to get a police sketch out? How long would it be before someone realized it was him?

He wasn't sure. At this point, he wasn't sure about anything. As he drew closer to home, he started to wonder what he would tell his wife. He was soaked from head to toe. He was supposed to be at Dave's place playing pool, so how would he explain being soaked to the bone to his wife? Lately, it seemed like he was always having to come up with excuses. He was growing tired of it.

As he pulled onto his road, his heart was still pounding. His mind switched to what the two policemen thought upon entering the house and seeing the man tied to the chair with his mouth covered with duct tape and marks around his neck from Cyrus choking him to wake him up. Would they ask, "Who would do such a thing?" Would they call him a monster? It's likely that is what he would have said a few weeks ago had he walked in on such a scene.

Cyrus pulled into the driveway and turned off his car. He almost felt like he should just go in and say goodbye to his family. It would only be a matter of time before the police found him.

Stepping out of his car, he headed to the door. Upon entering the house, he saw that his wife was seated on the couch.

"Babe, you're drenched," Sara said as she stood up

and walked over to Cyrus.

"Yeah, it's coming down hard out there," Cyrus said as he kicked off his shoes and removed his wet socks.

"What happened? How did you get all soaked?" She asked with concern in her voice.

"When I left Dave's, my car wouldn't start," Cyrus answered surprised that he was able to come up with an excuse on the spot.

"What was wrong with it?" She asked.

"The battery was low, so I had to have Dave jump-start it," Cyrus explained.

"In the rain? Isn't that a bit dangerous?" Sara enquired as her and Cyrus made their way upstairs.

"We were fine," Cyrus smiled. "Just got a bit wet," he added as he gestured at his entire body.

They got upstairs and Chris walked out of his room. "Dad, dang, you're soaked," Chris noted.

"Well, hello, what's your name? I don't think we've met. I never see you around here," Cyrus responded.

"Very funny, dad. I do have a life outside of you, you know?!" Chris laughed and walked back into his room.

"Well, that was fun," Cyrus laughed as him and Sara moved into the bedroom.

As Cyrus began to remove his wet clothes, Sara started going through the drawers looking for clothes for him to wear. Trying to pull the wet shirt off himself reminded him of when he had to take the blood soaked shirt off as it resisted, dragging across his back.

Sara was being extremely nice and helpful. Cyrus

wondered what she would say or do if she knew what he had become. If she knew what he had just done. He knew this was him now and he didn't know how to go back. In his heart, he didn't believe it was possible to go back.

"You know what I was thinking?" Cyrus enquired as he looked at Sara.

"What's that?" She asked.

"Sometime soon, you, I, and Chris should go on a vacation," Cyrus smiled.

"Oh yeah? To where?" She laughed entertaining Cyrus's idea.

"Anywhere," Cyrus replied as he wrapped his arms around Sara.

"Anywhere?" Sara reiterated.

"Anywhere but here," he rubbed his hands gently across Sara's bac

She just looked at him. "We could go right now," Cyrus continued only half joking. If he took off, perhaps the police would never find him.

Sara laughed loudly. "Oh, Cyrus, if only it was that easy," she responded as she turned back around to grab hold of some clothes for him to wear.

"You know what else I was thinking?" Cyrus took a step toward Sara.

Sara turned back around to face him. "Oh, what are you thinking this time?" She laughed at him with a big smile.

"I'm feeling lively," he said.

"Oh, lively? I like that," she replied.

"I want to make a change," he continued.

Sara just tilted her head and made a questioning face.

"I want to get a haircut. Can you cut my hair?" He asked.

"A haircut. Cyrus asking for a haircut!" She laughed.

"I might even shave to!" He sat down on the bed.

"And, what brought on this change of heart?" She giggled.

"My hair being all wet. It's almost long enough to get in my eyes! I think it's time for a change," Cyrus stood back up. "Babe, please cut my hair!" He begged only half seriously.

"All right, all right," Sara conceded. "Go get a chair and I'll do it right here," she waved her hand toward the door.

Cyrus smiled and headed out of the room. He didn't really want to have his hair cut, but if he was going to keep the police off his tail it would need to be done. Sooner or later, they were going to release a sketch of him and he needed to look as different from the sketch as possible. It was raining out when he had seen the face in the window. He was hoping she didn't catch a good glimpse of him. How good of a look could she have really got? On top of the rain, it's likely that she was scared. She must have been just as startled as he was. She couldn't have got a good look, could she?

10

"**YOU** know, I think I could get used to this," Cyrus said out loud to himself as he tilted his head and rubbed his newly-trimmed beard in the mirror.

He felt cleaner, sharper.

No one had shown up at his door trying to place him in handcuffs, so he was okay for the moment. How long that would last he wasn't exactly sure. There was nothing he could do except go about his daily routine, which of late wasn't even really his routine anymore.

How could he make a mistake as stupid as leaving the curtains open in the room in which he was carrying out a kill? Especially after vowing to himself that he would take extra precautions to avoid any slip-ups. The situation he found himself in was exactly the kind of thing he wanted to avoid.

He had to get to work. After feeling like he was already on the run, he now had to go and sit behind a desk for hours. He'd be surprised if he made it through the day.

On his way to work, Cyrus kept the radio on the news station in the hope he would hear something about the murder. He should have gone next door and just killed the woman that had seen him commit the act, but he was in too much of a panicked state to think clearly. His instincts told him to get out as quick as he could.

As he made his way through town, a strange feeling washed over him. There was a deep desire within him to head back to the house. He wanted to know if the cops were still there. They had probably moved the body a long time ago, however, if the woman hadn't already spoken to the sketch artist, it might not be too late. Cyrus had heard of criminals returning to the scene of the crime. He was tempted to do exactly that, but he wasn't stupid enough to go through with it.

As he drew closer to work and the scene of the crime, the urge was still there. He really wanted to drive by and take a look at the house, and see if the police were still there. They would be scurrying around trying to piece the puzzle together when the answer to the puzzle was driving by.

He passed by the road that would've taken him in the direction of the house and just kept going. The desire was still there, but it wasn't nearly powerful enough to put himself in jeopardy. He watched the road disappear in the rearview mirror.

Cyrus took a seat in his rotating chair and turned on his computer. Dave was there and so was everyone else, all clueless as to who was sitting just a few feet away.

"Cyrus," Cyrus turned around to see Joe standing behind him. "Come with me," Joe added.

He stood up and followed Joe, who didn't walk all the way to his office.

"Were you outside yesterday before break?" Joe asked.

"Yes, just for-," Cyrus was cut off by Joe.

"Don't do it again," Joe said before turning around and walking away.

Cyrus was surprised that was all that had come out of Joe's mouth. It was typical of Joe to go off like someone had just committed a crime and threaten them with dismissal, however, he wasn't about to fight or complain about it, so he made his way back to his desk.

"What was that all about?" Dave asked Cyrus before he even had a chance to sit down.

"Nothing, just Joe complaining that I stepped outside the other day," Cyrus explained.

Cyrus had a lot of work to catch-up on because he had been so preoccupied for the last few days. Luckily, just as he had suspected, nobody noticed. If anyone had spotted that his mind wasn't on the job, Joe would have made a point of mentioning it when he yelled at him for going outside.

There was no real point in working if the police were going to catch him. He was going to spend the remainder of his life in jail anyway, so why not just relax?

"Oh, yeah, I almost forgot," Dave turned around and handed Cyrus a box. "Here's that thing you ordered," he added.

"Oh, great, thanks!" Cyrus smiled excitedly.

"My wife wanted to open it," Dave laughed.

Cyrus took a gulp. "Did she?"

"No, I didn't let her," Dave replied.

Cyrus breathed a sigh of relief before once again thanking Dave. He placed the box on his desk, then spun it around and examined the sides. It was unmarked just as the site said it would be, with nothing on it but a barcode. He felt as excited as a child on Christmas Day wanting to open up the box and see what his purchase looked like.

"So, what is it?" Dave enquired.

"Just something for the bedroom," Cyrus replied.

"Oh, spicing things up!" Dave patted Cyrus on the back.

For once he had thought ahead, knowing full well Dave would ask him what was in the box. He had come prepared.

Cyrus placed the box to the side of his computer and started typing. He was typing away when some whispers caught his attention.

Stabbed…police…the guy again. He couldn't make out everything, but he caught bits and pieces coming from a couple of co-workers sitting adjacent to them.

Cyrus turned around, but Dave was gone. He turned back around and faced his computer so they wouldn't notice him eavesdropping. He was certain he knew what they were talking about, but he couldn't exactly understand what they were saying. He listened intently, but what he heard wasn't what his ears were expecting. They were saying something about coffee. Perhaps he had misheard them, or maybe they had moved on to another topic.

Upon hearing Dave sit back down, Cyrus turned around and whispered, "Dave."

"Yeah?" Dave enquired loudly.

"What were those guys over there talking about?" Cyrus asked Dave nodding his head in the direction of the people.

"I don't know?" Dave replied with a confused look on his face.

"I thought I heard them say something about a killing or a kill, or something," Cyrus continued.

"Oh, yeah, there was another killing yesterday just like the other ones," Dave explained.

The news made Cyrus feel good. He enjoyed being the topic of conversation.

"Really?" Cyrus asked as he tried to resist the urge to smile.

"Yeah, I guess this one was pretty messed up," Cyrus grinned at Dave's words. "Someone caught him, though," Dave added.

"Oh, they finally caught him?" Cyrus asked knowing that it was impossible.

"Well, not really, but someone did see him. They're supposed to have something about it on the news tonight," Dave said with a hint of interest in his voice.

"I wonder if they have a lead," Cyrus said in a vain attempt to make himself sound concerned.

"I'm not sure, but I heard they're supposed to have something big," Dave responded.

Dave's reply caught Cyrus off guard. He knew someone had seen him and there was bound to have been some sort of sketch released, but what if they had more? He wasn't there very long and was certain that he hadn't left behind anything incriminating. At least nothing that sprung to mind. If they had something else, would they even talk about it on the news?

Cyrus knew that Sara would definitely want to watch the news and that Chris would possibly want to as well. His only hope was that the sketch wasn't good enough for anyone to link it to him. He was nervous. If the sketch appeared on TV, Sara and Chris would look at him with their disappointed eyes and call him a murderer.

As the last minutes of the work day ticked away, Cyrus's heart began to pound faster and faster. Sara and Chris were sure to have heard about the news broadcast just as he had. It was time to go home and watch the news.

The car's engine sounded quieter than usual, as if it was giving Cyrus one last moment of peace before he had to drive home and face the music. Once again, he passed by the road that led to his last kill. By now, the cops would be long gone and the house vacant, lacking the life it once held.

Cyrus pulled up to his house, but didn't get out of

the car. Patting his fingers on the steering wheel to buy himself some time, he almost wished he could leave and show up after the news was over, but deep down he wanted to watch it.

As Cyrus made his way into the house, Sara and Chris were already sitting in the living room glued to the TV.

"Hey, guys, what's up? Cyrus asked.

"Waiting for the news to come on," Sara answered.

"They're supposed to be having something about that killer tonight," Chris added with a touch of excitement in his voice.

"I have never seen you this excited about the news," Cyrus said with a fake smile.

"Well, everyone at school has been talking about it. I have been waiting all day for this," Chris explained.

"Maybe they caught him, Sara," Cyrus said.

"We can only hope," Sara replied without breaking eye contact with the TV.

Cyrus made his way into the kitchen and opened the refrigerator, looking for the milk as he moved things around.

"What are we eating tonight?" Cyrus asked.

"I brought some burgers home," Sara shouted from the living room. "There should still be some in there."

Upon opening the refrigerator once more, Cyrus spotted the bag of burgers. They normally didn't eat fast food, so he didn't even give it a second thought when he first opened the fridge.

Looking at his watch, he noted that the news would be on in ten minutes. Cyrus wasn't actually hungry; he just didn't want to sit down yet as if it would stall the TV broadcast. His stomach felt sore and he was beginning to sweat. Perhaps he could lock himself in his bedroom and cut himself off from everyone including the police, but sadly that isn't how things worked in the real world. He was going to have to force himself through it.

Cyrus pulled a burger out of the bag and looked at it; it looked disgusting. After placing it back in the wrapper, he tossed it in the refrigerator. He tilted a cup high as he poured water down his throat, savoring every last drop.

Five-minutes left. He wiped sweat off his forehead and placed his cup in the sink, before resting his hands on the counter to hold up his body.

Three-minutes to go. It was time to take a seat next to his wife on the couch and wait. Wait for her to turn to him, confess her disgust at his actions, and turn him into the police.

One-minute left. He stared at the side of his wife's head before transferring his gaze to Chris. It was time.

The TV flashed and then a news anchorwoman appeared on the screen with a headline underneath her saying, "Man seen in house believed to be responsible for recent murders." Cyrus rubbed his hand against his cheek and waited for them to begin the report.

A suspect in the murder of a man is believed to be responsible for a recent series of murders.

Patrick Reuman

The screen then cut to footage outside the house in which he killed the man. He could still picture himself knocking on the door before striking the man in the face, leaving him there on the floor fighting for his life.

Last night, a man broke into this house, taking a man hostage. He was found tied to a chair, where he had been stabbed. Due to the family's wishes, his name is not being released at this time.

A person in the vicinity of the crime saw the suspect.

There it was. The news he had been dreading. It had finally come to pass. A picture was now going to be shown, and he would need to figure out what to do. He readied himself to run out the door.

The suspect is also believed to be responsible for a recent series of murders starting approximately a week ago, with the most recent murder having occurred last night. We are going to display an image of what we believe the suspect may look like. If you believe you have any information in relation to any of the recent murders, please contact us on the number shown at the bottom of the screen.

An image then flashed up onto the screen followed by a phone number. A mixed feeling of dread and relief had returned to his stomach as he stared at the image. In his opinion, it didn't even look remotely like him. He glanced at Sara before turning to Chris. Neither of them were looking in his direction or on their phone calling the police, so they must have both thought that it didn't look like him.

He just sat there waiting for one of them to say something before the news anchorwoman re-appeared on the TV.

If you recognize this man, please call the number shown on the screen immediately.

As the number re-appeared on the screen, Cyrus turned to Sara, who still hadn't said a thing.

"Well, there he is," Cyrus said as he looked at his wife.

"I expected something different, something worse. He looked too…. normal," Sara said as she rose to her feet.

"I guess they aren't always funny looking," Cyrus replied as he watched Sara walk into the other room.

Before she had made it all the way into the next room, someone else appeared on the TV. It was Detective Hughes.

We're going to catch whoever did this. Whoever you are, we will find you. Turn yourself in. If anyone has any information regarding the man's whereabouts, I ask you to contact the police immediately so we can take this criminal off the

streets.

Cocky little prick aren't you? Cyrus was beginning to grow tired of Hughes. *If he is going to catch me, he'd better do it soon because I'm starting to get sick of this guy.*

As Cyrus rose to his feet and followed Sara into the other room, Chris whizzed behind him and ran up the stairs. "I'll be upstairs!" He shouted from the top of the stairs.

Cyrus walked over and stood across the counter from Sara as she looked into a cupboard.

"So, what do you think?" He asked Sara.

"I just hope they catch him," she responded with a touch of anger in her voice. "Whoever he is, he's sick."

He felt like she was directing her anger at him, but he knew she wasn't as she'd be much angrier than this. Cyrus wasn't particularly concerned with how she was feeling. He was angry about what Hughes had said. Hughes came across as if he could catch Cyrus at any time if he wanted to, but there was no chance in hell of that occurring. Cyrus could do as he pleased and there was nothing Hughes could do about it. He had come agonizingly close to getting caught and still hadn't been found out. He had no reason to be afraid anymore.

If he wants to play, I'll play.

For the next couple of hours, Sara and Cyrus sat on the couch watching TV. He had to wait for her to head to bed. He had a plan. They sat there watching a boring movie about some basketball team, which he didn't really care for. Sara was at least a little talkative, so he was no longer worried about whether she suspected something was up. He just kept looking at the clock waiting for her to say she was going to bed.

Finally, the movie came to an end and Sara she was on her way to bed. Cyrus said he was going to stay up a little longer as he wasn't feeling tired. "The stuff on the TV about that killer has me feeling a bit on edge, so I'm going to stay up for a while," he told his wife.

"Thank you," she said with a smile as she hugged him.

She gave him a kiss and made her way upstairs to the bedroom. Now, he could get down to business. Hughes wanted to play, so Cyrus was going to play harder.

Sitting down at the computer in his living room, he opened up a Word document. He patted the tips of his fingers on the keyboard keys, plotting his next move.

My name-

He paused for a moment before deleting it. He rubbed his hands across the keyboard and continued to think.

If you want to find me, you will need my name.
That is your mission, this is your task.
But, I will not give my name, so don't even ask.
It rhymes with a car.
That I will say.
But, will you catch me? There is no way.

Before clicking the print button, he stared at the screen, a smile emerging on his face. The buzzing of the printer filled the air as he watched the riddle he had conjured up print out. One copy, two copies. The printer kept going until thirty copies had been created.

Getting to his feet, Cyrus opened a drawer in the kitchen, retrieving a box of envelopes and some latex gloves. He couldn't risk leaving behind fingerprints.

Cyrus grabbed the sheets of paper with the riddle on them and placed them in separate envelopes before sealing them. He took hold of a marker out of a cup that was in the middle of the table, then wrote on each envelope: **To the police**.

He wrapped a rubber band around them before placing them on the couch.

Cyrus began to creep upstairs as quietly as possible, then gently pushed his bedroom door open. Sara was laying there sleeping soundly under the blanket.

"Sara," he whispered to no reply. "Sara," he whispered again. She didn't move a muscle. She was fast asleep, so he turned around and headed back down the stairs.

Cyrus grabbed the pile of letters, then slipped out the front door. As he walked to his car, he repeatedly glanced back up at the upstairs window.

Cyrus looked behind him before reversing his car. He was unsure as to what street he was going down, so he just drove. He turned up road after road until he reached one that looked empty. The road looked silent. There was no sign of life whatsoever.

After parking at the end of the road, he started

making his way down the sidewalk. Silently, he walked slowly as he peered into the window of each house he walked by, watching for movement. Upon looking at his watch, he noted that it was 12.37am. Everyone should be in bed by now, but he had to be sure.

Cyrus reached the end of the road, then turned back around. Staring down the road, he took one final look around to check for any signs of life before beginning his mission. Quietly, he snuck up to the first house within his vicinity and placed a letter on the porch so it could be seen when they went to check the mail in the morning.

Thinking he had heard a noise, he jerked around but nothing was there. His mind was playing tricks on him. *I should probably just toss them onto the porches just in case there are dogs or something.* If dogs started to bark, everything would fall apart in the blink of an eye.

He hurried across the street to the next house in a desperate bid to get a letter to every house on both sides of the street. Thankfully, it wasn't that long of a road or he may have needed to bring more letters.

The final letter was dropped on the porch closest to his car. There was no movement or noises at any of the houses he had been to. He was proud of his handy work.

Cyrus kicked his car into gear and sped off. The police would fuss over this for days. He only wished he could be there to witness them open up the envelope. They would all huddle around trying to figure out the riddle. The riddle with no answer.

If Hughes thought he could toy with him, catch him with a mere sketch, he had another thing coming. Cyrus knew how to play the game, and he was prepared to do whatever it took to win.

11

CYRUS could hardly wait. With what the police would make of his letter at the forefront of his mind, it was a struggle for him to sleep. He wondered if it would be on the news. His excitement stemmed from someone calling him and telling him all about what they said after opening the letter.

His curiosity extended to what people would think upon opening their doors and seeing a letter on their front porch with the words, 'To the police' on the front.

It was still early in the day, and he was just getting ready for work, so it was unlikely anyone had seen one of the letters unless one of them had left early for work. If so, by now the street would be covered in police trying to plot their next move.

Cyrus was feeling good. He slid on some dress

pants, then put on a nice dress shirt and complemented it with a tie. He took a moment to admire his look. His clothes made a statement: Style, intelligence, intellect. They mirrored him perfectly.

He was far from done with Hughes. Cyrus felt like an animal had been unleashed inside of him. He wanted to rub it in Hughes's smug face that he had next to no chance of catching him.

It was still dark; the sun had yet to completely rise. Cyrus knew this time around he wouldn't be able to resist the urge.

He turned away from his normal route to work. His eyes were firmly fixated on the road. After making a few turns, he got closer to the road where he'd left the letters. He couldn't fight the urge to go back.

Slowing down a little bit, he let his car glide past the end of the road. As he cocked his neck and looked down the road, there was a single cop car near the end of the road, and a policeman on the porch engaged in conversation with an unknown person.

They must have found the letter. It wouldn't be long now until they realized there was one on each porch, and then a horde of police officers would show up.

Cyrus had one mission he needed to complete at work. He headed to his designated space in the City Hall Records Department and took his seat without speaking to a soul. Dave would always attempt to strike up a conversation upon his arrival. He was going to have to wait until he walked off to do something. He couldn't run the risk of Dave walking up behind him while he was engrossed in the task at hand.

Cyrus opened up a random file and left it open, so it didn't look like he was just sitting there idling away his time. Waiting for Dave to talk to him was strange. Lately, he was so used to avoiding conversation he had neglected the fact that they were close friends.

"Hey, man," Dave finally spoke.

"Hey," Cyrus said in an attempt to keep the conversation to a minimum.

"Work is going to suck today," Dave said. "You know that sketch that was on TV, I swear he looks just like my mail man," Dave laughed. "I think I might report him," continuing his joke.

"Maybe they have a reward you can collect," Cyrus laughed back. *It actually felt kind of good to laugh for once.*

Two hours had gone by and not once had Dave got up to use the bathroom. It was typical of him to get up and go to the vending machine or do something on a regular basis. Upon looking at the clock, Cyrus realized there was only five minutes remaining until their first break. If he was going to complete his task, he would need to skip his first break.

As was the norm, a bell dinged to signal them to go on their break.

"C'mon, man, break time!" Dave informed him.

"I'm just going to stay here and relax for now," Cyrus explained in a desperate bid to be left to his own devices.

"Well, all right, have fun," Dave said as he turned around and walked away.

Immediately, Cyrus spun around in his chair to face

his computer. He opened a box and clicked on a directory. A few more clicks and he had a window open that said, 'Phone number directory'.

Cyrus proceeded to open up a webpage and searched 'Detective Hughes' and 'Officer Lopez' followed by their city names. Their real names were Walter Hughes and Ricky Lopez.

He re-opened the directory and typed in their names. *Bingo*. Both of their phone numbers popped up. After jotting them down on a piece of paper, Cyrus opened a new window. This time, he was searching for them by name and phone number in an attempt to find one last piece of vital information.

Once again, Cyrus was successful. He had located their addresses and scribbled them down next to their respective names and phone numbers before quickly closing down all the windows.

Looking up at the clock, he saw that five minutes of his break remained. He was impressed at how fast he was able to locate the required information. If only the cops were as good as him, they may have caught him by now.

The bell rang, prompting everyone to return to their desks. Dave was still munching on a sandwich as he took his seat.

"I do wish I'd had something to eat," Cyrus said as Dave took the last bite of his sandwich.

The names, addresses, and numbers were now on scrap of paper in front of him, and he knew he needed to decide quickly what he would do with the newly-acquired information. He wanted Hughes to know that he couldn't mess with him.

He didn't want to kill him, though. At least not yet. Maybe scare him a little. He doubted he would be able to scare a cop, though. Hughes didn't look like the type that scared easily, however, he would be scared if he had a knife against his throat.

At times, Cyrus found himself wondering if other people had urges similar to the ones he had. Maybe they did, but perhaps they didn't succumb to them like himself. It wasn't that he was weak. Far from it. He just got enjoyment out of his heinous acts. Why fight something that gives you enjoyment?

As he made his way to his car, Cyrus examined the piece of paper. He didn't look up from it as he stepped inside and put on his seatbelt. He retrieved his cell phone and dialed Hughes's number. Taking in his surroundings, he watched the cars as they pulled out of the parking lot. He waited patiently until they were all gone and the coast was clear.

Once Cyrus knew he was alone, he clicked the call button. The ringing rattled in his ears as he prepared for Hughes to answer the phone.

Hughes picked up the phone. "Hello?" Cyrus didn't respond. "Hello?" Hughes continued.

"You're starting get under my skin," Cyrus said in a rough and muffled tone in a bid to disguise his voice.

"What? Who is this?" Hughes demanded.

"You think you can catch me. You think you can find me. You're sadly mistaken," Cyrus continued all the while not dignifying Hughes's questions with a response.

There was a brief pause on the line. The only noise on the line was the combined breathing of the two men.

"I'm going to put you in prison," Hughes broke the silence with a bold statement.

Cyrus laughed into the phone. "No, you won't."

"You can't run forever. We will find you," Hughes said firmly.

"Wherever you are, I will be there. I will haunt you until you die," Cyrus said as he hung up the phone, then the line went dead.

Now, he found himself sitting in his car in the empty parking lot. The roar of his engine broke the silence as he kicked the car into gear. Driving down the road with a smile firmly fixed on his face, he was proud of what he had accomplished. Just then, the newswoman on the radio spoke, breaking his train of thought.

Stay tuned for an urgent message; an update on the recent series of murders.

Already? He knew it would have something to do with his phone call. He wasn't even halfway home yet. What could they have possibly discovered?

He waited. A commercial about some new laundry detergent played. He assumed they had sent the channel to a commercial break to buy themselves some time as they set everything up at the station.

Like everyone else, he was eager to hear the news. He pressed hard on the gas in a desperate bid to arrive home before the newscast came back on, so he could sit in his driveway and listen distraction free. Driving while basking in the glory wasn't an easy task.

In the middle of a commercial, the newswoman chimed in.

And, we're back. This is Becky Towinski with Detective Walter Hughes who has a new update on the recent series of murders. Tell us what you have:

We have a recent voice recording of a phone conversation between a police officer and the suspect. Now, we want everyone to listen carefully. If you recognize the voice of the suspect, please contact us immediately so we can work toward making a quick arrest.

There was a brief pause, then the newswoman cut back in.

This is the recording:

A slightly fuzzy recording began to play.

"I'm going to put you in prison."

As he knew he would, Cyrus recognized the voice immediately.

"No, you won't."

"You can't run forever. We will find you."

"Wherever you are, I will be there. I will haunt you until you die."

Furious with himself, Cyrus punched his steering wheel. It was his intention to keep the phone call short enough to prevent them from tracking the call, but he hadn't anticipated Hughes recording the conversation. He had caught Cyrus off guard. Perhaps Hughes was smarter than he thought. He was fast, too. It couldn't have taken him any longer than twenty minutes to get the call on the air. Cyrus was almost home.

"Now, correct me if I'm wrong, but is that you on the recording?" The newswoman asked Hughes.

"It was," Hughes replied.

"How did this phone call come about?" The reporter asked Hughes.

"I received a restricted phone call and answered it," Hughes responded. He didn't stay on the phone long enough for me to track the call, but I was able to get this short recording."

"Is it true that you also received some other type of message from the suspect?" The reporter enquired.

"Yes, but as we are still working on the case we are

not able to discuss the matter in detail right now," Hughes explained. "If any progress has been made in the case, we will be sure to inform the public immediately."

"Is there any word on how he may have got hold of your phone number? Do you intend to change your number?" The reporter asked.

"At this stage, we don't have any leads as to how he came into possession of the phone number of a member of the police force, and it's not my intention to change my number. In fact, I welcome him to get in contact with me once more. I have a lot more I'd like to say to him," Hughes challenged Cyrus.

"Lastly, Detective, why did he call you?" She asked in a grim tone.

"It's my belief that he wanted to scare us, and myself in particular," Hughes replied. "He thinks he can intimidate us with idle threats. Well, let this be known, I know you're out there, I know you're listening to this, and I want you to know that it's just a matter of time. We have your picture, we have your voice, and next we will have you."

12

THE only noise filling the room was the clanking of Hughes's fork on his plate as he played around with his food. Something about the sketch released of the man responsible for the string of murders was bothering him, but he couldn't put his finger on what it was exactly.

Rising to his feet, he put his plate in the sink before returning to his chair and opening his phone. As he checked his incoming calls and gazed at the call from Cyrus, he wished there had been a phone number attached to the call.

The cap came off hard on the bottle of whiskey as he tilted it forward, filling up a glass. He slowly turned the glass, admiring the golden brown liquid inside. *Bottoms up*. He gagged and coughed loudly as it burned going down his throat.

The folder sat there on the table across from him barely within arm's reach, tormenting him into submission. It was filled with photographs of bodies. The man in the alley, the man in a garage, and another man tied to a chair in his own house, stabbed to death. They were all men. Was this a trend or merely a coincidence?

At first glance, he wasn't sure if they were all even connected, but then he called. The man on the phone called to tell him that he would never catch him. He was taunting him just as the folder was taunting him now. As he punched the table in frustration, the whiskey bottle tipped over, pouring out onto the table. *Fuck*. He hurried and grabbed it before too much escaped the bottle.

Hughes dried it up with a towel, then sat back down in the chair that he'd been seated in for the past hour. His sweaty fingers reached out and grabbed hold of the folder once more. He placed the palm of his hand on the outside of the folder before taking a deep breath.

As he opened the folder, the photos began to stare back at him. He always felt as if crime scene photos spoke to him, whispering their secrets, but this time he couldn't hear a thing. There were no fingerprints, no strands of hair, and no DNA left behind in a struggle that could help him pinpoint a suspect. There was nothing.

Hughes rose to his feet and stumbled to the bathroom. He couldn't even remember how many drinks he had consumed. Old habits seemed to be catching up to him quickly.

As he stumbled closer to the bathroom, the door swung open and he crashed into the wall. The last glass of whiskey had gone straight to his head. He began to urinate and missed the toilet. "Shit!" He shouted loudly as he stepped back. He tossed a towel on top of the toilet, then staggered out of the room.

After returning to his chair, he retrieved the sketch of the suspect and placed it on the table in front of him. *Who are you?*

Hughes had talked the talk, but at the end of the day they had nothing to fall back on. All the random calls in response to the sketch led to nothing. Half of them didn't even look like the sketch.

Hughes almost knocked over his chair as he pushed himself to his feet. He forced his way down a hallway and into his room where he fell onto his bed.

As he laid in bed, he pulled out his phone and stared at it once more.

"I'm going to put you in prison."

"No, you won't."

"You can't run forever. We will find you."

"Wherever you are, I will be there. I will haunt you until you die."

He played the recording on his phone, then transferred his gaze to the ceiling as he played the recording over and over. The voice on the phone echoed in his mind. *Who are you?*

Hughes kept rewinding the recording and playing the same part over and over. "Wherever you are, I will be there. Wherever you are, I will be there. Wherever you are, I will be there."

He paused for a moment, then rewound the recording once more. "Wherever you are, I will be there."

"Wait…you were there!" Hughes exclaimed as he sat up in his bed.

Rising to his feet, he bolted down the hall. He grabbed the sketch off the table and examined it closely. "You were there," he said loudly once more.

Retrieving his keys from the cabinet, he hurried to his car. After missing multiple times, he fumbled his keys into the lock and started his car, putting his seatbelt on as he pulled out.

Struggling to stay in his lane, he sped in and out of traffic. He turned down a road and came to an abrupt halt as he slammed on the brakes, jerking his head forward.

He tried to yank the seatbelt off without pushing the button, but failed. "Ahhh," he groaned as he smashed his finger down on the button before shoving the door open.

His face was greeted by the ground as he tripped himself up in the process of rushing out of the car. Pushing the dirt off with his feet, he forced himself up from the ground and stumbled to the front door of the house.

THUD! THUD! THUD! He pounded on the door. "Wake up!" Hughes shouted at the door.

A rumbling sound could be heard from inside as

someone approached the door.

"Wake up!" Hughes shouted once more.

The door swung open and Officer Lopez stood in the entry way wearing pajama pants and a t-shirt, looking puzzled and angry.

"Walter, I mean Hughes, what are you doing here?" Lopez demanded as Hughes pushed past him and entered the house.

"It's him," Hughes said.

"It's who? What are you talking about?" Lopez asked.

"The killer. The one committing all these crimes. It's that guy we questioned about a break in," Hughes explained spitting slightly as he spoke.

"Are you drunk?" Lopez asked as he leaned in to take a whiff of Hughes's breath. "Yeah, you've been drinking, you're drunk."

"No, that doesn't matter. I know who it is now," Hughes demanded in a desperate attempt to capture Lopez's attention.

Lopez transferred his gaze to his wife who was standing on the stairs witnessing the confrontation. Hughes looked up at her and threw his hands up in the air.

"You aren't listening," Hughes said with force.

"Did you drive here?" Lopez pulled the curtain to the side and looked out at Hughes's car which was parked awkwardly in front of his house and slightly on the curb.

"I'm going to have you stay here the night," Lopez said as he looked at his wife. "He can have the couch,"

Lopez continued.

"Fucking idiot," Hughes mumbled under his breath. He jerked the door open and made his way to his car.

"Hughes, what are you doing?!" Lopez shouted after him. "You can't drive."

"Fuck you," Hughes fired back as he hopped into his car and sped off.

What a dumb ass. Hughes put his foot to the floor, increasing his speed with every passing second.

A car came into his line of sight as he swerved, and he almost hit it. He caught control of his car just in time to avoid crashing into a fire hydrant and turned into a parking lot, coming to a halt in the middle of two parking spots. Hughes's head bounced off the steering wheel and his vision started to get blurry.

"Fucking idiots," he mumbled as his head fell from side-to-side like a bobble head doll.

With exhaustion slowly creeping up on him, Hughes's head fell back against the seat. His consciousness faded away as he drifted off to sleep.

The honking of a car horn snapped Hughes out of his daze.

KNOCK! KNOCK! KNOCK!

"Are you okay in there, sir?" An old man wearing a baseball cap asked as he tapped his hand on Hughes's car window.

Slowly, Hughes rubbed his eyes as if everything was gradually coming back into focus. As Hughes examined his surroundings, he realized he was in a parking lot, but remained unaware of the man camped outside his window. The bottle of whiskey was still on the passenger seat floor. He didn't recall bringing it with him.

As he rose from his slouched position, he finally made eye contact with the man outside his window. The window made a crisp sound as Hughes pressed down the button, rolling the window down.

"I am sorry, sir," the elderly gentleman said. "I saw you laying there before I headed into the store and you were still there when I came out, so I wanted to make sure that you were okay."

"Thank you," Hughes said as he reached out to give the man a handshake "It's appreciated."

"It isn't a problem," the man replied as he shook Hughes's hand before going on his merry way.

Upon looking down at his watch, Hughes noticed that he was late for work. He also smelled horrendous, but he had no time to head home and take a shower.

Everything from the night before came rushing back to him. He needed to make his way to the police station as soon as possible. Wasting no time, he put a small siren on the roof of his car, switched on the car, and sped out of the parking lot.

Hughes knew the killer was bound to strike again at any moment. He had to stop him in his tracks, and it needed to be done now.

As he stormed into the police station, the majority of the officers were engrossed in the letter Cyrus had sent, and were jotting down notes in a bid to make sense of the riddle.

"Stop! Everyone stop!" Hughes shouted as he

walked by and snatched the letter out from under someone's nose.

Everyone looked up at Hughes with confused expressions.

"This is garbage," Hughes said as he crumpled up the letter and tossed it in the garbage. "All of these are garbage."

The Captain got up and charged toward Hughes. "What do you think you are doing?" He shouted at Hughes in disbelief.

"The letter is fake," Hughes explained.

"What are you talking about? How exactly is it fake?" The Captain demanded a better explanation.

"His name doesn't rhyme with a car or anything remotely similar. His name is Cyrus," Hughes explained catching everyone off guard.

"How do you know this?" The Captain said as he reached over to grab a pen and paper from his desk.

"I just know," Hughes responded as he scrambled to his desk and started rifling through his drawers, tossing things to the side. "I have his full name in here somewhere. I got it from his neighbor the day of the robbery."

Lopez walked over and proceeded to grab Hughes by the arm. "Hughes, c'mon, stop," Lopez said with a degree of concern in his voice.

Hughes jerked Lopez's arm away and kept searching for the paper.

"Dude, we have no evidence pointing toward that guy," Lopez explained quietly as he tried to calm

Hughes down.

"You have no evidence?" The Captain shouted angrily. "You come in here acting like you have this killer on a leash and you have no evidence?" The Captain stated continuing his scolding.

"He looks exactly like the sketch, and I remember his voice," Hughes said as he retrieved a small notepad from his desk. "His name is Cyrus Barkley," Hughes added as he tossed the notepad onto the desk.

The Captain pointed at another police officer signaling the officer to commence typing into a computer.

"We need to arrest this guy. We need to get him in here now!" Hughes demanded in the Captain's direction.

The officer nodded to the Captain, prompting the Captain to walk over and examine the details on the computer. The Captain grabbed a piece of paper, then switched his gaze between the paper and the computer screen.

"This doesn't even look remotely like him," the Captain said with a touch of disappointment in his voice.

"The hell it doesn't!" Hughes fired back as he rushed over to the computer.

Hughes closely examined the picture of Cyrus on the computer, then switched his focus to the sketch on the desk.

"How do they not look similar?" Hughes asked. "They look similar," Hughes raised his voice.

"No," the Captain stated.

Sadistic

"This is our guy!" Hughes shouted in the direction of the Captain.

"Until you have sufficient evidence, he is nobody to us!" The Captain exclaimed. "We can't go around arresting people just because you think you recognize their voice. We have nothing on this guy. No criminal record, nothing."

Hughes slammed his hand down on the desk and turned around to grab his stuff before shouting, "Lopez, let's go!"

They walked out of the police station and hopped into an unmarked police car.

"We're going to grab some lunch," Hughes said.

"I'm not hungry," Lopez replied.

"Well, we're getting lunch," Hughes insisted as he pulled out onto the road.

They pulled up to a small diner and made their way inside.

"The usual," Hughes said as he walked past a waitress and made himself comfortable. Lopez took a seat across from him.

They engaged in small talk, discussing things such as the weather as they waited for the waitress to bring their food. Hughes waited until they were almost finished eating before bringing the topic of conversation back to Cyrus.

"So, you're telling me you think that sketch looks nothing like that Cyrus guy?" Hughes enquired as he set his focus firmly upon Lopez.

"You're on this again?" Lopez asked with frustration

in his voice. "Sure, maybe it does a little, but that doesn't make him our guy."

"It should at least make him a suspect, though," Hughes insisted.

"He has no motive, no criminal history, there's no evidence, and we found nothing at any of the scenes to indicate that he was involved. We have nothing. Unless we have something to give to the Captain, there's nothing that we can really do," Lopez explained apologetically.

"I know in my heart that he's the guy," Hughes mumbled.

They sat there in silence for a few minutes savoring the last few morsels of their food before handing the plates over to the waitress and thanking her.

"I'll get this," Hughes said as he handed the waitress enough money to cover the entire bill.

"Thanks," Lopez replied.

"I bumped into Cyrus at the store and he had a bunch of weird things in his shopping cart, and he acted strange when I asked him about it," Hughes said. "Then I saw him at the cash register and he pretty much refused to even talk to me. There's just something about him that irks me. I think he's our guy. I can't just let this go."

They both rose to their feet and headed toward the car. Silence filled the car for almost the entirety of the car ride until they reached the police station.

"Wait," Hughes said as Lopez reached for the door handle. "I'm going to go do something. I'll be back in a little bit," Hughes continued as Lopez just looked at him.

"Where are you going?" Lopez enquired.

"Just out on an errand," Hughes explained, even though he knew Lopez wasn't buying what he was selling.

As Lopez leaned back in his seat, he took a deep breath before returning his focus to Hughes.

"You know you're going to get us both in a lot of trouble. I've only been here a few months. I really don't need this," Lopez pleaded desperately.

"I won't be gone long. Just head out on patrol until I call you," Hughes instructed him.

"I know where you are going and I think it's a really bad idea," Lopez responded. "If the Captain finds out, you better have my back," he added, but he knew it was pointless trying to dissuade Hughes once he had his mind set on something.

"Just cover for me. I won't be gone long," Hughes answered.

13

MUD soaked her dress as she ducked behind a fence and frantically crawled under a table to escape the clutches of a man with a large blood covered knife. She ran as fast as she could, but every time she turned around he was right behind her.

She ran until she reached a house and pounded on the front door, but no one answered. The door handle wouldn't budge as she twisted and pulled at it. The man drew ever closer to her. In a desperate attempt to get inside, she picked up a rock and threw it at the window, but the glass didn't break. The man was now within striking distance.

"Please, no. Please, don't hurt me. I'll do anything," the woman begged as tears rolled down her eyes.

Ignoring her pleas, the man took a step closer and

thrust the knife deep into her chest until it came out the other end. Blood squirted all over the ground and onto the killer's coat. The woman fell to the ground, taking the knife with her.

Reaching for the remote, Cyrus turned off the TV. He hated horror movies with a passion. That wasn't how things went. The blood wasn't supposed to squirt all over like that. It would just drip down her chest. It's also unlikely the knife would've made it all the way through her. *What a stupid movie.*

He dropped the remote on the bed and sat up. He didn't have to head into work because it was his day off. Sara was at work and Chris was at school, so he had nothing to do. He could lay in bed all day if he wished, but he knew that wasn't going to happen.

As he walked over to close the window, Cyrus felt the cold wood under his feet. The breeze rolling in from outside chilled him to the bone. It was getting colder outside as summer began to draw to a close.

The stairs creaked as he made his way downstairs guided by his already rumbling stomach. Bacon was calling his name. It was nice to have the day off to spend some quality time alone.

He cracked open an egg and let it ooze out into the pan. Smoke rose up into Cyrus's face, causing him to cough, but that's how he knew they were going to taste good.

The eggs turned golden brown and looked ready to pop, releasing the bright yellow yoke all over. They were perfect. Cyrus scraped them out of the pan and placed them on the plate next to his bacon. Popping open the refrigerator, he grabbed a beer before making his way over to the couch.

"Shit!" A small drop of yoke fell off his spoon and onto his white t-shirt on its way to his mouth.

Cyrus placed the plate on the table and headed into the kitchen to grab a towel.

He rubbed the towel as hard as he could on the shirt to remove the slimy yellow mark, but it didn't want to budge. He wet the towel and tried again, but to no avail.

Fuck it. Just as he tossed the towel onto the table, his phone started to ring.

Hello?" Cyrus shoved the phone to his ear.

"Yes, Cyrus, would it be all right if you came in for a few hours today? We had some call offs."

"Sure," Cyrus responded with a hint of frustration in his voice. He couldn't believe they wanted him to come in on his day off.

He hung up the phone and shoved it back into his pocket. The last thing he wanted to do was go into work. He walked over to the sink to take care of his plate.

Just then, he heard a knock at the door. THUD! THUD! THUD! Picking up the towel, he wiped his hands before making his way to the door. As he pulled the door open and peered out, a look of disdain emerged on his face. Standing there in the doorway was Hughes, looking like he had just rolled out of a dumpster, staring Cyrus dead in the eyes.

"May I come in?" It wasn't a question. Hughes shoved right past Cyrus, catching him unawares, almost causing him to lose his footing.

Cyrus caught himself. "What the hell?" He asked as Hughes ignored him and made his way into Cyrus's living room.

"Let's talk," Hughes said as he sat down on the couch. "Please take a seat," he continued.

"What the hell are you doing in my house? You can't just walk in. What the fuck is wrong with you?" The intensity in Cyrus's voice quickly escalated.

"Please, let's just talk for a few minutes," Hughes said calmly as he gestured for Cyrus to sit down in the chair across from him.

"No, get the hell out of my house," Cyrus shouted again as he pointed toward the door.

Hughes rose to his feet. "Just sit the fuck down and talk to me!" He shouted.

Remembering who Hughes was, Cyrus made his way over to the chair. With Hughes being the lead Detective in the investigation into the recent series of murders, arousing suspicion by causing a scene was the last thing he needed to do. The smartest possible thing he could was to appease Hughes and then get him out of his house as quickly as he could.

Slowly, Cyrus walked over and sat down in the chair. For a brief moment, the two men stared at each other like a showdown in the old west. Cyrus reached for the TV remote and turned off the TV.

His elbows rested on his legs as he leaned forward. "All right, Detective Hughes, what is it that you would like to talk about?" Cyrus asked.

Instead of responding to Cyrus's query, Hughes took in his surroundings before rising to his feet and making his way toward the hallway, looking in both directions. Cyrus just sat there watching Hughes examine the room, then Hughes turned back around and returned to the couch.

"Where's your dog?" Hughes asked.

"Dog?" Cyrus wasn't sure what Hughes was talking about.

"Oh, you don't remember?" Hughes leaned back. "The dog you were buying those things for at the store the other day."

The trip to the store had slipped Cyrus's mind. He never thought Hughes would turn up at his house and bombard him with questions.

"Turns out he was very sick, so we had to put him down," Cyrus said in an attempt to cover his tracks.

"Was it?" Hughes smiled.

"Yes," Cyrus answered.

Hughes took another quick glance around the room. "I don't think this house looks like a dog ever lived here," Hughes fired back as he rubbed his hand on the couch, then caressed the carpet. "I don't see any dog hair on anything, which is rather unusual for a house that supposedly had a dog."

"We clean a lot," Cyrus responded in a desperate bid to bring an end to Hughes's inquisition.

"You see, I don't think there ever was a dog here," Hughes said as he placed his hand on his chin before pointing at Cyrus. "Wanna know what I think? I think you lied."

"Why are you here?" Cyrus asked no longer trying to conceal his frustration.

"I want to know what else you might have lied about," Hughes responded as his face shifted to a much more serious expression.

"I think it's time you left," Cyrus said.

"Let's play a game. I say something that you said and then you tell me if it was a lie, deal?" Hughes suggested as he mocked Cyrus with a fake laugh.

Cyrus didn't answer Hughes. He just stared at him, wondering what he was going to ask, and trying to come up with a way to get him out of his house.

"You were at the store getting some cleaning supplies for your dog, correct?" Hughes fired the first question in Cyrus's direction as he stared him dead in the eyes like he was trying to pry the answer out of him.

"Well, since we both already know the answer to that one, let's try a different one," Hughes added as he put his hands together. "You weren't awake the night your neighbor's house was broken into and it wasn't you that their kid thought they saw, right?"

Once again, Cyrus didn't respond so Hughes continued his line of questioning. "Well, are you going to answer? I am rather curious."

"I was in bed sleeping. I don't know what the kid saw, but it wasn't me," Cyrus fired back defending himself.

"If it was you he saw I wonder what you were doing out that late?" Hughes enquired. "But, you aren't going to answer that now are you?"

"It wasn't me, so I don't know," Cyrus answered as he looked up at the clock on the wall. "Look, I am due in at work soon, so you're going to have to leave."

"All right, just one more question," Hughes said with a confident smile etched on his face.

Cyrus couldn't wait for Hughes to leave. If he wasn't a member of the police, he would've thrown him out by now and with force if needed. He only had to keep his cool for a few more minutes.

"You see, when those sketches were released, the ones of the killer, which I'm sure you've seen, I could've sworn I'd seen that person somewhere before," Hughes said as Cyrus's hands began to sweat. "I couldn't put my finger on it, but the face looked familiar," Hughes continued.

"All right," Cyrus said simply acknowledging Hughes.

"Did you recognize him?" Hughes asked.

"I don't think so," Cyrus responded. He had a feeling he knew what Hughes was referring to, but he hoped like hell that he was wrong.

"Then, this 'suspect' as we like to call him chose to contact me. I'm not sure how he got hold of my number, but he did and he called me," Hughes said as he gave Cyrus a questioning look.

"Yeah, I heard about that on the radio," Cyrus responded.

"Did you?" Hughes asked. "Well, he said some pretty negative things. He said I'd never catch him and that he would haunt me until I die. Rude, right?" Hughes continued and laughed.

"What are you getting at?" A clearly frustrated Cyrus demanded.

"Well, just like the sketch, I thought I recognized the voice that called me," Hughes continued.

"So, who was it then?" Cyrus enquired.

"Well, that leads me into my final question," Hughes said as he moved in a little closer to Cyrus in an attempt to intimidate him.

"Tell me if this statement is true or false," Hughes said. "You're the one responsible for the recent string of murders."

Furious, Cyrus immediately stood up and gestured toward the door. "Get the hell out of my house!" Cyrus commanded.

Hughes shot to his feet. "We both know it's you. Just say it is so we can get this over with. You tied a man to a chair and killed him, you sick fuck!"

"I told you to get the hell out of my house!" Cyrus exclaimed as he stormed toward Hughes and shoved him back onto the couch.

Hughes instantly stood back up, grabbing Cyrus by the shirt and driving him into the wall. "You fucking bastard, how could you kill those people? Who else have you killed?" He shouted into Cyrus's face as he forcefully pressed him against the wall.

"I didn't kill anyone!" Cyrus shouted as he pushed Hughes off him.

Both men stood there, hands on their knees exhausted from the sudden altercation.

"Get out," Cyrus said to Hughes as he pointed at

the door.

Hughes lifted himself up and started making his way toward the door. He reached for the door handle and opened the door, but stopped before walking out.

"I'm going to catch you. You will go to prison," Hughes said defiantly. He walked out, slamming the door behind him.

Cyrus peeked out the curtain, waiting for him to leave. After Hughes was gone, he sat down and tried to regain his composure. His heart was racing at a mile a minute.

What the hell just happened? In a state of disbelief, he looked back out the window at the point where Hughes was parked only moments ago. *How the hell?* Cyrus had underestimated Hughes. He had linked Cyrus to the sketch after meeting him twice, albeit briefly.

Now, he was fearful that he would come back again, but next time his wife might be home. He didn't want to risk the possibility of Sara or Chris putting two and two together and pinning him as the killer. Coming to the realization that the one they had feared all along was actually living in their home.

He needed to conjure up a way to get Hughes off his back, or at the very least buy himself some much-needed breathing space. No one is perfect, not even Hughes.

Cyrus pulled up to work shocked that he'd arrived on time given the morning's incident. He knew he wouldn't be able to handle a confrontation with Joe following the encounter with Hughes earlier in the day. Not both in one day.

Sadistic

"Hey, man!" Dave greeted Cyrus as he did every other morning. "You look a bit rough, man. Fall out of your car this morning?" Dave asked with a laugh. If he only knew the half of it.

"I just wasn't expecting to be called in today, so I hope they don't expect too much of me," Cyrus laughed as he took his seat.

"As if you ever do anything anyway," Dave spun around in his seat laughing before sinking his teeth back into his work.

As was the norm, Cyrus opened up a work folder before examining his surroundings. With the coast clear, he clicked on the web browser. *Now what?*

He clicked on the search bar and typed in ***Walter Hughes***. Multiple links popped up, most of which were social network sites or advertisements. As he scrolled down, he didn't find anything that was worth his time.

He tried ***Detective Walter Hughes***. More links came up. Some were police cases and others were spam links or more social networks.

As Cyrus scrolled down, he spotted a link titled, **Detective brings down small-time drug ring**. According to the article, a Detective had single-handedly brought down a small drug ring by going undercover and gaining the trust of the leader. He scrolled down further until he came across a photograph of the Detective in question, revealing that it was in fact the same Detective Hughes that had interrogated him earlier in the day.

Backing out of the page, he scrolled down further.

Much to his disappointment, he could only locate articles about police activity involving Hughes and other articles involving a different Hughes.

There was nothing he could use to gain an edge on Hughes. Sitting back in his chair, he contemplated for a moment before shifting his gaze back to Dave, who was busily typing up a report.

Detective Walter Hughes….. Gets Arrested. Three links down and there was an article titled, **Local Detective gets caught up in what he is detecting.** *Perfect.* As Cyrus got further into the article, a smile emerged across his face.

The article made reference to a man named Walter Hughes who had gone undercover into a drug ring, and somewhere along the line he got caught up in the murky side of things. After another member of the police force became aware that Hughes wasn't doing as he was supposed to, he brought him in for a urine test and it was revealed that his urine contained various illegal substances. As a result, he was kicked off the force and incarcerated for a short period of time.

The news was music to Cyrus's ears, but he wasn't exactly sure what he could do with this information. The police must have already known about what had transpired, so it would be pointless trying to blackmail Hughes with information that was public knowledge.

Once more, Cyrus glanced around to make sure the coast was clear, then thought for another moment. *If he has this on his record, how the fuck is he still on the police force?*

Cyrus went to the Police Department website and had a look around. He wasn't even sure what he was looking for.

"What are you looking at?" Dave enquired as he stuck his head over Cyrus's shoulder.

"I just had some trouble with a police officer this morning and I was trying to figure out who I should contact about it," Cyrus explained.

"You could try the Police Chief. His name is Nathan Hughes, I think," Dave muttered.

That had to be it. The Police Chief and Hughes shared the same last name. It's likely that they were related.

"Thanks, man!" Cyrus exclaimed happily. "You probably saved me a lot of time!" He continued.

"Glad I could help, dude," Dave said sounding somewhat surprised at Cyrus's level of excitement.

Now, he was curious as to whether the remainder of the police force knew about Hughes's interesting past, especially his drug abuse and arrest.

After Dave had returned to his seat, Cyrus went back to work. *Police Chief Nathan Hughes*, he typed. A police profile immediately popped up. There was also an article about the impending retirement of the long time Police Chief, Nathan Hughes, and it was questioning who would take his place. It wasn't his brother. Nathan Hughes must have been Walter Hughes's father. He hoped that everyone didn't already know about this so that he could use it to get Hughes off his back.

He wrote down the name of the Police Chief before closing down the page.

"I'm going to need you to stay until tonight," Joe said seemingly out of nowhere.

"Are you kidding me?" Cyrus replied angrily.

"No, I need you until at least ten," Joe responded.

"That's longer than my normal shift and today is my day off," Cyrus groaned.

"Not everything always goes the way we want it to," Joe said as he turned around and walked away.

Cyrus remembered he didn't have the chance to tell Sara that he had been called into work, and now they were going to make him stay back late. He had been so pissed off, and still was, that he had neglected to inform his wife. After ensuring Joe wasn't within earshot, he dialed Sara's number and waited for it to ring.

"Hey," Sara answered.

"I got called into work," Cyrus said sounding less than pleased.

"Aww, really? That sucks. I wanted to order some pizza and relax with you tonight, and maybe watch a movie or something," Sara responded with a hint of sadness in her voice.

"Even worse, they're making me stay late," he replied.

"How late?" She asked.

"Ten," Cyrus answered.

"Ugh," she sighed "I'm feeling pretty tired, so I will probably be asleep by the time you get home."

"I'm really sorry, but Joe didn't even tell me I had to stay late until I was already here," Cyrus explained.

"It's not your fault. Well, I'll talk to you later. Love you," she said.

Sadistic

"Love you, too," Cyrus replied before hanging up the phone.

First Hughes barges into my house, then Joe forces me to work more hours, and now Sara is pissed at me! Fuck!

This drug stuff wasn't going to be enough to get back at Hughes. Cyrus could tell by how Hughes had acted this morning, but what else could he do? He had to come up with something.

Cyrus spent the majority of his remaining time at work trying to devise a plan to get back at Hughes. He was still pissed off. Perhaps he needed to do more than scare him. The only problem was that there was the possibility that he had already mentioned Hughes to someone, and if Hughes were to suddenly go missing he would be suspect number one.

The streets were poorly lit as he made his way down the dark roads. It wasn't typical for him to get out of work this late. As he drove, he remembered he had Hughes's address on a piece of paper in his center console. Perhaps he should pay him a surprise visit just as Hughes had done to him.

It didn't take long to reach Hughes's house. Sitting in his car, he couldn't help but notice an old-looking house with a terribly maintained yard. *What a pigsty.*

He emerged from his car and stood there gazing at the house. Never in his life had he broken into a house. He wasn't sure if he'd be any good at it. He might a make noise and set off Hughes, who most probably had a gun in his possession.

Standing there, he contemplated what he should do.

He took a few steps, then looked around the corner into Hughes's driveway. There was no car in sight. Hughes must be out. A smile came across Cyrus's face as an idea popped into his head. He knew exactly what he could do.

14

DARKNESS fell over the street as Cyrus stood at the edge of the curb readying himself to enter Hughes's home. For all Cyrus knew, Hughes could be home at any time, so he needed to be efficient.

Silently, he stepped across the street and approached the front door. Even though he was wearing latex gloves, the rocks were cold as he felt around, lifting them up and checking underneath them. He picked up the dirty welcome mat and peeked under. *Hmmm*. He looked around the door. Standing on his toes, he reached above the door to feel around the small ledge.

There it was. He pulled down a small, rusty key. Quickly, he squeezed it into the lock and silently cracked the door open just enough to look inside. The light from the street lamps poured inside, lighting up a narrow path, allowing Cyrus to spot various things scattered across the floor. He pulled out his phone to light the way and closed the door behind him.

Moments after having closed the door, Cyrus's foot got tangled up in a shirt and he almost stumbled over. *Dammit.* He shook it off and flashed the light around him. It appeared as if Hughes wasn't the type that cleaned often, if ever.

Cyrus knew what he was looking for and needed to find it quickly. He stepped over more obstacles as he passed by doorways. The bathroom seemed to be nowhere in sight. Time was rushing by at a fast rate. He had already been in the house for five minutes. A flash of light rushed in through the windows. Cyrus ducked down, but the light kept going as a car passed by the house.

As he rose to his feet, he noticed beads of sweat had formed on his forehead. The latex gloves felt tight as the sweat began to fill the gap between his hands and the gloves. *I need to speed things up.* He jerked up and started through the house again.

Almost walking right by the door, he turned around and noticed a toilet through a slightly opened door. Pushing the door open with his foot, he looked in and saw a towel on the floor and toilet paper on the sink.

Flashing the light on the sink, he intently scanned the contents before transferring his gaze to the floor. The cabinet creaked as he opened it. If medicine was what he was searching for, he would have just hit the jackpot. He closed the cabinet and picked the towel up off the floor; it was clean, not what he was looking for.

Time wasn't on his side. He needed to get a move on. Examining the room with his light, he spotted a small case containing a shaver. He grabbed it, removed the shaver, and looked inside the holder. *Bingo*. He tipped it over, dumping a small pile of hair into his hand. Now, he needed to get out as fast as possible.

Ensuring he left the house exactly as he had found it, he closed the bathroom door slightly before hurrying down the hall all the while being careful to avoid garbage and piles of clothes. Upon reaching the door, he looked out the window to make sure no one was outside.

His heart began to race as he closed the door behind him and placed the key back on top of the door. *Home free*. He darted toward his car and climbed in.

The car engine blared like a thunderstorm coming out of nowhere to disrupt the silence of the night. He pressed hard on the gas and sped off, putting as much distance between himself and Hughes's house as quickly as possible.

As he turned a corner, he looked at his watch. He had enough time to get home without arousing suspicion. A car drove by, and at a quick glance it almost looked like Hughes. He tried to look in his rearview mirror to see what kind of car it was, but it was too late.

He unclenched his fist and looked down at the hair in his hand. His problem with Hughes may have just been solved.

Upon arriving home, Cyrus saw that all the lights were turned off. Finally, something seemed to be going right for him. As he hurried his way into the house, he tried to keep as quiet as possible so as not to wake his wife, but every single one of his movements were magnified in the silence of the night. He opened drawers until he located a box of sandwich bags. Carefully, he opened a bag and dumped the hair into it.

With the coast clear, he made his way back out to his car. He wanted to put the hair alongside the rest of the things in his trunk. He was starting to build up quite a collection of items.

Despite still being pissed off about his confrontation with Hughes, he felt a wave of excitement rush over him. He might be able to put a mile between himself and the only thing standing in his way without even having to kill.

I deserve a new bed was Cyrus's first thought as he rolled over to silence his alarm. He hadn't had a decent night's sleep since the day he committed his second kill. When he stood over the body of the man he had killed, he felt free. It was a piece of art that was of his own creation. His life now was nothing but stress and frustration at every turn. There were people threatening to take away his happiness and his family, and others wanted him in jail and were labeling him a monster.

His idea of a monster was vastly different to that of most. His boss, Joe, was a monster. A monster he had to go and deal with. As he stretched his arms, he resented the fact that he had to head into work shortly. At least he would have Hughes off his back in the near future.

All he needed was for an opportunity to present

itself. With a little luck, he hoped a chance would arise before Hughes magically found evidence to link him to the recent series of murders. He wasn't sure how long he would be able to keep Hughes at bay.

As he zipped his way to work, the breeze flowed through his hair. His anger levels had been somewhat subdued by his excitement. The radio blared and he bobbed his head to some classic rock.

"Hey, man!" Dave greeted Cyrus.

"You know, you say that same exact thing every morning," Cyrus laughed.

"Yeah, I know. I never really thought about it, though," Dave returned Cyrus's laugh. "Guess what?" Dave continued.

"What?" Cyrus replied.

"I and some of the other guys are going to grab some food at the diner across the street for lunch today, and you're coming. You've been fucking around for too long."

"A-," Cyrus was immediately cut off.

"Nope, you're coming. End of discussion," Dave laughed.

"All right, all right," Cyrus conceded.

He couldn't recall the last time he'd sat down with some friends and enjoyed a bite to eat. After all the dramas he'd encountered recently, he felt as if he deserved some downtime. Plus, he couldn't deny the fact that he was feeling pretty damn hungry. He had forgotten to eat before leaving for work this morning.

As he flipped through his work folder on the

computer, he realized how far behind he was in his work. Cyrus was starting to wonder if his work was falling onto others. They never really discussed what they were working on. Usually, it was just making sure complaints were filed and records were kept. Nothing overly interesting.

The final minutes on the clock before it was time to go to lunch ticked away. Since his conversation with Dave, he had gotten significantly hungrier and was looking forward to filling his stomach with some much-needed food.

"Ready to go?" Dave asked just as the final minute before lunch ticked by.

"Hell yeah," Cyrus responded with a smile.

They met up with a Mark, Greg, and Steve, and ran across the street to the diner. It was a small diner that got the majority of its business from people working at City Hall and other companies lining the road across the street.

The diner looked decent enough. It was what McDonald's probably looked like at some point, with red and yellow tables. There was nobody there aside from a few older people and the staff, who looked as if they would rather be elsewhere.

"What can I get you?" The waitress enquired.

Everybody began to place their orders one by one as the waitress tried her hardest to keep up with a pack of hungry animals. After the final order had been placed, they started talking. Much to the surprise of Cyrus, the conversation centered mostly on work. If this is what he was missing out on at lunch breaks, he was fine not going out with them for lunch.

"Are we going to be able to make it back in time?" Cyrus asked with a hint of nervousness in his voice. The cook had five orders to prepare and they only had half an hour to get the food, eat it, and head back to work.

"Yeah, probably," Mark said.

"Maybe," Greg laughed.

"What's Joe going to do, fire all of us?" Dave laughed.

"I wouldn't be surprised," Cyrus said as he laughed in an attempt to allay some of his concern.

As they waited for their food to arrive, all the men sat around jokingly discussing their work and home lives. Greg did most of the talking, and since he never shut up they all sat and listened. Cyrus wondered why they even invited him along, or maybe he was the only one that found Greg irritating.

The food came. French fries piled high covered in ketchup and artery clogging burgers ran for miles. They all dug in, stuffing their faces without even coming up for air. It was like a scene from a documentary on Animal Planet about the eating habits of lions.

Cyrus's phone interrupted him, forcing him to part ways with his food. It was Sara. He leaned away from the guys and answered his phone, trying to talk as low as possible so no one would hear him.

"Hey," Cyrus said.

"How's work?" Sara asked.

"It is fine, we're just at a diner having lunch," Cyrus explained as he shoved a French fry into his mouth.

"I will have dinner ready by the time you get home!" Sara exclaimed with frustration in her voice.

"Well, I didn't know," Cyrus said as he tried to keep his voice down.

"We were also going to watch that movie tonight," Sara continued.

"What movie?" Cyrus asked.

"The one about the hooker that you said you would re-watch with me when it come back on, and I told you that today was the day that it was coming back on," Sara continued sounding annoyed.

"That was a while ago. How would I remember that?" He asked.

"Just head straight home after work. Don't stay late," she continued.

"Don't worry, I'll be there," Cyrus replied as he hung up the phone.

"Whoa, what was that all about?" Dave asked. Clearly, they had all been listening in on the conversation. "Sara?" Dave continued.

"Yeah, she was just mad that I was eating because she was making dinner and wanted to make sure I wasn't staying out late," Cyrus explained.

"That sucks," Dave said with his mouth full of food.

They all stacked their plates up and made their way back to work. They arrived late, but were able to sneak in quietly, managing to avoid Joe's wrath. By the time Joe had arrived, they were all in their seats and looked as if they were in the middle of doing work.

After the manner in which Sara had talked to him earlier in the day, Cyrus was in no rush to get out of work. A part of him wanted to stay late at work. He wasn't sure why she seemed so angry. It wasn't like he had done anything wrong or at least nothing she was aware of.

Cyrus turned on some relaxing music to accompany his ride home. He needed a clear train of thought to come up with a solid plan to take care of Hughes, avoid getting yelled at by Sara for eating out with the guys, and get out of spending the night watching a movie about some abused hooker.

Just as Cyrus pulled up to a red light, his phone started to ring. Cyrus yanked his phone out of his pocket and realized the call was from a restricted number.

He looked at the phone for a moment, letting it vibrate in his hand. It vibrated and vibrated until it finally stopped. One missed call the phone said.

The light turned green and Cyrus placed the phone on his lap, and started to drive. He never answered restricted calls. No one ever restricted a call for a positive reason. Chances are that it was just a bunch of bored teenagers dialing random numbers.

The phone started to vibrate again. *Restricted number again*. Finally, he gave in and answered.

"Hello?" Cyrus said expecting a group of obnoxious kids to start shouting into the phone.

"What are you doing?" The voice on the other end asked.

"Who is this?" Cyrus asked annoyed that his gut instinct about the call was on the money.

The phone went quiet for a moment. Cyrus kept his eyes on the road to make sure no police cars passed by.

"If you are doing anything, you might want to stop and take a seat," the voice on the other end of the line continued just as Cyrus was about to hang up.

"Excuse me?" Cyrus asked angrily.

"Unless you want a serious problem, I wouldn't hang up," the voice responded.

Hurriedly, Cyrus turned into a store parking lot and parked his car.

"All right, I'm sitting down. Who is this and what do you want?" Cyrus demanded.

"I know who you are," the voice said. Ignoring his questions, the voice continued, "I know what you've done."

The voice now had Cyrus's full attention. It must be Hughes. Who else could it possibly be? Maybe it was just a prank call and they weren't talking about what he thought they were referring to.

"And, what is that exactly?" Cyrus asked as his heart began to race.

"Let's not play games. You know exactly what I'm talking about," the voice continued.

Cyrus didn't bother entertaining the person on the other end of the line with a response. He just sat there waiting for the unknown person to speak.

"The way you wrapped that rope around the man's neck, I bet you loved it, didn't you?" The voice enquired all the while laughing.

It must be that woman that saw me in the house. But, it can't be because the voice was clearly a guy and the strangulation was mentioned on the news, so anyone could've known that.

"Who the hell is this?" Cyrus asked with nothing else to say.

"Okay, now that I have your attention-," the man said before Cyrus cut him off.

"Listen, I don't know who you think-," Cyrus shouted, but was also cut off.

"Don't interrupt me! Enough. I told you, I'm not here to play games. I know who you are and I know what you've done!" The man shouted.

Cyrus wanted to reach through the phone, grab the man by the throat, and end his life. The voice didn't sound remotely similar to that of Hughes. Whoever this person was must have spoken with Hughes at some point because no one else could have any reason to suspect that he was the one responsible for the murders.

"I hope I have your attention this time because I'm not repeating myself again," the voice went on.

It was obvious that whoever was on the other end of the line was disguising their voice. Maybe he knew him. Why else would this person feel compelled to disguise their voice?

"I'm going to kill," the voice said catching Cyrus off guard. "And, you're going to take the blame for it," the voice continued.

"No, I'm-," Cyrus began before he was cut off once more.

"Nobody else knows who you are, so YOU won't be taking the blame. The killer will be taking the blame.

That is unless you refuse, then everyone will know," the voice explained. "I am going to kill people, I don't know how many, and you are going to take the blame for it. You don't even have to do anything."

"You're messed up," Cyrus said. He didn't know what else to say. He couldn't say no, and he didn't want to acknowledge the fact that the man on the other end of the line was correct about him being the killer. It could still be a trap from Hughes.

"Do you agree with my plan?" The voice asked "Wait, I don't care because you have no other choice. You will hear from me again," the voice warned chillingly, then the line went dead.

Cyrus looked at the phone as it blinked signaling the end of the phone call. He looked out his front window into the cloudy sky. *Who the fuck was that?*

Consumed with frustration, he began to punch the steering wheel. Right after sorting out one problem this happens. He didn't have the time nor the patience for this. Who was he even going to kill? What sick act was he about to be blamed for?

This must be what it felt like for the police. He had no suspect and no leads. Nothing to work with to find out who the man was. The man knew his secret and could reveal it at any time. The man had the power to ruin his life.

He turned the key and started his car. After taking one last look at his phone, he stepped on the gas. He had to get home to watch the movie with Sara and play the waiting game. All he could do was sit and wait.

15

IT felt like the walls were closing in on him as he drove to his house. In his mind, it seemed as if everyone was staring at him. Any one of them could be the mystery caller.

After he hung up the phone, Cyrus could picture the man laughing. He was going to go on a killing spree and pin it on Cyrus. Until Cyrus found out who the man was, he had full control over him. He could do as he pleased and get away with it.

He needed to find this guy quickly and put his life to an end.

As he pulled into the driveway, he saw the light of the TV reflecting against the window. They must already be in there waiting for him. Sara was going to force Chris to watch the movie as well. He was probably even less excited than Cyrus.

"I'm home!" Cyrus announced as he walked through the door.

The smell of chicken and mashed potatoes greeted him before Sara had a chance to reply.

"Dinner is on the stove," Sara said as she looked back at Cyrus.

"I know I can smell it. Wow, this is going to be good," Cyrus said as he kicked off his shoes and headed over to the stove.

"Are you sure you're still going to be hungry?" Sara asked in a sarcastic tone as she looked into the kitchen to see that Cyrus already had his head buried in the cupboard looking for a plate.

He lifted up the saucepan and dumped gravy onto his potatoes. "Ahhh!" He yelled as some gravy managed to land on his arm.

"What happened?" Sara shouted into the kitchen.

"I spilled some gravy and managed to burn myself, but it's all right," he replied.

"That's impossible, honey. The food was prepared like an hour ago. It shouldn't be hot anymore," she answered.

As he rubbed the gravy off his arm with his finger, he noticed that it wasn't hot. Was he going crazy?

He carried his plate out and sat down on the couch next to Chris. Sara began clicking buttons on the remote, bringing up menus on the TV.

"Here we go," Sara said as she turned on the movie.

The movie came on. Cyrus had remembered bits and pieces about the beginning, but he couldn't keep his focus on the movie. Everything around him was beginning to resemble a blur and the words emanating from the TV sounded muffled.

The anonymous man's threat kept playing over and over in his head. If he didn't do as instructed, he was going to be turned in to the police and his life as he knew it would be over. This isn't how things were supposed to go. Cyrus is the killer. He is the one who dishes out the threats. Apparently, there was another person with bloodlust and he was going to use Cyrus as a scapegoat. What if he did all the killing he wanted, then still chose to turn him in? No one would believe that he wasn't the one that had committed all the crimes.

"Cyrus, are you even paying attention?" A visibly angry Sara cut into his daydreaming.

"Yes," he answered.

"What's going on then?" Sara persisted, but Cyrus didn't utter a word. He had no clue what was going on in the movie and he didn't particularly care.

"Exactly," Sara continued.

Sara continued to talk, but the words just floated in the air bypassing Cyrus. In Cyrus's mind, everything had started to sound muffled and a loud ringing filled his ears. He wanted to cover his ears. He wanted to escape.

"Shut up!" Cyrus shouted cutting Sara off and shocking everyone in the room in the process.

Everything came to a standstill, and Chris and Sara stared at Cyrus in awe.

"Now is not the time," Cyrus said.

Sara picked up the remote and turned off the TV before proceeding to smack the remote back onto the couch.

"When is the time then?" She asked. "It's like you're never around anymore. Even when you're here it's like you aren't. You don't think I notice?" Sara continued.

"I feel like you've been gone for days," Sara added.

"It's just been a long day," he said quietly.

"It's just been a long day," Sara repeated mockingly as she rose to her feet and headed toward the stairs.

Cyrus transferred his gaze to Chris who didn't let a word pass his lips. Rising to his feet, Chris followed Sara up the stairs without making eye contact with Cyrus.

"Babe! Sara! C'mon!" He pleadingly shouted up to her.

"No, just go. Take your long day somewhere else and come back when you're ready to actually be here," she said as she forcefully closed the bedroom door.

"Argh!" Cyrus loudly groaned barely concealing his desire to smash his hand into the wall and throw everything in sight.

Swinging the door open, he headed to his car. *I'm sick of all this fucking shit.* He climbed into his car and slammed the door. *When I need my family the most, this is how they fucking treat me!*

He pulled out of the drive and sped off. The stupid movie was a waste of his time anyway. He needed to be out trying to figure out who the anonymous caller was and come up with a plan to get Hughes off his back.

Cyrus drove until he reached the edge of the city. It had been so long since he had last been out there, but he needed to release his anger somehow, and there was only one way he knew how to rid himself of his frustration before it boiled over.

Just as he was about to get one person off his back another decided to start meddling in his business. He wanted them both wiped out. Both of them dead at his feet.

The loud sounds of the city were soon replaced with silence as he left the city in his rearview mirror. Turning down roads that led to more trees and fields, he couldn't recall the last time he was in this area.

He spotted someone walking alone up ahead of him. His rage had been bottled up for so long that it was ready to burst out at any moment. Cyrus put his foot on the gas in readiness to speed up and flatten the person there and then. He had never seen a person bounce off the front of a car before, but then he would have blood on his car. He couldn't risk the possibility of getting blood on himself.

As he closed in on the man, he slowed down to contemplate what he would do. When he got close enough, he pulled over to the side of the road and stepped out of the car, feeling the rocks under his feet.

"Hello!" Cyrus shouted loudly at the man that was now just thirty feet away from him.

The man turned around and looked at him. He pointed at himself to see if he was the one that Cyrus was talking to.

"Can you help me?!" Cyrus enquired loudly. "Something is up with my car!" He knew car trouble was the oldest trick in the book. It might not work, but it wasn't like he had any other ideas up his sleeve.

Slowly, the man made his way toward Cyrus. "Did it stall out?" The man asked as he drew ever closer.

This is the part where a car drives by and ruins everything.

"Well, I don't know much about cars, but I can try to help," the man said as he closed to within half a dozen feet of Cyrus.

As the man got to within striking distance of the car, Cyrus opened his passenger seat door and leaned inside to retrieve his knife. He got back to his feet, and before the man had a chance to process what was going on, Cyrus plunged the knife as hard as he could deep into his upper chest. He yanked the knife out of him and stepped back, waiting for the pain to force him to the ground.

"A- a- plea-," the man tried to speak as one knee dropped to the ground. He leaned over and coughed up some blood, but still didn't fall.

Cyrus walked around to the back of him and drove the knife into his back, pushing him to the ground. The man's hands grasped for anything within reach, grabbing at dirt and rocks that proceeded to fall between his fingers. He tried to push himself up, but every last bit of strength had already escaped him.

Just then, a burst of rage filled his head as he thought about why he was here in the first place, then he dropped to the ground, stabbing the man in the back repeatedly until his entire back was covered in wounds. The man's shirt began to fade to red as blood soaked it.

Cyrus wiped the blood off the knife onto the man's

pants and rose to his feet, towering over the man. Not wanting to risk getting blood on himself, Cyrus left the body where it was. The trunk popped and he tossed the knife into the back. As he climbed back into the car, he felt a sense of relief. The anger had been replaced with hunger as his stomach was beginning to rumble.

As Cyrus continued to drive, the city came back into his line of sight. It rose up and over the trees like a beast in hiding. He had somewhere to go, but it wasn't home. He had a stop to make.

Making his way down the road, the sky grew increasingly darker. He continued his journey until a familiar sight came into view. After parking on a different street, he made his way toward Detective Hughes's street. Just as he had hoped and expected, Hughes's car wasn't at his house. He stood almost directly across the street from Hughes's house as he looked around for a place to hide.

Cyrus ventured from yard to yard looking for a way to get to the next road over and to his car quickly if needed.

He found a spot and crouched down. Sometimes he surprised himself. A whole hour had passed before Hughes arrived home.

Pulling out his phone, Cyrus went to his previous calls before landing on Hughes's number. As soon as Hughes stepped out his car, Cyrus clicked CALL. He noticed that Hughes had come to a halt and pulled his phone out of his pocket. At first, it appeared as if Hughes would ignore the call, but he answered it just as the call was about to go to voicemail.

"Hello," Hughes said.

"Hello, Detective Hughes," Cyrus said in the same muffled voice.

"You again?" Hughes said as he started to pull the phone away from his mouth.

"Don't do that!" Cyrus exclaimed.

"Do what?" Hughes asked.

"Start recording, I'll hang up," Cyrus said.

"What makes you think I was about to do anything?" Hughes said as he examined his surroundings.

"Just don't do it," Cyrus answered.

"Can you see me?" Hughes asked as he continued to look around in an attempt to spot Cyrus.

"You see, we aren't as different as you would like to think," Cyrus said matter-of-factly.

"I know this is you, Cyrus," Hughes responded as he stopped looking around.

"You think you know who this is, but you know nothing. You are nothing. You think you are above me when in reality you're trash just like me," Cyrus said as the anger rose in his voice.

"I am nothing like you. You're filth. You deserve to rot in prison or die just like your innocent victims!" Hughes shouted down the phone.

"We both have an addiction," Cyrus continued all the while ignoring Hughes's berating.

"Where are you?" Hughes asked as he started looking around once more.

"I am everywhere," Cyrus answered mockingly.

"Where the fuck are you. You coward. Show yourself," Hughes demanded.

"You have your alcohol addiction and I......I'm addicted to killing. I need the feeling of watching the life fade away in a person's eyes as they take their last breaths," Cyrus said.

"You're nothing but a freak," Hughes said sounding more enraged than ever.

"An animal. That's all you will ever be, and when I prove it you will spend the remainder of your life behind bars rotting with the rest of the animals I've put away," Hughes continued.

For a moment, the line went silent as Cyrus sat there hiding behind a bush while Hughes looked around trying to locate him.

"I gave up drinking. I didn't let it consume me," Hughes broke the silence.

"Or, did you give it up after you realized it had consumed you? What about the drugs? Did you have any family before the drugs?" Cyrus taunted Hughes.

"Fuck you!" Hughes said before dropping the phone to the side and shouting, "Where the hell are you, you coward?!"

As he watched Hughes shout angrily into the street, Cyrus couldn't help but grin. The feeling of power consumed him. It was lovely.

Suddenly, the line went dead. Hughes hung up the phone and made his way toward his front door. Cyrus knew he had won. He had got the better of Hughes and loved every second of it. He had to leave before Hughes decided what his next move would be.

Slowly, Cyrus crept back and started walking between houses, through the dark, back toward his car. *That's right, Hughes, you need to go to bed. You've got a body to take care of in the morning.*

16

SHE looked so beautiful laying there covered by just a blanket, with her hair spread across her pillow as she slept. If he found her to be so beautiful, why didn't he regret leaving early instead of trying to fix things with her? Sara had been visibly angry about Cyrus being absent minded whenever he was home, but he didn't particularly care. He preferred to be gone. Her sadness was none of his concern.

There was no reason for her to be sad in the first place. Everyone is guilty of being a little absent minded from time to time. Sometimes people just get caught up in their own things. He used to regret committing that first kill and revealing that part of himself, but now he loved it. He questioned how he had got this far in life without the pleasure of the kill.

It seemed like eons ago that he carried out his first kill when in reality it had not even been two weeks since he created his first piece of art. In his eyes, killing had made him a new and improved person.

The alarm started going off on Sara's phone. She quickly turned it off so as not to wake up Cyrus. Quickly, he closed his eyes in a desperate bid to avoid a conversation with her. He wanted her to hurry up and leave, so he could get up and get ready alone. There was no need to talk.

The bed shook as she sat up and hopped out of bed. Cyrus cracked his eye open to see if she was going to walk out of the room. She stood there wearing nothing but her blue lace underwear and her white tank top as she looked through her drawers for clothes.

As she turned around, he closed his eyes again. He could hear her making her way toward the bed and sitting down. Cyrus cracked his eyes open again as she walked naked into the bathroom. He closed his eyes and tried to picture her in the shower, but he started seeing himself instead. Blood was flowing down his body and into the drain. He could remember that night like it was just yesterday. The blood stuck to his body like it never wanted to leave.

As he imagined himself slowly bathing off the blood, he slipped back to sleep before waking to another alarm, his alarm. He opened his eyes and looked at the bathroom. The bathroom door was now open and the light was off. Upon glancing at the clock, he noticed that it was now his turn to get ready for work.

As Cyrus readied himself for work, he remembered

a thought he had a couple of days earlier. He had come to the conclusion that it would be a good idea to get a gun. Cyrus wasn't a fan of guns, but he figured it'd make sense to have one to prepare for the unexpected. There was the possibility that he would be confronted by the police or lose control of a situation during a killing. He couldn't run the risk of being arrested or overpowered by someone, but he was hesitant about getting a gun because he wasn't sure whether guns could be traced.

He needed to be more professional. A long time ago, he'd read that people like himself would select a victim, stalk them for days or even weeks before even giving consideration to moving in for the kill. He hadn't done anything like that. To this point, the longest he had waited was a couple of hours and that kill went horribly wrong, resulting in a sketch being released. Even though that was the only time he tried to plan a kill, he clearly didn't give sufficient attention to the planning process. At some point, he would need to do some research to see how other killers went about their work. He didn't want to make the same mistake that others had, and part of him wanted to top all of them, set himself apart from the rest as the killer that could never be caught.

As he made his way out the door and to his car, he couldn't help but notice that the morning was colder than usual. He rubbed the crusts out of his eyes and switched on the car. When he turned the key, the radio immediately turned on. He reached for the knob to change the station, but what was on caught his attention.

This is Channel 4 Morning Talk News reporting.

Susan: It's a grim morning, with a body discovered off Route 142 heading eastbound out of town. What should we make of this, Linda?

Linda: It's horrible. The condition the man was found in, and he was in plain view for everyone to see. His family went looking for him when he didn't come home. All they had to do was drive down the road and they would've come across his body. Truly heartbreaking, Susan.

Susan: The victim was stabled multiple times in the front and back. I cannot imagine what was going through the victim's mind as this was occurring.

Linda: Well, I know what everyone is wondering. Is it safe to assume that this attack is related to the recent string of murders that have been linked to one person?

Susan: I don't see why not, Linda. It was carried out in a similarly brutal manner as the other murders.

Linda: This victim was a little different, though. It has been reported that he was a pastor at an area church.

Susan: This person is a monster. Satan. This person is Satan himself. Ruining lives, taking away precious loved ones, and now he has violently murdered a pastor.

All for what? His own sick satisfaction? Does he think he is above the law?

Linda: Those are all questions we would love to have answered. If you're listening to this, we invite you to call in and chat to us, and explain why you feel compelled to take these people from their loved ones.

They would like that wouldn't they? Cyrus didn't know that the man was a pastor, but it didn't matter to him. He needed to satisfy his appetite to kill and that man just happened to provide him with the opportunity. *They think they can call me Satan? They think they can decide what I will be called?* Cyrus was beginning to get angry. *This is my game and I make the decisions.*

Turning down the radio, he spent the rest of the ride in silence. He felt on edge. Others were trying to put their claim on his legacy.

After pulling into the parking lot at work, Cyrus examined the building before deciding he wasn't in the mood to deal with Joe and everyone else. This place was not worth his time. The car rattled as it pulled back out the other end of the parking lot. *Fuck this.*

He chose to head back down the road, returning in the direction he came. *I have no reason for being here. This is not where I belong.*

As he drove away from City Hall, he wondered whether he needed to send another message. Upon his arrival home, he made his way over to the computer.

Cyrus's phone began to vibrate. It was just Dave

wondering where he was since he hadn't shown up to work. He slid his phone back into his pocket. After opening a document, he stared at the screen. *What to say?*

I am not Satan, Cyrus typed before transferring his gaze to the window.

He patted his fingers on the keyboard as he stared at the words he had put on the screen.

But, I am powerful. I can do what I want, whenever I want. No one will ever stop me.

He sat there for a few minutes looking at his finished message. He felt like something was missing.

But, I can be Satan if you want me to be.

Cyrus clicked on the enter button and proceeded to print out the papers. Thirty copies just like last time. He put on his gloves and placed the letters in separate envelopes with the message: **To the police**.

This seemed boring and repetitive to Cyrus. He didn't want to do the exact same thing again. There was nothing impressive about that. He rose to his feet.

Something intimidating. He made his way into the kitchen and opened the freezer. After grabbing a couple packages of meat, he put them on a plate and then into the microwave to thaw them out.

The microwave beeped, then he pulled the plate out with a big smile. He grabbed the envelopes and put them in the empty sink before picking up the thawed plate of meat.

As he held the plate over the letters, he let the blood slowly drip off the meat and onto the letters until every one of them had the taste of blood on them. It was exactly what he needed.

This time, he wanted the letters delivered straight to the police station. After retrieving a box from the attic, he returned to the computer, stacked the letters in the box, and closed it. He placed all the letters in the box except one. That letter had an extra special destination.

On the front of the letter, which he left blank, he wrote: **To the Channel 4 News station**. With a grin firmly etched on his face, he headed toward the door. The box landed softly as he tossed it on the passenger seat along with the extra letter, which sat neatly on top.

The box bounced on the seat as he made his way down the road. There were still traces of blood present on his gloves as he had forgotten to change them. The letter started sliding off the box, but he reached out and put it back in its rightful place.

He pulled up to the police station and parked around the corner. As he examined his surroundings, he began to devise a plan. There were pedestrians walking past the building. He saw a young boy of about 13 years of age walking down the road in the direction of the police station. Cyrus put on a pair of sunglasses and grabbed a hat off the backseat before opening the door.

He took hold of the box and hurried down the street. The boy turned as Cyrus approached him with box in hand.

"Hey, can you do me a favor?" Cyrus asked the boy.

"Why would I do that? Who are you?" The boy asked rudely.

"If you take this box to the police station, I'll give you ten dollars," Cyrus continued.

"Ten dollars? Just for bringing this box to the police station?" The boy's attitude quickly changed.

"Yep, just take the box to the station and then meet me back here. That's all you have to do," Cyrus added.

"Fine, I'll be right back," the boy replied as he took the box out of Cyrus's hands before running down the road.

Cyrus bolted back in the direction of his car as quickly as he could. He had to be long gone before the boy told the police where the box came from.

As he drove down the road toward his next destination, Cyrus couldn't help but be impressed by his ingenuity. The circumstances probably wouldn't align as well for him at the news studio as they did at the police station, but he had to get his message across.

The news station was within his line of sight. There was nobody out the front this time. He was going to have to do the dirty work himself, which was fine by him as he wasn't as concerned about being seen here as he was at the police station. After putting his sunglasses back on, with his head facing the ground so there was no possibility of him being caught by security footage, he ran to the front door, dropped off the letter, and darted back to his car desperate to get out of there as soon as possible

It was likely the police had already got the message and had begun searching the area for Cyrus. He didn't care, though. Just like the letter said, they would never find him.

17

THE yellow cheese glistened as Hughes stirred his freshly made cup of microwavable mac and cheese at his desk. These sorts of meals had become the norm as he began spending more of his time at the station searching for a killer that he already knew the identity of.

Lopez sat across from Hughes examining a folder of notes gathered from the various crime scenes. Lopez reasoned that if he kept looking at the crime scene photos he might pick up on something that everyone else had missed. Hughes knew Lopez wasn't going to find anything. He wouldn't find anything because Cyrus wasn't leaving anything behind for him to see.

Cyrus had killed again. This time, judging by the estimated time of death, it occurred in broad daylight and they still had nothing to pin Cyrus as the killer. He found a man and stabbed him to death on the side of the road, and no one saw it. His luck would run out eventually, but how many people would lose their lives before that happened? When was Cyrus going to slip up and make a fatal error?

As Hughes looked across the room, he could see the Captain speaking to someone in his office. It was evident they were arguing about something. It was likely the source of the heated conversation was the body they found that morning. The victim this time was a pastor, which seemed to have struck a chord with everyone as the Captain and the other man shouted back and forth.

Some of the police officers sat around waiting for the impending media frenzy. The press would be expecting answers, but this time they would have none to give.

Hughes looked over and saw an officer talking to a boy. The boy handed the officer a box, which he proceeded to place on the table before examining his surroundings.

"Hughes, get the Captain over here!" The officer shouted to Hughes.

Hughes stood up to try and gain a better view of the box, but the officer had already nodded his head in the direction of the Captain's office. Hughes hurried to the office and informed the Captain they had something he needed to look at. They both ran out to the officer.

"This boy just came in with this box," the officer said as he pointed at the kid standing in front of him. He says a man gave it to him and told him he'd give him money if he brought the box to us."

"Where was the man?" Hughes asked the boy.

"At the corner over there," the boy replied as he gestured out the door.

"What was he wearing?" The Captain enquired.

"Blue jeans and a green long sleeve shirt," the boy answered.

"Go and have a look," the Captain ordered. A few men proceeded to march out the door in the direction the Captain pointed.

"Now, it's important that you think carefully," Hughes said as he reached over and grabbed a piece of paper off the desk. "Did the man look like this?" Hughes asked as he pointed at the sketch of their suspect.

"No," the boy answered.

"What did he look like?" Hughes asked.

"He had short hair and he was wearing sunglasses," the boy responded.

"I knew it," Hughes replied as he ran over and grabbed hold of the picture of Cyrus that he had printed out. "Was it this man, but with shorter hair?" Hughes showed the boy the picture of Cyrus.

"No, I don't think so," the boy replied.

"Are you sure? Are you positive it wasn't this man?" Hughes continued frantically.

"I'm sure. Can I go now?" The boy asked.

"Hughes stomped on the floor and threw the picture at the table. "Fuck!" He exclaimed.

"Just give me your name and your parents phone number, and we will give them a call and get them to pick you up," the Captain said as he handed the boy a piece of paper and a pen.

As the boy made his way over to a bench to wait for his parents to pick him up, the police shifted their attention back to the box.

The police officer that first talked to the boy picked up the box, tilting it from side-to-side.

"I can hear something sliding around inside. I don't think it's a bomb. It's really light," the officer explained.

"I'll open it," Hughes said as he rejoined the circle of people. "Let me see it," he continued as he took the box out of the officer's hands.

As Hughes tilted the box back and forth, it was apparent that the contents were light as the officer had said. Sliding the drawer open, Hughes pulled out a box cutter and placed the box on the table. Knowing who had given the box to the boy, his heart was racing at a mile a minute.

Slowly, he slid his hand across the box until he reached the edge, then wrapped his fingers around the corner, tightly holding it in place. He cut the tape with the razor and dragged it across the box, releasing it open. Hughes grabbed the flaps and opened the box.

As he opened the box and revealed the blood soaked letters, groans of shock emanated from the crowd of officers behind him.

"Somebody get me a glove," Hughes said as he looked at the letters with dismay.

An officer handed him a pair of gloves and he put them on. He placed his hand into the box and pulled out a letter, holding it in the air for everyone to see.

"Is that blood?" A voice from the crowd asked.

"It looks like it," another voice responded.

After examining the letter, Hughes noticed that it said: **To the police** just like the previous letters they had received. Hughes looked at the letter. He placed the letter on the table and retrieved another out of the box. This one was stickier, but had the same words written on the front: **To the police**.

"Someone get bags or something so we can secure these," Hughes ordered.

The Captain came in closer and examined the contents of the box before transferring his gaze to Hughes.

"I guess we know who these came from," the Captain muttered.

"I'm going to open one," Hughes said as he reached in and picked one up that wasn't completely soaked with blood.

Hughes got to his feet and walked over to a table with a roll of paper towels on it and tore off a strip. After he had wiped the blood off the letter, he headed back over to the Captain. The lip of the envelope pushed up as Hughes dug the end of his finger into it in a desperate bid to force it open.

The envelope opened and Hughes reached in, pulling out a piece of paper. He examined the envelope to make sure there was nothing else in it, then sat it down on the table with the other two he had pulled out. Slowly, he opened the folded paper and revealed its contents.

I am not Satan, but I am powerful. I can do what I want, whenever I want. No one will ever stop me, but I can be Satan if you want me to be.

Reaching into the box, he pulled out another letter and wiped it off. Just as he had anticipated, this piece of paper had the same message.

"Satan?" Hughes muttered "What is he talking about?" He continued.

For a brief moment, the Captain and Hughes looked at each other in confusion, then Hughes sat the letter down on the table.

"It was on the radio," a voice from behind them said.

Hughes jerked around and looked at the man.

"What was?" Hughes asked.

"The Satan thing. I heard them call this killer Satan on the news this morning on the radio. That might be what he's talking about," the officer continued.

"Why the hell are these people feeding this guy's ego?!" Hughes shouted angrily. "Someone needs to get on the phone with these guys and tell them to quit airing things like that. That's the sort of thing that motivates these kinds of people."

"It's too late," an officer said as he made his way over to them. "They just called. They received a letter, too."

"Someone go and get that letter," the Captain ordered.

"And, no more giving him names!" Hughes shouted in the officer's direction as he hurried out the door to retrieve the letter from the news station.

"I was going to say that we can't let the media get ahold of this, but he sent a fucking copyright to them," the Captain said in frustration. We need to get all this in for DNA testing. I want some answers, dammit!" The Captain continued to shout as he headed toward his office.

Just before he reached the office, the Captain turned around, "Well, c'mon! We need answers, let's go!" The crowd of officers started to swarm around.

Hughes signaled for Lopez to follow him, and they walked off into another room.

"I still think it is Cyrus, so we need to look into him further," Hughes said as he closed the door behind them so no one could listen in on their conversation.

"Just give up on this, man, before you get yourself in trouble," Lopez begged.

"You know what, maybe you're right," Hughes conceded. "I'm probably just on a wild goose chase with this guy."

"All right?" Lopez responded.

"I'll talk to you later, all right?" Hughes said as he opened the door and walked out.

Hughes knew there was no point in trying to reason with Lopez. As long as the Captain said it wasn't Cyrus, Lopez would persist in saying it wasn't Cyrus. It was like talking to a brick wall. This was one case he would need to figure out on his own. He had to do some personal investigating.

Sadistic

Not wanting anyone to catch onto the fact that he was doing outside research, Hughes left the station and headed for the library. He figured it would be the safest place for him to learn a little more about Cyrus and what made him tick.

The library was silent as Hughes made his way passed shelves of books looking for a computer that was in a private area, allowing him to do research without someone looking over his shoulder.

He sat down at a computer in the corner of the building facing the wall. He wasn't going to leave without something. *No one just comes out of nowhere and becomes a killer like this guy.*

Upon opening a web browser, he typed in Cyrus's full name, **Cyrus Barkley**, then clicked enter. As he didn't see anything noteworthy, he typed in **Cyrus Barkley News**. He scrolled through the links, but once again nothing piqued his curiosity. Sitting there for a moment in deep thought, Hughes knew there had to be some dirt on Cyrus.

Hmmm. Desperate to find something on Cyrus, he typed in his full name once more. As he scrolled down, he noticed Cyrus's social media page. His page was active, but he hadn't used it in months. He was about to click off the page when **Rosburg** caught his eye. The information section said Cyrus was from **Rosburg, Ohio**.

Heading back to the search page, Hughes typed in **Cyrus Barkley, Rosburg, Ohio**. He scrolled down, but there was nothing that looked like a possible lead. No crimes had been committed by someone going by that name.

He was running out of options. He typed **_killers_** into the search bar and clicked enter. A page called 'Inside the Mind of a Killer' claimed to describe what went on inside the head of a killer. With nothing to lose, he skimmed down the page taking in the information as fast as he could.

Apparently, a troubled childhood was a common theme among killers. The text said there was usually something off about these types of people from the start, but everyone often missed it or didn't catch on until it was too late.

He typed in **_Rosburg Ohio School_**. A page came up. The town was small, meaning every school-aged child attended one large school after second grade. Hughes looked at the school information, then pulled out his phone. He dialed a number and placed the phone against his ear.

A woman answered the phone. "Hello, this is Rosburg Central High School, Mary Roberts speaking. How may I help you?"

"Yes, this is Detective Hughes calling from Maysville Police Station. I was wondering if I could ask you a few questions regarding a former student," Hughes said in as professional a tone as possible since he wasn't authorized to make this call.

"Let me forward you to the Principal," the woman said before placing him on hold.

Hughes looked around the room, then up at the

clock. He needed to get back to the police station before Lopez started questioning his whereabouts.

Another voice came onto the line. "Hello, this is Principal Mike Moores speaking, how may I help you?" He asked.

"Hello, this is Detective Walter Hughes from the Maysville Police Department in New York," Hughes explained. "I'm calling to enquire about a person who I believe may have been a former student of yours."

"All right, I will help the best I can," Moores said.

"I'm not sure how long you have been Principal, but do you know of a person that goes by the name of Cyrus Barkley?" Hughes asked. "He is 42, so it's my belief he would've attended the school sometime in the 1980s."

"Let me see," Moores said.

Hughes could hear him clicking away at the keyboard in the background. As he waited, he tapped his finger on his leg.

"Ah, yes, here we are, Cyrus Barkley," Moores said. Upon hearing this news, Hughes cracked a smile. "You were right, he did attend here in the 80s. So, what is it about him that you'd like to know?" Moores asked.

"Was he ever in any kind of trouble? Perhaps anything out of the ordinary?" Hughes enquired.

"Well, he did get sent to detention a few times for getting into fights, and he had to spend some time with the student counselor. Let me see what else I can find," Moores continued typing.

"Maybe this is what you're referring to," Moores

said immediately capturing Hughes' attention. "It says here that in the fourth grade he had to be removed from school," Moores continued.

"For what?" Hughes chimed in.

"It says that he was caught," the Principal stopped and quietly coughed, and groaned before proceeding. "It says he was caught torturing a squirrel he had somehow caught in the recess yard. A student reported him because it made her feel uncomfortable."

The line went quiet for a moment. "Anything else?" Hughes persisted.

"It says he refused to give up possession of the dead carcass of the squirrel, insisting that it belonged to him. He tried hitting anyone that attempted to take it away from him. They had to wait for his mother to get there and calm him down. Eventually, his mother took it away from him," Moores responded.

"All right, thank you," Hughes said.

"After that, he was required to visit a counselor twice a week for one year, and after that nothing like this occurred again," Moores added.

"All right, that's all I needed. Thank you," Hughes said.

"May I ask what prompted you to have a look into the background of a former student, Detective Hughes?" The Principal asked.

"I'm sorry, but I cannot reveal such details," Hughes answered.

"It's all right, I understand," the Principal replied.

"All right, thanks for all your help. Have a nice day," Hughes responded before hanging up the phone.

Hughes knew Cyrus wasn't right in the head. He had a feeling he would find something like this. The guy had been an animal torturer, and now he was targeting people.

Quickly, he made his way back to the police station and quietly slipped in so nobody would notice his absence. The box was still sitting where it had been previously, with some of the letters in plastic bags and others nowhere to be seen.

"Do you know where Officer Lopez is?" Hughes asked an officer.

"Yeah, I just saw him walk into another room. He mentioned something about being hungry. If I had to take a guess, I would say he's at one of the vending machines. He's your partner, shouldn't you know where he is?" The officer responded all the while glaring at Hughes.

Instead of dignifying the officer with a response, Hughes turned away and headed toward the break room, where the vending machines were located.

Hughes popped his head into the break room "Lopez," he said.

"Yeah?" Lopez replied as he turned around and sighted Hughes. "Where did you go, man?" Lopez continued.

"Come here for a minute," Hughes insisted.

"All right," Lopez said as he nodded at the other men seated at the table who weren't particularly paying attention.

Hughes directed Lopez back to the room where he

had talked with him earlier in the day.

"Why are we going in here again?" Lopez asked as Hughes closed the door.

"Just take a seat," Hughes insisted.

They both sat down, then Hughes looked at Lopez.

"Just listen to me, all right," Hughes said.

Lopez tossed his hands up in the air in dismay because he knew what words were going to pass Hughes's lips.

"All right, let's hear it," Lopez agreed.

"I called Cyrus's school," Hughes whispered.

"You what?" Lopez said sounding shocked.

"I called his old school. I had to look into him a little more," Hughes explained.

"Yeah, you just had to," Lopez said sarcastically.

"I talked to the Principal and it turns out Cyrus was once required to leave school and start seeing a counselor on a regular basis because he was caught torturing a squirrel on the school playground," Hughes explained.

"Torturing a squirrel?" Lopez laughed.

"I'm not kidding. He had to see a counselor because of it," Hughes added in a desperate bid to indicate the seriousness of the situation to Lopez.

"What else did he torture?" Lopez asked still unable to take Hughes completely seriously. "Any singing chipmunks by any chance?"

Hughes slammed his hand down on the table in frustration. "This is serious, man. This is our guy. The fucker tortured animals! He's sick!" Hughes shouted.

"He may be a little messed up in the head, but that

doesn't mean he's our killer," Lopez said trying to calm Hughes down.

"All right, this is pointless. You aren't going to listen. This is just a waste of my time. If you aren't going to help, I will find a way to get this guy on my own. There is no doubt in my mind that it's him," Hughes said as he rose to his feet.

"I wish I could help, man," Lopez said as he followed suit and stood up. "But, even that kid said Cyrus doesn't look like the guy that gave him the box. I mean, what more do you need?" He continued.

A clearly frustrated Hughes opened the door and headed out of the room. Even if he presented what information he had found, the Captain was bound to tell him not to bother Cyrus. For Hughes, that was not an option.

18

SARA had no clue that Cyrus had skipped work, and she didn't make mention of the argument they had last night before they went to bed. He couldn't be sure if that was a good thing or a bad thing. It was good for now that she hadn't brought up the fact that Cyrus had seemed so distant lately, but he knew she would eventually bring the subject back up, and next time she might be even angrier. He didn't want to talk about it, and he had no interest whatsoever in any of her concerns.

As he rolled over, he gazed at his clock and watched as the minutes slowly ticked away. The alarm would soon sound and he would have to get up and ready himself for work. The agony of having to resume his daily life of sitting in a chair filing records pained him no end. Since his hobby wasn't one he could make money from he had no other choice.

The whole room seemed black in comparison to the brightly lit red numbers on the clock. Sitting alone in a room filled in virtual darkness, his mind began to plunge even deeper into the darkness when his alarm began to loudly buzz. It was time.

He didn't want to shower or eat. Neither of them seemed like activities particularly worthy of his time, but he knew both were part of his humanly duties and must be done. After he slid on his shoes, he buttoned up his red plaid dress shirt. He enjoyed looking professional. The look demanded a certain level of respect from others.

The creak from the stairs and the sound of the TV were the only things cutting through the silence of his nearly empty house. Being home alone was quickly becoming one of his favorite things. A clear train of thought and no stress came with having no one around.

He opened a cupboard and scanned for something to eat. Cereal sounded good. He couldn't recall the last time he sat down and enjoyed a nice bowl of cereal. Cyrus poured himself a bowl of Fruit-O's and flopped onto the couch. As always, the TV was on and the news was playing. He put a spoonful of cereal in his mouth as he waited for something about himself to come on the TV. Lately, he had been the star of the news and he was loving it.

It didn't take long for Cyrus's wish to be granted. A

newswoman appeared on the TV.

"A town outraged, people in fear. When will something be done? Today, at 4:30pm, there will be a live interview with the Captain of the Police Department on the series of murders that have rocked this town to its core. As it stands, the public has seen no direct action whatsoever taken by the Police Department to stop this monster in his tracks. It's time for action." Then, the screen cut away to further news.

Interesting, the police are finally going to make a more formal statement about the murders. They have nothing on him. They must have fabricated some evidence to reassure the masses. *Whatever helps people sleep at night, I guess.*

Cyrus turned off the TV and rose to his feet. *I could kill someone and leave the body at the very spot where they're going to stage the interview. That would show them how much control the police have and how safe they all are.*

"I don't think I want this job anymore," Cyrus said to Dave as he leaned back in his chair.

"Right," Dave laughed as he typed on his keyboard.

"It's so dull and boring. It really seems like a big waste of time," Cyrus continued as he stared at the ceiling.

"Do you have a better job in mind lined up for us?" Dave laughed.

"No, not really, but just about anything is better than this," Cyrus continued.

"I don't know, man. This job is really easy. I get to sit down and do almost nothing all day. To be honest, I don't mind it," Dave replied.

"Well, we could actually be doing something that mattered instead of being bossed around by someone like Joe. I want to be the one bossing people around," Cyrus said.

"Well, let me know when you find that job and I'll quit and come work with you," Dave laughed before heading back to his work.

Cyrus placed his hand in his pocket and pulled out his phone. No texts or calls. It reminded him that he hadn't heard back from the anonymous man that threatened to ruin his life if Cyrus didn't allow him to kill under Cyrus's name.

Cyrus thought he was sick in the head, but this guy took things to another level. If Cyrus was going to kill, it would be done his way and not in the vein of some other person.

He wasn't naïve enough to think he was off the hook. Not by a long shot. Nothing had happened yet, but something was bound to pop up. Someone doesn't go to such lengths to send a threat like that then not bother to follow through.

It was only a matter of where and when. What was this person going to do that was so bad that the blame had to be pinned on someone else? He could just want to get someone in his own life out of the way without any repercussions, which was pretty smart but he still wanted no part of it.

Cyrus had come to grips with the fact that there was no way to stop this mystery man from doing as he pleased; at least not in the short term. He would have to play the waiting game until he made an error. Everyone slips up, even Cyrus.

It wasn't so much that this man was going to kill under his name, but the manner in which or who he was going to kill. Who would be this man's first victim and how would he carry out the act? If it was a simple stabbing or something of that nature, then it wouldn't be so bad, but Cyrus had already learned that things are never that simple.

It was almost 4:30pm. He wanted to watch the interview on TV, but he couldn't because he intended to call Hughes during the interview. There was no possible way that he could pull off the call at home given that Sara and Chris would be watching the interview as well.

The break room at work was a possibility as there was a TV in there. It might be risky, but there was no other option if he wanted to watch the interview, so it was worth a shot. It wouldn't be quite as satisfying if he didn't get to see Hughes's reaction on TV.

The bell rang over the loud speakers telling everyone it was time to switch shifts. Cyrus hung back and waited for everyone he knew to leave before making his way to the break room. He squeezed by people as he walked down the hall. Pushing the doors open, he walked into the break room, where he saw multiple people that he didn't know sitting around waiting to punch in for work.

Luckily, the TV station was already on the news channel. He didn't want to be the one to tune the TV to the news station and arouse suspicion.

Cyrus walked to the corner and sat in a chair by himself. He didn't want anybody to attempt to strike up conversation with him or notice that he was there. It felt like he was waiting for the opening kick-off of a football game. Just as he had hoped, everyone around him was talking and not paying the slightest bit of attention to his presence.

"Hold on, guys, the thing is on," someone said, and then silence filled the room.

The person they were all so curious to hear about was in the room. The person that brought fear to them and their families was behind or to the side of them. As the newscast commenced, a smile emerged across Cyrus's face.

There was a man standing in front of a podium, with an American flag to the side of him. He was on the older side and wearing a different version of a police uniform. He stood there looking tall and proud as he prepared to speak. The cameras flashed all around him.

"Hello, I'm Captain Stevens with the Maysville Police Department." Stevens paused. "I'm here today to speak about something that has been on everyone's mind. Who is committing these crimes? We are working as best and as fast as we can to answer this question. We ask for the full cooperation of the civilians of this town and your patience."

Immediately, everyone started throwing questions at him. Only some of the questions could be heard over the TV, and the Captain only answered a few of them.

"How can we be patient when there is someone going around killing innocent people?" A reporter asked.

"We understand your concern. We too have families that we care about. We are working around the clock analyzing all possible evidence to determine the identity of the killer," Captain Stevens responded.

"Do you have any clues as to who may be behind all of this?" Another reporter shouted from the back.

"At this stage, we do not have any suspects," the Captain answered.

"Is there any profile yet on who or what type of person this killer goes after?" A blonde reporter in the front enquired.

"No. Next question," the Captain said.

"Since there is the chance the killer could be watching this, what would you say?" Asked a reporter in the back.

"I would want him to know that we will never stop looking for him. This is not your city, these are not your people, and you do not have the right to do what you are doing. The people of this city have the right to live their lives in peace without having to worry about who might be around the corner, or who might come into their house and try to take their family away from them. You need to stop what you are doing. When we find you, and we will, you will get what you deserve and spend the remainder of your days behind bars," the Captain said in a firm, clear voice.

It was nothing Cyrus hadn't heard before. The Police Department's classic claim that they would find him and put him behind bars. He had already heard it a few times before and they were still yet to pin him down. He didn't want to get too cocky for fear of slipping up, but he couldn't help but let out a small laugh upon hearing the Captain's statement.

Some of the people in the room turned and looked at him when he laughed. He looked away from them and back at the TV. Cyrus needed to do what he came to do before the chance passed him by, but he still didn't see Hughes on the TV. Hughes had to be there or his call would be pointless.

Cyrus was going to try anyway. He rose to his feet and passed the horde of people mindlessly staring at the TV. It was almost as if no one had noticed he was walking right in front of them.

He escaped the room, then looked around. There was no one there. The clock indicated that he only had a few minutes before everyone would come pouring out of the break room and head back to their respective stations. He wanted to get it over and done with so he could get back in and witness everyone's reaction if anything happened.

Upon exiting, he walked a little way down the side of the building so that anyone that walked out the front door wouldn't be able to hear him. He opened his phone and clicked on Hughes's number. The phone didn't even complete a full ring before Hughes picked up.

"Hello," Hughes said.

"Hello, Detective Hughes," Cyrus replied.

"I had a feeling it was you," Hughes continued.

"He says I need to stop what I'm doing. I will stop what I'm doing when it stops feeling so damn good, and

I want to feel good right now," Cyrus said.

He immediately hung up the phone and hurried back into the building. Quietly, he stepped into the break room hoping not to capture anyone's attention. Thankfully, for him, their attention was still firmly fixed on the TV screen.

"I'll take one last question," the Captain said.

Just then, Hughes came into shot and whispered something in the Captain's ear. As the Captain grabbed the microphone, a smile appeared on Cyrus's face.

"That will be all," the Captain said before heading off the stage and out of view of the camera. Whispers erupted in the room all around him. "I wonder what happened," a voice asked from across the room.

With a smile still firmly etched on his face, Cyrus walked past the room of people and out the door. He got to his car and climbed in. Driving away from work, he didn't head in the direction of his house. He had informed Hughes that he was going to do something, and he was going to follow through on his promise.

"He told me it felt good and that he wanted to feel good right now,'" Hughes explained in a panicked tone to the Captain as they headed off the stage.

"What are you trying to say, Hughes?" The Captain asked sensing the distress in Hughes's voice.

"I think he is going to kill someone right now!" Hughes exclaimed. "We need to do something; we need to stop him!" He began to shout.

"How do you suppose we stop him when we don't even know who he is," the Captain stated.

"I do," Hughes continued.

"Who is it? Don't tell me you're still caught up on that one guy, whatever his name was," the Captain responded with a hint of anger in his voice.

"You don't understand, I looked into his past," Hughes fired back as he stopped and faced the Captain.

"What did you find? What charges does he have? What criminal past? What motive? What evidence? What did you find that gives us the right to storm into his house and interrogate him?" The Captain demanded.

"The possibility that it could save a life. He killed an animal when he was in middle school," Hughes answered back.

"This is what you're basing it on?" The Captain said with intensity. "If you can find one single piece of evidence on this guy, then bring him in, but until then you're to leave him alone. I don't want to hear another word of this. You are staying at the station until we sort this out, and whoever it actually is must have seen you on that first interview and he might target you. He clearly knows who you are," the Captain continued.

"Don't worry, I can handle myself. Let him come after me," Hughes responded as he gestured toward his gun holster.

19

SATAN, Satan, Satan. The name bounced around in his head, refusing to leave. Cyrus drove down the road mumbling to himself as he stared back and forth at the sides of the streets looking for someone to satisfy his hunger. A scapegoat he could use to show everyone what Satan was really like.

As he slid his hand across the steering wheel, a streak of sweat followed closely behind. Looking up and down the street at the numerous people going about their day, none of them piqued his interest. They were missing something. He couldn't figure out why, but none of them felt like they were calling out his name.

Cyrus pulled up to red light and sat there. A woman reached out and grabbed her son by the shirt as he almost ran out into the street. "Be careful, don't get hurt," she said to him as she wrapped her arm around him. "Be careful, don't get hurt, don't get hurt," Cyrus whispered to himself as he stared at the young boy who wore an ashamed look on his face for almost getting himself hit by a car.

A loud honk whaled behind him as a truck loudly revved its engine. Upon looking up, Cyrus realized the light had already turned green. As he transferred his gaze once more to the boy, he noticed the young child was looking back at him from the other side of the road, waiting for him to proceed.

His mother yanked at his arm "Let's go!" She said.

For a brief moment, Cyrus and the boy broke eye contact before the boy looked at him one last time as Cyrus pulled away.

"Where are you?" Cyrus asked himself as he drove down the road. The sound of an engine broke his train of thought as a truck tailed him closely. It was the same truck that had been behind Cyrus at the stop light. The truck driver was revving the engine and honking the horn, but Cyrus was already exceeding the speed limit.

The road changed into a two lane road, so Cyrus moved over to allow the truck to pass. He didn't have time to deal with someone's road rage. His undivided attention needed to be on the task at hand.

As the truck moved into the passing lane, the honking ceased. Cyrus began scanning the streets for someone to share his moment with. Whoever he chose to rid of life would go down in history with him. He felt as if he would be doing someone a favor, putting them alongside himself in the history books. The moment had to be perfect. They had to be perfect.

Cyrus's brakes squealed as the truck cut out in front of him, causing him to swerve. "Fucking asshole!" Cyrus shouted at the top of his lungs. Gripping the steering wheel tightly, Cyrus quickly regained control of the car. He was the one. The person in the truck needed to die.

Cyrus reduced his speed, allowing another car to get between him and the truck. The truck was blue with white rims, and there was a red baseball logo on the back window. The right side of the fender had rusted away and the license plate read ZRT-7637. He repeated the license plate over in his head to make sure he wouldn't lose the identity of the truck.

The ugly roar of the truck's engine was loud enough to ensure he knew the whereabouts of the truck even when it wasn't in his line of sight. A wave of excitement was washing over him in anticipation of putting his plan into action. The feeling of finding the right person was akin to falling in love.

The sky was already beginning to turn dark. The truck pulled into a store. Although he had parked far away, the truck was still within his line of vision. A relatively well-proportioned man wearing a dirt red shirt with some sort of tractor on it stepped out. He was larger than all of Cyrus's previous victims, but he still had nothing on Cyrus.

Cyrus's patience was in short supply as he eagerly sat in his car waiting for the man to exit the store. He didn't have time for this. For all he knew, the police could be out patrolling after the message he sent out during the interview. It was unlikely they would locate him, but he didn't want to run the risk of being found out by sitting in the parking lot any longer than he needed to.

The man left the store with just one small bag in hand. *All that time and only one damn bag.* Looking at his watch, Cyrus noted that the man had only been in the store for twenty minutes, but it felt like a whole lot longer. He tapped his fingers on the steering wheel as he waited for the man to get back into his truck.

The roar of the truck's engine was similar to that of an old man choking on food as the man started the truck, and then pulled out of the parking lot. After waiting a brief moment, Cyrus started his car and began following him. Cyrus was surprised that the driver had yet to notice him as he had been tailing him for some time.

Street after street, Cyrus tailed the truck until they arrived at their destination. Not wanting to arouse the suspicion of the truck driver, Cyrus parked down the road. He saw the man step out and greet a woman and child. The truck driver handed the bag to the woman before the woman and the child got into a car. *Perfect, we get to be alone.*

As soon as the car pulled away, the man disappeared out of Cyrus's view. Cyrus stepped out of his car and made his way toward his trunk. Upon opening the trunk, the light lit up revealing his tools of choice. He grabbed a bag and started filling it with chloroform, rags, and other equipment.

His excitement levels were bubbling over because

this would be the first time he would be presented with the opportunity to put the chloroform to use. He pulled out a pair of gloves and put them on. The gloves were becoming a ritual for him signaling his intent to kill. Slowly, he poured chloroform onto one of his rags. He quietly closed the trunk and stepped out onto the sidewalk with bag in hand.

As he made his way to the door, the cobblestones rattled under his feet. The house was a lot nicer than Cyrus had expected going by the man's previous behavior and the condition of his truck, but that was irrelevant. There was light pouring out of his window at the point where a TV was playing a loud movie.

He placed his finger on the doorbell and rang it. The sound echoed throughout the house as he waited for the man to answer the door. As the familiar sound of footsteps making their way to the door entered his ears, Cyrus pulled out the rag and prepared himself.

The door opened and a man came to the door.

"Hello?" The man said.

"Hey, I'm here," Cyrus said as he pushed himself into the door.

"What the-," the man responded as reached up and put his arm on Cyrus' shoulder.

Before the man had a chance to react to what was going on, Cyrus pulled his hand out from behind his back and pushed the rag on the man's mouth, shoving him and pinning him up against the wall. The man fought back as hard as he could, but only for a brief moment before he fell to the ground. "Don't you dare put your hands on me," Cyrus whispered.

Sadistic

Stepping over the unconscious body, Cyrus walked into the next room. There was an old western movie loudly playing on the TV. He would leave it on as cover noise just in case the man woke up and tried screaming.

Upon entering the kitchen, Cyrus noticed that everything was spotless except a few bags of groceries sitting on the counter. He must have interrupted something. He followed the blue carpet leading down the hallway, peering into rooms as he went.

He came across a room with pink wallpaper. Stuffed animals were scattered around the floor, and there was a large pink princess blanket stretched across a bed that was also covered in stuffed animals. Cyrus walked over to the closet and looked in. He rubbed his hand across his chin hair. *All right*.

After placing his bag down, he pushed all the stuffed animals off the bed and onto the floor, kicking them up against the wall. The wooden legs scraped against the carpet as Cyrus dragged the bed away from the wall. He took a deep breath, then scanned the room.

He exhaled, then headed out the door and darted back into the hallway. Cyrus made his way down the hall and looked into an even bigger bedroom. It was much cleaner. It was hard for him to comprehend that the grubby-looking man lying on the floor owned such a house. It didn't stack up.

As he approached the bed, he looked down at the blanket and pillows that were all neatly lined up as if someone was preparing the scene for a picture. With knife in hand, he took hold of a pillow, slicing it wide open, letting its stuffing fall out onto the covers. He turned and looked back at a blanket that wasn't covered in fluff from the pillow. He thrust the knife down into the bed, stabbing repeatedly before dragging the blade across the bed, cutting it to shreds. He smiled at his work. "Much better," he said as he turned and walked back out of the room.

Cyrus kicked at the man's body to make sure he was still out cold. Taking hold of the man by the boots, he started dragging him down the hallway. He stopped and turned, dragging the body into the pink colored room.

The man's body felt heavy as he reached under him, lifting him up onto the bed. He retrieved a rope and took hold of the man by his left arm. Cyrus wrapped the rope tightly around the man's limp arm, then wrapped the other end of the rope around the corner of the bed. He did the same to the man's other arm and both of his legs, tying them as tight as possible, giving the man no room to move.

Cyrus turned and walked over to the closet and reached in. He pulled out a small purple shirt and went back over the man, who looked so weak and pitiful as he laid on his daughter's bed. Cyrus wished the man's family could see him tied up begging for mercy.

He wrapped the shirt around the man's head, gagging him in the process. "Stay here," Cyrus said as he headed out into the hallway. He made his way into the dining room and grabbed a chair, dragging it down the hallway until he reached the bedroom.

Taking a seat on the side of the bed, Cyrus rested his elbow on his knees and held his head in his hands as he

Sadistic

leaned in closer to the man.

"If you hadn't been such an asshole, I would never have been aware of your existence. If you hadn't cut me off, you wouldn't be here right now tied to the bed like a helpless animal," Cyrus said as he stared intently at the man's pale face.

"You did this to yourself, and now you have to live with your decision for the rest of your life. Luckily for you, that won't be very long," Cyrus continued as he picked up his bag and reached inside.

As Cyrus sat back down, he scooted the chair closer to the bed. He grabbed the man's arm and turned it, observing it from all angles before swatting off a small piece of dirt.

"What…are… you… do-," the man quietly mumbled as he attempted to regain consciousness.

"Oh, we're awake are we?" Cyrus happily enquired.

"What are you doing? He asked with one eye slightly opened.

"We're just going to have a little bit of fun. No big deal. Just relax," Cyrus answered.

As both of the man's eyes opened, he started to examine his surroundings. He looked at his arms, then transferred his gaze to his legs. Still not having regained his energy, the man lightly tugged at the rope in a desperate attempt to break himself free. He pulled at his arms, then started shacking violently, pulling in every direction.

"Let me go, what is this, who the hell are you?" The man demanded as he tried to break free.

Reaching back into his bag, Cyrus poured a little more chloroform onto the rag.

"I'm the person you cut off in traffic not too long ago. The one you were rudely honking at. Now, you have to stop shacking. I can't have you bothering me anymore," Cyrus said.

Disobeying Cyrus's orders, the man started shacking even harder, but Cyrus calmly reached over and placed the rag on the man's face.

"Now, go back to sleep," Cyrus said as the man quickly stopped shacking as his body went limp. "If you wake up again, I'm going to get mad," he continued as he dropped the wet rag into his bag.

"Now, where was I?" Cyrus asked himself as he picked the knife back up.

Sticking the tip of the knife gently into the top of the man's wrist, blood started oozing out as Cyrus pressed the blade in deeper. Cyrus cracked his neck, then started moving the knife from side-to-side, with the blade an inch into the man's arm.

He pushed the blade in with even greater force, then pulled it out in a sawing motion, slowly cutting open the skin. He kept pushing and pulling the blade, but the skin was resisting the cut.

Cyrus yanked the blade out of the man's arm and then stuck it back in facing the opposite direction before beginning to saw again. The skin still refused to cut as he pushed the knife back and forth. Increasing the intensity of his sawing, the skin broke but not in a straight line as he had hoped. *What the fuck.*

"You're lucky today," Cyrus said as he turned his

Sadistic

head to look back at the man's face. "It's not as easy to skin someone's arm as you might think," he continued as he pushed the skin on the man's arm back down.

The man didn't respond as he laid there unconscious with bloody slowly dripping out of his arm.

"You're lucky I didn't hit anything because you're barely bleeding," Cyrus said as he laughed.

Reaching into his bag, he pulled out a rag and wiped off the blood before it could drip to the floor. Briefly, he stopped and took in his surroundings.

"You know, that gives me an idea," Cyrus continued talking.

Rising to his feet, Cyrus headed to the kitchen and started opening drawers. *There must be one around here somewhere.*

"Ha!" He shouted as he pulled an empty bucket out from under the sink.

Hurriedly, he made his way back into the bedroom and sat down in the chair.

"You know, the body has approximately five and a half liters of blood in it," Cyrus said as he retrieved some more rags out of his bag. "There is also an artery in your arm called the brachial artery. I read about it on the internet. You see, you will die in a matter of minutes if I cut you open. There isn't enough blood in our bodies to accommodate this kind of blood loss, so you will die. It's actually quite beautiful," he continued.

Cutting the man's arm free, Cyrus let it dangle to the side of the bed. He angled the bucket below the arm, rose to his feet and towered over the man.

"I know exactly where it is," Cyrus said as he leaned forward.

Sticking the knife into the man's arm, he dragged it along the length of his arm as blood poured down the man's arm and into the bucket. Once the bucket was sufficiently filled with blood, Cyrus pulled the bucket out from under the man's arm, allowing the remainder of the blood to flow onto the floor.

"Now, I'm going to paint a picture for your lovely daughter to see," Cyrus informed the man as he lifted up the bucket and started splashing blood along the wall. Slowly, the blood dripped down leaving trails in the carpet. He made his way back over to the body, which was now hovering above a pool of blood.

"You should really clean up this mess, but instead I'll leave it for your family," Cyrus said as he removed his bloody gloves and put them inside a plastic bag along with the remainder of the items. After putting on a new pair of gloves, he rose to his feet and headed into the living room, quickly scanning for a pen and a piece of paper.

Returning to the bedroom where the man laid lifeless, Cyrus sat down, using his leg as a table as he wrote a message on the paper: **You wanted Satan**. He dropped the note on the man's chest, then took hold of his bag. Just then, he remembered something.

Sitting the bag back down, he started digging through the contents until he retrieved a small plastic bag. Upon opening the bag, he dumped a clump of hair into his hand. As he turned and looked at the lifeless body before him, he reached down and pried one of the hands open before gently laying the hair in the man's hand, then closing it back up. Cyrus looked around to make sure he hadn't forgotten anything, then took off out the door.

20

SADLY, witnessing the looks on the faces of his wife and daughter as they entered the room to find the man they loved tied to the bed would be a pleasure that would allude him. He had yet to see the face of terror. It was something he craved. The blood stretched across the wall and trailed down to the floor. He was hoping some of the blood would work its way onto the stuffed animals.

He wished he would have stayed within the vicinity of the house to hear the screams that would emanate from them mouths upon the discovery of the body, but it was far too dangerous to do so.

Cyrus sat at the side of his bed staring gun barrel straight into the darkness. With so many thoughts filling his head, sleep was something that escaped him. It was his day off, and normally he would sleep in, but he didn't want to miss the morning news. His most recent kill would be on the news, and there was the possibility that it would kick-off the broadcast.

As he stood up and walked over to the window, his mind drifted back to the moment when he looked out the window after he started his killing spree. It seemed like a lifetime ago. He was no longer the same person

"Babe," A yawn erupted quietly behind him "What are you doing over there?" Sara continued.

Cyrus looked back at her and smiled, "I was just having a bit of trouble sleeping."

She looked over at the clock, then back at Cyrus. "You have today off, right? Get over here and get some sleep," she responded as she patted her hand on the bed.

He walked over and laid down in bed.

"I still have twenty minutes before I have to start getting ready for work," she said as she put her arm around Cyrus.

This was the first time they had shown each other even the slightest bit of affection in days. At times, he had almost forgotten she existed. Placing his hand on hers, he slowly rubbed it back and forth.

He kept quiet and pretended to start falling asleep, but there was no way he was going to let himself fall asleep. The news was always on in the morning as he got ready for work. If he missed the broadcast, he would have to wait until later in the evening to see if they mentioned him. He wouldn't be able to enjoy it anywhere near as much with Sara and Chris by his side.

His eyes were firmly fixed on the clock, watching the minutes count down until Sara would up and leave, leaving him free to watch the news in peace.

As he laid there, a thought popped into his head. It had been days since Sara last made mention of the killer. She had been so worried before, but now it seemed as if the recent series of murders was nothing more than an afterthought. Perhaps her and her work friends had calmed down about the whole situation. Regardless, he was glad she had settled down. It had been quite a juggling act constantly worrying about her and satisfying his urge to kill.

Ten minutes had elapsed. Chris was almost non-existent around the house these days. He was usually at a friend's house, and when he wasn't he would confine himself to his room. Cyrus only saw his son for brief moments, and on the rare occasions when they did make contact barely a word was uttered between the pair of them, although that wasn't much different to how things normally were. Teenagers were just like that.

Five minutes remained on the clock until the alarm would sound. Cyrus desperately wanted to reach over and click the button, making the alarm go off. Sitting around waiting was driving him crazy.

His mind drifted to Sara and what she was thinking as she laid there. Perhaps she had fallen back to sleep already or maybe she had just wanted to cuddle. Contact between them had been minimal lately, and it was obvious that it upset her. Cyrus couldn't put his finger on why he didn't feel the same. Well, he had an idea but he chose to ignore it.

He just didn't have time for that kind of thing. There were far too many things he needed to get done. He didn't even have time to go to work.

Only a minute was left on the clock. As he stared intently at the clock, the numbers began to form into one blurry light until the alarm went off. It rang loudly, echoing throughout the room and waking up Sara.

"I don't want to get up," Sara groaned as she stuffed her face into the pillow.

Laying there with eyes closed, pretending to be asleep, Cyrus listened to her sit up and start moving around as she talked to herself.

"Cyrus," she said as she rubbed her hand on his shoulder.

"Have a good day, babe," he mumbled in his best fake tired voice as she lightly shook him.

Accepting the fact that he was sleeping, she rubbed his shoulder and got out of bed to prepare herself for work. Cyrus cracked open his eyes and peeked at the clock. Only twenty minutes left.

He heard the door close behind him, then the shower started. Immediately, Cyrus flipped over and looked at the ceiling. He couldn't recall feeling this eager since waiting to commit his second kill.

Now he would be exactly what they told him he was. Since they saw him as Satan, that's exactly what he would be. The difference between him and the devil was that he existed. He could do what Satan couldn't, and that was strike real fear into the hearts of the masses.

He heard the squeak of the shower turning off and quickly rolled over to pretend he was sound asleep. Cyrus knew she would be leaving soon because he would usually be up in about ten minutes, and she was always gone by the time he had woken up.

He could hear her fiddling around with things, then step out of the bathroom before walking out the bedroom door. She left the door cracked open so he listened closely for movement downstairs.

After a brief silence, he heard the front door close as she left. *Awesome.* There was less than ten minutes remaining until the news came on. Springing to his feet, he slid on some shoes before opening his drawer in search of a pair of pants.

Cyrus hopped on one foot across the room as he tried pulling on his pants before slipping out the bedroom door. He flopped onto the couch and switched on the TV. There was still a few minutes before the news would come on. Preparing for his moment in the sun, he turned to the side and reclined his chair.

The news finally began. His gaze was firmly fixed to the TV. A reporter came on and they started talking about the weather. This wasn't what was supposed to be first. His news was first, not the weather. *No one gives a fuck about the weather.*

Finally, another newsperson came on announcing that there was breaking news. **THREE MORE MURDERS ROCK MAYSVILLE**.

"Three?" Cyrus asked out loud in a surprised tone as he jerked up from his slouched position.

Sadistic

The TV cut to a scene outside a house Cyrus had never seen before. Slowly, the newswoman walked toward the front of the house.

"This was the scene of another gruesome murder yesterday as a woman and her young child were brutally murdered," the newswoman said as she pointed toward the house.

The bodies were found badly bruised. These and the other murder take things to a whole new level," the newswoman added as she made her way into the living room of the house.

"The young child was found hanging from a rope right here from the ceiling fan. It appears as if both victims were beaten to within an inch of their lives before the perpetrator proceeded to put an end to their existence," the newswoman continued.

"Now, we take you to the scene of another terrifying murder. We must inform the audience that the following footage is not suitable for children, and we advise that you prepare yourself for what is to come," the newswoman warned before the screen cut to another location where another reporter was on standby.

"Imagine walking into your house and finding blood all over your child's bedroom wall. Today, that is what this family was forced to endure after they returned home from visiting a relative. Due to the graphic state of the room and the fact that it's still being treated as a crime scene, we cannot take you in, but we do have in our possession an audio clip of the 911 call from the victim's wife:

"Oh my god, please help me, my husband, there is blood everywhere, help. I think he's dead, oh my god," the voice said in between sobs.

One officer was quoted as saying, "This is the worst thing I have ever seen in my career. You can't train for something like this, you just can't," the woman read aloud.

"There has been no mention made of whether they have any evidence or a suspect in mind, but I think we all know who is responsible for this," the newswoman put her hand to her ear before talking once more. "We have a new detail in this story. It appears that a note has been left on the body that read: You wanted Satan. We aren't entirely sure what it is supposed to mean."

Cyrus was too distracted by the news of the other murder to fully enjoy the reporting of his own killing. This had to be the work of the mystery caller. He had viciously beaten a child before hanging her by a ceiling fan. Cyrus was furious. He didn't want credit for such an act.

"This makes seven deaths that are believed to be attributed to this mystery killer, correct?" The newswoman asked a police officer at the scene.

"Yes, that is correct. We will be putting in place a 10.00pm curfew, and anyone without legitimate cause for being outdoors after this time will be subject to a potential arrest. We are not impinging on your rights. We are merely looking out for the safety of the general public and taking any and all necessary precautions," the officer explained before walking away.

"That was Officer Hitchens and this is Channel 4

News," the newswoman said before the broadcast cut back to the main studio.

"On behalf of the team at Channel 4 News, we would like to send our deepest condolences to the families affected by this terrible tragedy. This is a terrible event, and as a community we must support one another and stay strong," a newsman said before handing the show over to another reporter that was reporting from a local shop.

In a fit of rage, Cyrus slammed his hand down on the table. "That fucking bastard!" He exclaimed. He didn't kill children. He hadn't killed any children. This anonymous man wasn't entitled to put this on him. This wasn't supposed to be a part of his legacy.

He had an overwhelming desire to slit open the man's throat. As he aimlessly walked around, it came to Cyrus that he would need to send a message indicating that he wasn't the one responsible for this. He and he alone got to add to his kill count.

Cyrus picked up his phone and clicked on an old call to Hughes. The phone began to ring.

"What do you want you sick fuck?" Hughes demanded already knowing who it was.

"The woman and her child, that was not me," Cyrus said in a calm tone.

"Is that supposed to make things better? Am I meant to get down on both knees and thank you, and let you off the hook? So, are you saying the other one was you? Not the child and her mother, but the murder of that man was you? You are sick!" Hughes exclaimed.

"I wouldn't do that to a child," Cyrus continued.

"Fuck you," Hughes responded.

Cyrus hung up the phone and sat down. The call had made no difference whatsoever. Hughes would never tell anyone the woman and her daughter were not his work. He could contact the station, but it felt too risky.

Cyrus was angry. He wanted the man to come and knock on his door right now so he could cut him open. Make him scream for mercy, then cut his wind pipe and watch him flop around in pain as the last ounces of life drained out of his body.

Cyrus rubbed his hand through his hair. The freak was probably watching the news at the precise moment he was, soaking in his accomplishment at Cyrus's expense. The sick bastard needed to be torn apart, ripped from limb to limb.

Taking a seat on the couch, Cyrus knew if the man's mind worked in a similar manner to his own he wouldn't be able to resist giving him a call and throwing the kill in his face.

Now, all he could do was sit and wait. He stared at the clock on the wall as the minute hand moved around the circle, causing the hour hand to slowly follow. The hour hand's chase was similar to the one Cyrus found himself in. He was the hour hand and he would patiently wait as the man made his way back around to him, and then he would catch him and make him pay.

Sitting on the couch, he waited as the minute hand made its way around, and the TV filled his ears with white noise as he stared at the wall, blocking out everything as he stood by waiting for his phone to ring. His heartbeat echoed in his head, almost in sync with the ticking of the clock.

RINGGG! RINGGG! RINGGG! The room filled with noise as his phone blared, bringing Cyrus's anger back to its peak. The number on the phone was blocked.

Cyrus picked up the phone and slammed it against his ear. "I'm going to fucking kill you," he let out before even asking who it was.

"Now, that's not a very nice way to answer the phone," the voice on the other end of the line said in a mocking tone. It was the cold, rough voice that had taunted the darkest corners of his mind.

"When I find out who this is, you're dead," Cyrus continued not acknowledging the man's statement.

"Judging by your response, I take it you've seen the news," the voice laughed.

"You're dead," Cyrus repeated.

"I would have thought that you of all people would show some appreciation for the art of killing," the man went on.

"The art of killing? You beat a little girl to within an inch of her life, then strung her up to the ceiling fan!" Cyrus shouted into the phone.

"Yes, it was amazing, wasn't it?" The man asked as he shoved his smile through the phone.

"You are seriously messed up," Cyrus said.

"Like you're any better. You killed a pastor. If this makes me messed up, then what does that make you?

Also, you've killed more people than I have. If I'm a monster, then you're the boogie-man himself," the man said sternly.

"Fuck you!" Cyrus exclaimed.

"Oh, shut up. Now, here's what's going to happen-," before the man could continue Cyrus cut him off.

"No, you're done. No more killing under my name!" Cyrus demanded.

"No, I have more people I want to kill. You have no damn choice. Either you go along with it or spend the rest of your life in prison. Or, how would you like it if I went to your house and told that wife and son of yours, Sara and Chris, what kind of person you really are?" The man asked threateningly.

"Don't ever speak of them again. Don't even say their names. You aren't worthy of mentioning them. If I find you anywhere near my house, you will die," Cyrus continued no longer afraid of the man's threats.

"Enough with the threats. If I need you, I will contact you," the man warned, then the line went dead.

Shaking with anger, Cyrus stared at the wall. Just then, the phone rang again. He took hold of it and was ready to lash out, but the number was not the man's, it was his wife. He picked up the phone.

"Yeah?" Cyrus answered.

"Hey, babe, I'm just calling because I received this weird call," Sara replied.

"A call?" Cyrus asked sounding puzzled.

"Yeah, it was a man's voice, but I couldn't make out anything he was saying. The only thing I could hear was 'Cyrus', so I thought perhaps it was you and your phone line had lost service, but the number was blocked," she continued.

In his heart, Cyrus knew who it was. Anger filled his mind like never before. Not only did the man fail to heed his warning, but he had contacted Sara and tried telling her god knows what. Filled with rage, his fingers crunched together and scraped against the couch.

"It was probably nothing," Cyrus muttered.

"What?" Sara asked.

"It was probably nothing," Cyrus repeated this time more loudly.

"Well, all right, I just figured I should let you know. I'll talk to you later, all right? I have to get back to work," Sara responded.

"All right, love you," Cyrus replied.

"Love you, too," she said.

21

CYRUS was living in a nightmare. Being hunted, controlled, and loved. As he sat outside City Hall, he stared at the building that consumed so much of his life. He spent his time there desperately trying to disguise a life he wasn't certain he was cut out for anymore.

It had been almost 24 hours since he received the call from the mystery man, and since then that was all he thought about aside from the *I love you* exchange with Sara. The conversation felt refreshing, but somehow distant. It was like he was listening through a long pipe and she was a million miles away.

Getting out of his car, he entered the building, took his seat, and quickly turned on his computer.

"Hey, man," Dave said.

"Hey, what's up?" Cyrus turned around and replied.

"Nothing, dude, just a bit freaked out about this killer shit. I'm probably going to get my wife a gun. You should get one for Sara. We can teach them how to shoot. You can never be too careful these days, especially with some psycho going around killing people," Dave continued.

For once, Cyrus didn't want to talk about the killer, himself. He wanted to put as much distance between himself and the whole thing as he could. He wanted to get Hughes, the mystery man, his family, and everything else as far out of his mind as he could, but he knew that would be impossible as it would mean getting killing out of his head, and that was an addiction Cyrus simply couldn't shake. The same addiction that was causing all these problems to begin with.

"Yeah, that might be a good idea," Cyrus replied.

"It would definitely make my wife feel better, even though she's never been a fan of guns," Dave nodded.

"Sara isn't either, but I wouldn't be surprised if she had one lying around the house already after all this craziness," Cyrus joked grimly.

"Yeah, these are crazy days," Dave said as he swung his chair back around to the computer.

Just as Cyrus was about to turn around as well, Dave swung back in his direction. "Actually, I wonder if they have any sort of reward out on this guy because I'd shoot him for ten bucks," Dave laughed.

Cyrus laughed with him as best as he could, then transferred his focus back to his computer. He wasn't sure how he felt about his best friend talking about killing him, even though Dave didn't know it was actually him they'd be buying the gun for.

Looking at the document he had opened up on his screen, Cyrus noted that some of the documents were financial statements of some sort, but he didn't take the time to read them in detail. He never did. He knew what things to look for and knew where to file them, so there was no real need for him to read them in-depth. Some of them had addresses on them and other information. If he ever felt the desire to do so, he might be able to use the information to pinpoint a good victim. He needed to improve his process somehow and all ideas were still on the table.

Time dragged on. Aside from short exchanges with Dave and scattered conversations throughout the office about the recent series of killings, nothing of note happened at work. It still felt somewhat strange hearing groups of people talking about the murders with him so openly.

As the work day drew closer to the end, Cyrus emptied folders and tidied up his desk. Just as he looked down at his phone to check for text messages, a voice captured his attention.

"Yeah, I'm about to get out now…No…No…I'll do it," Cyrus heard.

No fucking way. It can't be. But, there was no mistaking it as the words bounced around in his head. The voice that was a mystery to him. The one that had haunted his every thought every waking hour was coming from right behind him.

Turning his head around in disbelief, he stared at

Dave who was in the process of hanging up his cell phone. Cyrus's mind bounced off the walls as he contemplated the moment in disbelief. Closing his eyes, he imagined the terrible voice that was making his life a living nightmare, then opened them again to look at Dave who was just sitting there examining his phone.

Dave looked up at Cyrus who was glaring at him with an unbreakable stare.

"You all right?" Dave asked jokingly.

"Who was that?" Cyrus asked.

"Just my wife," Dave answered.

Cyrus sat there in silence for a moment. He couldn't believe it, but he knew what had to be done. "Hey, you should come over tonight and play some cards or something," Cyrus suggested.

The work bell started to ring signaling to everyone that it was time to go. Quickly, Dave stood up. "I would, but I-,"

Cyrus cut him off, "I insist, man, it has been too long since we had some chill time. Get away from the wives for a minute. Come on, man."

Dave just looked at Cyrus for a moment, then looked away and then back at Cyrus. "You know what, you're right. I'll be there," Dave said as he let out a smile. "Even if the wife gets a little cranky about it," he continued laughing.

"All right, great," Cyrus said returning Dave's smile.

"Just let me run home really quick, get changed and talk to Judy, and then I'll be over. Sound good?" Dave said as he started making his way toward the door.

"Yeah, of course. See you then," Cyrus said as he started following Dave out.

They both got in their cars. Cyrus watched as Dave pulled out and started down the road. How had he not noticed it before? He had worked next to him every day and it took until now to connect his voice with that of the mystery caller.

Stepping on the gas, Cyrus hurried home. He pulled into the driveway and stepped out, and hurried to the door.

"Oh, Sara!" Cyrus shouted as he made his way into the house.

"Yeah?" Sara said as she hurried down the stairs.

"How are you?" Cyrus asked.

"You scared me a little, I thought something was wrong," Sara said half smiling.

"How would you and Chris like to go to the movies?" He asked with a big smile on his face.

"The movies? Why?" Sara asked sounding confused.

"Well, Dave asked if he could come by and play some cards or something," Cyrus explained.

"So, you want us to go to the movies?" Sara asked still sounding uncertain.

"Well, he really emphasized the 'just me and him' part. I think he's having some problems at home and wants to discuss it with me or something. I'm not really sure," Cyrus continued.

"I guess we could…Chris!" Sara shouted up the stairs.

Chris came walking down the stairs. "What's up, mom?" He asked.

Sadistic

"Dad's friend is coming over, so we're going to go to the movies," she explained.

"Why does it matter if dad's friend is coming over?" Chris asked sounding disinterested in the idea.

"They are going to have some 'man time'," Sara explained to Chris as she held her hands up making fake quotation marks in the air.

"That's dumb," Chris went on.

"Is it such a big deal to have to spend a little quality time with your mother? That wasn't a question by the way, so go and get ready," Cyrus said as he gestured Chris toward his bedroom door.

Angrily, Chris stomped back into his room as Sara put on her shoes. Cyrus stared out the window hoping Chris and Sara would be gone by the time Dave arrived. He looked back at Sara and wanted to tell her to hurry up.

"I didn't make anything, so we might go grab something to eat after the movie. Is there anything you want?" Sara asked breaking the silence.

"A cheeseburger sounds good," Cyrus said.

Walking over to his wife, Cyrus wrapped his hands around her and gave her a kiss. "Have fun at the movies," he said as he gently rubbed her back.

"We will. You have fun, too," she responded. "Chris, let's go, I'm ready!"

Chris came storming down the stairs and headed out the door without uttering a word to either of them. As Sara smiled and walked out the door, she said goodbye to Cyrus.

Cyrus watched them step into the car, then drive away before he walked outside. Now, he had to play the waiting game. He had to wait for the mystery man, his best friend, to arrive so he could get rid of him. He wasn't sure if Dave had caught on to his motive for inviting him over, or if he actually thought Cyrus wanted to hang out and play cards.

He headed to his car to grab his kill kit. For days, he had dreamed about torturing his captor, but never in his wildest dreams did he think it would be like this. He never would have given a moment's thought to it being his own friend.

Having already decided upon what he was going to do on the ride home, he grabbed the table from the kitchen and dragged it down the basement stairs. There was a drain built into the floor in the basement that would come in handy.

Tilting the table sideways, he was able to force it through the door. He slid it to the middle of the floor above the point where the drain was located. Looking back and forth around the basement, he walked over to a pile of big boxes and started foraging through them until he found a large blanket.

Lifting it into the air, it fell over the top of the table. He made his way back upstairs and toward the back of the house where he found the hose. After making sure it was properly screwed in, he dragged it down the stairs and into the basement, tossing it to the side.

As he observed the area he had set up, he heard a loud pounding coming from upstairs. It was the door. Dave must have arrived. He hurried up the steps and quietly closed the basement door behind him.

"One second!" Cyrus shouted as he looked around.

Cyrus spotted his bag on the floor where the table was located. He had forgotten it. He was going to have to do this quickly. After pouring some chloroform onto a rag, he put on his gloves and headed toward the door. Holding his hand behind his back, he opened the door to allow Dave to step inside.

"Hey man," Dave said as he walked in.

After allowing Dave to walk past him, Cyrus reached out and wrapped his arm around him, pressing the chloroform soaked rag against his mouth. Cyrus heard a rattle, then Dave began sliding down to the floor.

There was a large knife on the floor at Cyrus's feet. Cyrus breathed heavy as he let Dave fall to the floor. Just like Cyrus, Dave came with the intention to kill.

Cyrus picked the knife up off the floor, tossed it in the garbage, and threw a bag on top of it to hide it. Unsure as to how long Dave would be out for, Cyrus knew he had to hurry. After retrieving Dave's keys out of his pocket, he took hold of Dave and slowly inched his way over to the basement door. As Dave was heavier than he looked, Cyrus had to take small steps down the stairs.

Dropping Dave onto the table with a loud thud, Cyrus almost thought the table would give way under Dave's weight. Wasting no time, he ran back upstairs to grab his bag. The door was still wide open. He glanced out the door and then locked it securely.

Closing the door behind him, he headed back to the

basement to lock the basement door. In the unlikely event that Dave would escape his restraints, there was no possible way that he would get out of the house.

Cyrus wrapped the rope around Dave and the table, tightly locking him to it, then wrapped the rope around both of Dave's wrists and pulled his arms underneath the table, before tying a rope between his hands. To finish the job, he wrapped the rope around Dave's ankles and then around the legs of the table. Placing his hands on Dave, he shook him to make sure the rope was secure.

A box slid across the dusty concrete floor as Cyrus dragged it underneath him and took a seat. Looking at his watch, Cyrus saw that he still had plenty of time. As he examined Dave's unconscious body lying on its side, an idea came to his head.

He pulled out his knife and placed it on the old porcelain sink that was built into the wall a few feet from where Dave laid helplessly on the table. Cyrus wanted Dave to wake up and see the knife just out of reach and think he had a chance of escaping. He wanted to witness the desperate look in his eyes as he attempted the impossible and fought to get the knife.

The tiny rocks crunched beneath Cyrus's feet, and he began to slowly push them around as he became increasingly tired of waiting for Dave to regain consciousness. He didn't think it would take this long. It felt like an eternity, but after glancing at his watch it had only been seven minutes.

The box slid backward as Cyrus abruptly stood up. Lightly, he kicked the table. "Wake up," he said. He kicked the table again, but this time with a little more force.

A dazed and confused Dave started moving his head around in a manner that suggested that he was waking up with a hangover. Cyrus stepped out Dave's line of vision.

"Cyrus?" Dave said as he opened his eyes.

Silently, Cyrus took another step back to ensure Dave couldn't yet see him. Looking left and then right, Dave noticed his hands and feet were tied up, and began to panic and shake around.

"Ahh!" Dave shouted at the top of his lungs as pain shot down his back. With his hands tied under the table, struggling would only hurt him. It was as if his arms were being pulled back like someone was digging their knees into his back.

Slowly, a smile emerged across Cyrus's face as he saw Dave switch his focus to his side and sight the knife on the sink. In a desperate bid to break free and reach for the knife, Dave started pulling at his right arm. That wasn't working, so he started shaking his body in a bid to get the table to slide closer to the sink, but that quickly failed as well.

As the reality of the situation sunk in, Dave's body began to relax. Letting out a quiet laugh at Dave's expense, Dave suddenly became aware of Cyrus's presence. Cyrus took a step toward Dave.

"You were watching the entire time!" Dave shouted.

"Of course I was," Cyrus responded. "You don't think that knife got there by accident, did you?" Cyrus continued all the while laughing as he slowly inched his way closer to Dave.

"You fucking bastard," Dave said angrily. "Let me go. Why are you doing this?" He pleaded.

"Oh, you don't think I'm going to let you go, do you? We both know why you are here. Let's not play kid games," Cyrus said as he finally stepped into Dave's line of sight.

"Just let me go. We can both go on with our lives and pretend none of this ever happened," Dave begged.

"You know, I'm surprised. You walked right into the door and didn't even notice I had gloves on. You'd think that would be some kind of warning," Cyrus said as he towered over Dave.

"Let me go," Dave said breathing heavily.

"You showed up a little bit before I had expected. I didn't have time to get completely ready. I had to just throw some gloves on and hope for the best," Cyrus continued ignoring Dave's pleas.

"My wife knew I was coming. She will call the police if I don't come home," Dave explained.

"No, you never made it here. I was worried, but just assumed you lost track of time or something," Cyrus said with a smile firmly planted on his face.

"Fuck you!" Dave said with force as he started to violently shake around.

The table shook back and forth, but Dave couldn't break free.

"Are you done yet?" Cyrus asked.

Dave took a deep breath, then looked at Cyrus. "Dude, just let me go. We're friends. Please don't do this," Dave continued to beg.

Cyrus let out a loud fake laugh. "HA! Friends? Do friends blackmail each other and use them? Do they also threaten to turn them in to the police?" Cyrus asked sarcastically.

"What did you even do? How did you get me down here?" Dave asked as he took in his surroundings.

"Chloroform can be your best friend when you're a killer," Cyrus explained.

"What?" Dave replied.

"I noticed you didn't come un-prepared either," Cyrus laughed. "That was a big knife you had, maybe you should get better at using it and you won't end up down here next time. Well…..now that I think about it there won't be a next time," Cyrus continued as he picked his knife up off the sink.

"It's funny how you would talk with all of us about the killer as if it was nothing when it was you all along. How many have you killed now?" Dave asked.

"It's funny how you would talk about gunning down the killer while talking to me as if all along you didn't know that I was the killer," Cyrus fired back ignoring Dave's question.

Everything went silent as Cyrus began walking around Dave, looking him up and down.

"I know why you do it. Taking a life feels so good. I've never experienced such a thrill," Dave said breaking the silence.

"You sick fuck!" Cyrus yelled as he brought the knife down into Dave's leg.

"Ahhh!!!" Dave shrieked as the blood started seeping out of the wound. Tears started coming out of Dave's eyes as he groaned in pain.

"You beat a little girl to death, then hung her!!" Cyrus shouted.

"No…," Dave said as he tried his best to hold back the pain. "She was still alive and kicking when I hung her," he continued as he began to laugh.

"Shut up!" Cyrus shouted as he brought the knife down into Dave's other leg.

"You're just as bad as me. You kill, too!" Dave fired back with tears rolling down his face.

"I don't beat children," Cyrus said as he worked his way around the table.

"No, you just leave their father's blood all over the wall for them to find when they get home. That's a whole lot better!" Dave continued.

The first drop of blood made its way off the table and dripped to the floor.

"And then you used me, you used me so you could satisfy your own desire to kill. Your best friend. You threatened to get me thrown in jail if I didn't let you!" Cyrus shouted furiously in Dave's face as he circled passed.

"Like you wouldn't have done the same thing. I wanted to kill. I saw an opportunity so I took it. What was I going to do, just ask you for permission?" Dave asked as he let out a cough.

"It looks like you have a bleeding problem there," Cyrus said gesturing toward Dave's legs.

"Just let me go. I'll just leave and never utter a

word," Dave said in a desperate bid to escape with his life.

"Too late for that," Cyrus said as he stopped circling right in front of Dave's face.

"Fuck this. You're dead when I get out of here," Dave lashed out at Cyrus.

"The problem with that is that you won't be getting out of here," Cyrus laughed.

Dave started jerking at the ropes again as hard as he could, but still they didn't budge.

"It was good, though. I must admit I didn't expect it to be you," Cyrus said.

"Well, you made things so easy. When I heard you talking on the phone when we all went out to lunch at work, I immediately recognized the tone as you, and then I saw the picture and that was it," Dave answered.

"That's funny because I figured out the same way when you were on the phone today at work. I was pretty surprised," Cyrus replied.

"Congratulations," Dave said.

"Well, I really would love to continue this conversation, but Sara and Chris will be home soon, and I can't exactly have you tied to a table in the basement when they show up, so I'm going to have to end this," Cyrus said.

Dave eyes grew wide, but before he could even let a word pass his lips, Cyrus silenced Dave with one swift cut across his neck. Dave's head dropped the side and fell still. Blood began forming a puddle next to Dave's neck as it made its way to the edge of the table.

Cyrus checked Dave for a pulse, then cut his hands free. Fearful of hair or something else getting on him, Cyrus proceeded with caution. He straightened Dave up, then began to pull off his shirt. Next were his pants. He tossed Dave's pants into a garbage bag he got from his bag, then looked around for anything else that needed to be disposed of. He didn't see anything, so he wrapped Dave's shirt around Dave's neck, then picked him up. Looking behind him to make sure no blood was escaping the shirt, he worked his way up the stairs.

After a brief struggle, Cyrus managed to get the front door open. With his wife and son due home at any time, he needed to be efficient. He examined his surroundings, then bolted to Dave's car and pushed the body onto the passenger's seat. Cyrus climbed into the driver's seat, placed the garbage bag on Dave's lap, and started the car and quickly pulled out.

He already knew where he was going to take Dave's body. There was an old pier Dave used to talk about from time to time that was only about a mile away from Cyrus's house. He knew it was nearly impossible to make it look like Dave had committed suicide, but he could at least try.

Pulling up to the pier, he popped the door open. After stepping out, Cyrus reached in and dragged Dave's body into the driver's seat, before placing him in the driving position. He got out and looked around. Taking hold of the garbage bag, he hurried his way over to the pier, dropped to his knees, and started filling the bag with rocks.

Once he had enough rocks in the bag to weigh it

down, he charged back toward the dock and hurled the bag as far into the water as he could before watching it slowly sink. He darted back to the car, then removed the shirt from around his neck, and ran as fast he humanly could back to his house.

Panting, he closed the door and hurried into the basement. His family could be home at any moment. Taking hold of the hose, he started washing all the blood off the table. It hit the ground and seeped into the drain. *Almost done.*

Cyrus noticed some blood still remained on the table. He tried spraying it again, but the water did nothing. It must have been sitting there too long and stained the wood. Taking hold of the table, he carried it to a corner of the basement. He pushed some boxes to the side to make room for the table, then began stacking things on top of the table in a bid to keep anyone away from it until he came up with a way to get rid of it.

He knew he would need to get rid of it as quickly as possible because as soon as Detective Hughes caught wind of the fact that Cyrus was one of the last people to talk to Dave he would be all over the place searching with a fine tooth comb.

In a moment of frustration, Cyrus smacked himself in the head. He had committed a cardinal sin in killing someone he knew personally. He had messed up big time, but Dave had left him with no other choice. "Fucking hell, Dave. Why did you have to go and screw shit up?" Cyrus said to himself as he stacked the final box onto the table.

The stairs creaked as he hurried his way back upstairs. Needing a moment to regain his composure, Cyrus flopped onto the couch and turned on the TV. He wiped the sweat off that had built up on his forehead.

As time passed, Cyrus began to calm down. Sara had texted him and said they were on their way home. They would be there any minute.

Cyrus heard the clunking as Chris and Sara approached the door. The door cracked open and they entered the house.

"So, how did it go?" Sara asked as she kicked off her shoes.

"I don't know. He never showed up," Cyrus said with his legs resting on the couch.

"Never showed up?" She asked sounding confused.

"Yeah, he must have got caught up or something," Cyrus explained as he shrugged his shoulders.

22

ANOTHER adversary defeated. *Am I unstoppable?* Cyrus asked himself as he laid in bed. His alarm had gone off a half an hour ago, but he had no interest in getting ready for work. He was done with work.

At some point during the day, the police would rock up and question him about Dave's whereabouts, which of course he would have no clue about. More than likely they would haul him off to the police station for interrogation.

If he did head into work, he would be forced to listen to constant questions about Dave from his co-workers. Where's Dave? When did you last speak to Dave? Those were the type of questions he would expect to hear. The same sort of questions he would most likely be asked by the police.

To this point, he had met every challenge thrown in his path, and he wasn't afraid of this one, especially after he had been able to seek out and destroy Dave. Nothing could stop him in his tracks. He was a god among men. He was forced to kill his best friend and came out feeling fine. His potential was endless.

As he sat up in bed, he looked at his phone. He had already missed a call from work. *No*, he thought to himself as he dropped back down to his pillow and quickly fell back to sleep.

Cyrus arose from his slumber a few hours later. The floor boards creaked as he made his way to the center of the bedroom. Laying down face first in the middle of the floor, he pushed himself up with his arms, then went back down and pushed himself up again. He gradually performed push-ups faster and faster until his muscles grew sore.

Flipping over, he laid on his back and began doing sit-ups. Relentlessly, he pushed on until he reached 100 sit-ups all the while never breaking his stare from the same area on the bedroom wall. Energy was surging through his body.

Standing up, he grabbed a chair and took a seat. A part of him wanted to call Hughes and reveal his true self, and admit that Hughes was on the money from the get go.

Cyrus sat around in his bedroom doing next to nothing for a short while. He didn't want to start any project because he figured the cops would turn up at any moment. He was surprised there hadn't been at least a phone call to ask him a few questions. Surely, Dave's wife would've contacted the police by now.

Dave's wife had called the previous night asking if he knew of Dave's whereabouts, and he told her that he hadn't shown up. He explained to her that he figured Dave had been so worn out from work that he had fallen asleep or had simply forgot about their plans. He assured her that he hadn't seen or heard from Dave since they both departed work earlier that day.

The whole situation clearly had her broken up and she had most likely contacted the police immediately after the phone call. The only thing he could think of was that perhaps they were yet to come across Dave's body. He should have set the car on fire, destroying all the evidence in the process, but he didn't have the time.

Either way, there hadn't been any police at his door yet, so he couldn't complain. He had only ever met Dave's wife once, but he could still picture the wonderful look of despair on her face upon hearing the fate that had befallen her beloved husband. He wanted her to know that Dave was the one that killed the woman and her child, but he couldn't disclose such information without revealing how he knew about it.

His train of thought was interrupted when he heard the downstairs door slam. Cyrus shot up from his bed and stormed out the door ready to hit somebody, but upon reaching the stairs he was confronted by Chris marching to his room in a fit of rage.

"What are you doing home?" Chris asked.

"What are you doing home is the real question," Cyrus responded.

"Don't worry about it," Chris said as he walked past Cyrus and into his bedroom.

"What the hell do you mean don't worry about it?" Cyrus asked as he followed Chris into his room.

Just as Cyrus was about to enter his room, Chris came walking back out, pushing by Cyrus and starting down the stairs. Cyrus turned around to follow him.

"Don't talk to me like that," Cyrus said with force as he followed Chris. "Did you get kicked out of school?" He continued

"No, I just got sent home early," Chris answered as he opened up the refrigerator.

Placing his hand on the refrigerator door, Cyrus pushed it shut before Chris could even look inside.

"Why were you sent home?" Cyrus asked.

"They said I was misbehaving and not paying attention. I told them I called you and that you said it was okay for me to walk home," Chris explained.

"They let you do that?" Cyrus asked in disbelief.

"Apparently," Chris said as he avoided Cyrus's glare. He just turned and opened a cupboard.

"You can't be behaving like this," Cyrus declared.

Chris turned around and stared at him for a moment. Cyrus wasn't sure what Chris was doing, but returned his angry glare.

"You want to know why I can't focus in school?!" Chris asked, then stormed off in the direction of the stairs.

Standing there in confusion, Cyrus awaited Chris's return. He walked over and closed the cupboard door, then heard Chris coming back down the stairs.

"This is why," Chris said as he held up a piece of paper.

Cyrus's heart plummeted as he realized the piece of paper in Chris's possession was the list of items he purchased to assist him in the killings.

"I found it yesterday when I was poking around in your room for money to go and do shit with my friends. It was on the floor between the dresser and the bed," Chris continued.

Not a single word left Cyrus's mouth. There was nothing he could say. Time came to a standstill. He had absolutely no idea what to do.

"It might not be a big deal on its own, right? Just a list of items?" Chris asked.

Chris stared intently into his father's eyes waiting for some kind of response, but Cyrus didn't have one. Cyrus was motionless. Tears began streaming down Chris's face as he took a step closer to Cyrus and held the piece of paper up close to Cyrus's face.

"I have known for a while now. I just didn't want to know. I didn't know what to do," Chris said as he took a backward step.

"I knew from the moment the phone recording was played on the news, and then when they showed your sketch on the TV," Chris continued as he fought back his tears.

Leaning forward against the kitchen counter, Cyrus wanted to say something, but no words would form in his mouth. He couldn't translate his thoughts into coherent sentences.

"Then, last night when I went downstairs I saw the table in the basement that you told mom you got rid of because you accidently broke a leg on it," Chris said as his voice rose in intensity. "Another bullshit lie!" He continued.

"Chris-," Cyrus began, but Chris continued over him.

"I couldn't just walk away. I had to look, and then I saw the red marks on the table. Was that blood? Is that why you hid the table, dad?" Chris shouted at Cyrus desperate for a response.

"I don't know," was all that came out of Cyrus's mouth. It was all that he could think of saying.

"You don't know! Who's blood was it, dad!?" Chris continued shouting. "I don't know how mom didn't notice. I kind of think she did, but she didn't acknowledge it. How could she not notice, though? How could either of us live in a house with you and not recognize your face and your voice? Did you really think we wouldn't?" Chris went on.

"I don't want to lose you or your mother," he continued.

"You're a serial killer, dad!" Chris pointed at Cyrus, losing all control of his tears. "You've been taking people away from their families."

Cyrus was fully aware of what he had been doing, but it felt different hearing it from his son. Seeing him point out the things he had done. Telling him how messed up it was. Chris thought of him as a monster.

"I have to tell mom. I just have to," Chris continued his eyes completely red and glassy.

"No, don't!" Cyrus shouted "I can't let you!" He continued as he took a step toward Chris.

"What are you doing to do, dad? Kill me too? Kill me if I tell mom? Are you going to kill me for telling her something she probably already knows?" Chris asked as he walked toward Cyrus.

Cyrus turned and ran to the door. He didn't know what else to do. He hopped into his car, started it up, and drove away as fast as he could.

Tears flooded his eyes, blurring his vision as he flew down the road. *What just happened?* He was angry. Why did Chris have to tell Sara? Couldn't they just talk it out? Things could be just fine, but Chris was going to tell Sara and tear his family apart.

Driving at full speed, Cyrus didn't stop for stop signs. The sweat was pouring off him and his heart was racing. He knew of only one way to make this feeling go away, and that was to kill.

23

THE paper floated down to the floor as Hughes tried tossing it onto a pile of papers. "Dammit," he said as he leaned to the side of his desk to pick it up. Placing it down hard on the pile, he started on the next paper. He had stacks of paperwork to fill out on the two most recent incidents.

He was frustrated at being tied to a desk while Cyrus walked around a free man. After all these murders, Cyrus was still out there living his day-to-day-life, while the ones he killed would never get to experience that luxury again.

Hughes shot up from his chair shoving it backward, causing everyone within earshot to look at him. Turning around, he walked to the bathroom. He was frustrated. To him, it seemed as if no one was doing anything of worth on the investigation. It was as if they didn't care at all.

Resting his hands on the sink, Hughes propped himself up as he stared into the mirror. His eyes looked dark and saggy. Hughes had barely slept since this all began, and significantly less after it became apparent that Cyrus was the killer. To Hughes, it seemed unfathomable that Cyrus had yet to slip up. *He should have by now.*

After wiping his hand across his face, Hughes walked out of the bathroom. It seemed like his desk was mocking him as he made his way back to it. He was certain that every time he got up out of his chair the Captain was eyeballing him. Four years ago, Hughes pursued a bad lead too long and it almost resulted in one of the biggest drug dealers in the state getting away. Silently, the Captain has held it against Hughes ever since.

He was beginning to wonder why the Captain even kept him around if that was how he was going to act. To Hughes, not examining a lead further because of something that happened four years ago was childish. He was supposed to be one of the lead investigators in the case and the Captain treated him like he was just some kid there along for the ride.

As Hughes took his seat and started filling out some paperwork, Lopez walked over and took a seat next to him.

"What's up, man?" Lopez asked.

Lifting his head, Hughes just looked at him with a

deathly stare as if to call him a moron without letting the word pass his mouth.

"How do you think?" Hughes asked as he glared in Lopez's direction.

"Relax, man," Lopez said as he took a sip of soda.

"Relax?" Are you kidding me?" Hughes said. "After that asshole called me, I knew something bad was going to happen, but these dipshits forced me to stay at the station, and you know what happened? Three more people died!!" Hughes continued angrily.

"Look, I made mention of Cyrus's past to the Captain and he looked into it. He only had one incident like that. Not even a parking ticket after that. We still can't use it to bring him in. I wish we could," Lopez explained.

Hughes leaned in toward Lopez. "You want to know why this person keeps calling and taunting me? Saying all these messed up things to me? It's because he knows that I know who he is. That's why!" Hughes said with force.

"If he was aware that you knew who he was, why would he keep calling you? Doesn't that seem like a bad idea?" Lopez asked.

"It's because he's a damn lunatic and doesn't care. He probably watches all of our broadcasts about him and jerks off to them. He's sick in the head," Hughes explained.

As they sat there for a moment, Lopez looked around as if he was trying to think of something to say. Hughes looked at him, but didn't even care what Lopez had to say anymore.

"You know, he was at my house one time," Hughes said immediately catching Lopez's attention.

"What?" Lopez asked in disbelief.

"He called me while I was outside my house. I'm pretty sure he was watching me. He was saying weird shit about what I was doing," Hughes quietly said to Lopez.

"What the hell?" Lopez said.

Lopez's reply sounded like he was surprised, but Hughes could tell Lopez was looking at him as if he was some kind of crackpot who belonged in a straitjacket.

"Whatever, man," Hughes said as he grabbed his pen and pulled a piece of paper toward him.

"What?" Lopez asked.

"You are looking at me like I'm some kind of nutcase," Hughes said.

"No," Lopez answered.

Two police officers walked over, tapping Lopez on the shoulder.

"We're going to look into a disappearance over on Fourth Avenue," the first officer said.

"Disappearance?" Hughes asked curiously before Lopez could form a response.

"Yeah, this lady reported her husband missing last night after he was supposed to have left to go hang out with some friends for a bit. Someone popped over there and took down some general information, but enough hours hadn't passed for it to be called an official missing person's case, so we are going to go back and check things out, and see if there has been any sign of him," the officer explained.

"Who was the friend?" Hughes asked.

"We're not sure," the officer answered. "Off we go," he continued.

They turned around and walked away. Hughes needed to find something to do before he went crazy. He should just sneak off and shoot Cyrus right now and get it over with, but this was reality and that was cold-blooded murder, even if he did deserve it.

"I don't know, man," Lopez said as he placed his hand on the desk and pushed himself up.

Hughes went back to filling out the paperwork for a brief moment before his pen ran out of ink. *Are you kidding me?* He shook the pen and tried again, but to no avail.

Tossing the pen onto the desk, he took hold of his gun. Hughes was sick of sitting around. He wasn't sure what he was going to do, but he needed to do something. Hughes intended to drive around in the hope that he could come up with a reason to go back and question Cyrus that wouldn't see him get into trouble with the Captain.

As he walked over to the door, the Captain stopped him in his tracks.

"Hughes! Wait up!" The Captain shouted as he hurried over to Hughes.

"What?" Hughes asked frustrated that he couldn't make it to the door without someone hassling him. He was starting to feel like he was being watched more than Cyrus.

"I have to talk to you," the Captain said nudging

Sadistic

Hughes to the side away from everyone else.

"Okay, what about?" He asked as he moved in the direction the Captain was heading.

"Well, the evidence from the last crime scene just returned," the Captain explained.

"Which one?" Hughes asked.

"The Satan one," the Captain replied.

"All right? So? Did they find anything useful?" Hughes asked.

"Well, we found some hair in the hand of the victim," the Captain answered.

"That's great!" Hughes shouted. "Let's fucking nail this guy then!" He continued.

"Well, the problem is that it's your hair," the Captain said.

"What the hell do you mean it's my hair? I didn't even go to that crime scene, I was tied up at the other one," he answered angrily.

"It was your hair," the Captain insisted.

Hughes turned around, then returned his gaze to the Captain.

"So, what the hell? Do you think it was me? You think I killed those people?" He asked glaring into the Captain's eyes.

"No, I don't know," the Captain said.

"So, now what?" Hughes said demanding an explanation.

"For starters, we have to take you off the case," the Captain responded.

"That fucking bastard!" Hughes shouted "You have

got to be kidding me!" Hughes shouted in frustration.

He knew Cyrus was responsible for putting the hair there. *That asshole. He must have found some way to get inside my house and grab a sample of hair, but how and from where?*

"So, I am under arrest then?" Hughes asked.

"No," the Captain replied.

"I'm getting out of there then," Hughes responded as he made his way toward the door.

"Wait, I need your gun," the Captain said prompting Hughes to turn around.

Hughes pulled out his gun and tossed it in the Captain's direction, and walked out the door.

Visibly pissed off, Hughes stormed to his car. How the hell could he let Cyrus get by him? He had been inside Hughes's house. Who knows what else he messed with or took?

He flung open the car door and climbed in. What was he supposed to do now? He couldn't let Cyrus get away with this. Turning on the car, he sped out of the parking lot.

Before long, he was at his house. He got out and hurried inside. Pushing open the door, he entered his bedroom. Reaching into the drawer by his night stand, he took hold of a cold, black M1911 pistol in his sweaty hand and hurried back outside to his car.

Hughes tossed the gun onto the passenger seat and pulled away from his house. He needed to do something. Without him on the case, they were going to let Cyrus get off the hook. As it was, they weren't even acknowledging the fact that Cyrus was a legitimate suspect.

Sadistic

He went into my house, my home, and got me thrown off the case. Heading in the direction of Cyrus's house, he wasn't sure what he was going to do, but he knew he had to catch Cyrus doing something. Something that would help bring him down. This was a battle he wasn't going to lose.

24

AS Cyrus tore down the road, tears streamed down his face as the realization of what was happening around him sunk in. His family would be gone forever. His wife, the woman he had loved for so long, and his son, Chris, his only child. Neither of them would acknowledge his existence again. *They would have to put their heads down when my name was brought up, and pretend they never had anything to do with me.*

Cyrus hadn't experienced emotions like this in a long time. He didn't want them. He didn't want them anywhere near him. They were tiny little parasites slowly sucking the life out of him.

The only way rid himself of these emotions was to do exactly what had brought him to this point in the first place. He had to witness someone else's pain to take away his own.

Pulling up to a stop light, he took in his surroundings. Who could he kill? He hadn't felt this type of need before. He had yet to kill for this reason. It was as if he needed a certain type of kill for each emotion he wanted to get rid of. Anger could be removed with something ruthless. Sadness could be removed with a slow and painful death, but there were so many emotions running rampant in his head. How could he get rid of them all simultaneously?

An addiction he had grown to love wasn't coming in clearly anymore. Desperate for help, he wanted someone to tell him what to do. He needed someone to walk up to him and clear out his distorted mind.

The roads were lined with people walking around in the night, running across the street from bar to bar. It reminded him of the first time he killed, when the drunken man stumbled out of the bar and challenged him. The first time the demon inside him had been awoken. The one that took control of him in the blink of an eye.

Someone ran across the road right in front of Cyrus. He came to a quick stop before hitting him. Cyrus could have easily continued on and ran him over. He should have. It might have helped him. It would have got him arrested.

At this point, letting himself get arrested was probably the best option. He could bypass the man-hunt and skip straight to sentencing. If he was lucky, Sara and

Chris wouldn't even attend his court hearing. He couldn't bear the prospect of seeing the disgust in their eyes. The same disgust that would consume Sara after Chris told her the truth about her husband.

So many things could be easier if he just let himself get arrested. No more looking over his shoulder waiting to get chased and forced into custody.

By morning, he would be on the news. They would happily announce that they had finally uncovered the identity of the one they called Satan. The one that had been terrorizing them for what seemed like an eternity. His neighbors and work colleagues would tell everyone stories about how normal he seemed, and tell them all about how shocking it was that he was so close to them this whole time. He would be remembered as the killer that got caught because he dropped a list on the floor, and couldn't keep his double life a secret from his family.

Slowing down, he came to the realization that he had been going in circles. The time had come. He absorbed his surroundings in search of his pray. He was looking for that one person to satisfy his hunger or perhaps he could just kill them all.

The sun had gone down and the street was shrouded in darkness. His headlights helped him pierce his way through the darkness to Cyrus's house. Hughes was determined to bring Cyrus down. He wasn't a killer, but if push came to shove he would end Cyrus's existence. He almost wanted Cyrus to test his patience so he would have a legitimate excuse to draw his gun and put a bullet in his head.

His mind began to wander as the road's center strips came and went in the blink of an eye. Hughes knew he was going to lose his job, but he couldn't let Cyrus get away. He was due for a job change anyway, and he wanted to prove to all the guys at the police station that he was right all along. From the start, they had never taken his accusations seriously, even when lives could have been saved.

Hughes turned onto Cyrus's road and slowly crept his way along. He wanted his presence at Cyrus's house to be completely unknown. As he drew closer to his destination, only the rocks crumbling under his tires broke the silence of the dark road.

Quietly, he pulled up and switched off the ignition. Light from a lamp and the TV poured out of the living room window. Hughes could somewhat remember a partial layout of the house directly inside the front door. If he had to go in, he wanted to be prepared.

Taking hold of his pistol, he rubbed his hand along the barrel, then pulled out the magazine, making sure it was loaded. After placing the gun on his lap, he reclined the seat preparing himself for the stake out. Aside from a slight breeze pushing leaves through the yards, the road was empty and motionless.

Cocking his head, he tried to peer to the side to get a better view into the house. All looked quiet, but if Cyrus tried to leave the house he wasn't going to get by Hughes without being noticed. The window squealed as he rolled it down to let a light breeze enter the car. Resting his head back, he got himself comfortable, preparing for the long-haul.

There was nothing specific about the killing process. It wasn't about race, gender, or how tall or short they were. The person just had to give him that feeling. He couldn't find the right words for it. Certain people sent a chill down his spine, and he knew he had to kill them.

Cyrus craved that sensation. He needed them to call out to him. Between his frustration and his thoughts, he couldn't focus on any one person for more than a mere moment.

Pulling over to the side of the road, his hands clenched down hard on the steering wheel. Feeling tense, he needed to get out and walk.

As he stepped out into the dark, it became apparent that in an area like this his knife would most likely be used in self-defense than to kill someone. Placing his hands in his pockets, he slowly started up the road. As he passed by people, he kept his head down almost sniffing them out. He felt like a lost dog sniffing around for its owner.

Eventually, he stopped and observed the people as they walked by. Each and every one of them were oblivious to the fact that they were being tracked, but only one of them had anything to worry about.

A group of people quickly walked by chatting away, paying no attention to his presence, then a minute later another man walked passed. He was wearing a black coat similar to a trench coat, which struck Cyrus as odd given how warm it was, and dark red pants and a hat. Cyrus's body fell cold, chills moving through him from head to toe.

Sadistic

The feeling flooded him out of nowhere, just as it always did. Even the very first night it happened, even though he hadn't noticed it at the time. It pulled him in the direction of the man, yanking him with all its might.

Walking softly so as to not arouse suspicion, Cyrus began to follow the man. He planned to follow him until they arrived at a place where it was safe for him to commit the kill without being seen, which could take any amount of time because the streets were far from empty.

The thought played back through Cyrus's head once again. It was likely Chris had already told Sara of the monster he had become, and they were well on their way to alerting the police. It was possible they were on the phone with family members expressing their shock, and telling them they never saw something like this coming. Even Cyrus wouldn't have seen this coming a few weeks ago.

Everything was over. Suddenly, Cyrus stopped his pursuit and fell against a dirty brick wall, sliding to the ground. As he dropped, his head fell into his arms and tears rolled down his face. *This shouldn't be happening. I should be getting ready to go watch Chris's next football game or figuring out how to keep food on the table. Maybe then Sara wouldn't been feeling so…* "Ahh!" He grunted to himself as he threw his fist into the brick wall.

Maybe they hadn't called the police yet. Maybe it isn't too late. We can figure something out. Rising to his feet, he hurried back to his car, turning corners and avoiding people. Cyrus needed to get back to his house before

Sara contacted the police. He didn't have any missed calls from her, so perhaps Chris hadn't told her yet, or maybe she was too afraid to call him. Either way, he had to hurry.

A significant amount of time had passed, and the sound of leaves rustling poured in as Hughes slowly drifted off to sleep. Just as the last bit of consciousness was about to leave him, a loud noise went of shooting Hughes to attention.

As he cracked the door open, the noise went off again before he could step out of his car. It was the sound of a gunshot ringing from Cyrus's house. Stepping out, he bolted toward the door. Glancing through the window, he saw a man in the living room doorway. Desperate to get inside, he twisted the front door repeatedly but it wouldn't budge. He stepped back and kicked the door as hard as he could, sending it flying open and smashing into the wall.

The man was already gone, and there was Cyrus's wife lying on the floor with a gunshot wound to the chest. She laid there gasping for air as she tried to roll over, but try as she might she couldn't. Next to Sara, a kid was laying on the ground with a gunshot wound right under his neck

Hughes ran to Sara, dropping down to his knees. "Hold on! Hold on! I'm calling 911!! Hold on!" He said as his phone fumbled out of his pocket and onto the floor. He picked it up and yelled into the phone, "Emergency! A shooting! Two down!" He provided the man on the phone with the address, then dropped the phone to the floor.

He looked around, then ran into the kitchen, taking hold of a small towel off the counter before scrambling back to Sara.

"They're on their way! Stay with me!" He shouted as he pressed the towel up against Sara's wound.

Blood soaked through the towel as it made its way to the floor.

"Chris… caught him…. in the room," Sara forced out before letting out a rough cough. Her eyes began to roll back, then her head slouched to the side.

"Stay with me, c'mon, god dammit stay with me!" Hughes shouted as he increased the pressure on the towel in a desperate attempt to control the bleeding.

25

THE garage door lit up as Cyrus pulled into the driveway. He was going to see if he could talk Sara out of contacting the police. There had to be a way for them to work through this. If he couldn't, he would leave of his own accord. If Chris had yet to talk to Sara, he would try and convince him to not utter a word. Perhaps if he promised that he wouldn't kill again everything would go back to the way it was.

Stepping out of his car, he took a deep breath to prepare himself for whatever was going to happen. *What the hell?* As he drew closer to his house, he quickly saw that the door had been smashed in.

Cyrus charged into his home, quickly noticing Hughes standing there with his shocked gaze firmly locked on Cyrus. Cyrus's stare broke away and shifted toward the floor, where he saw Sara and Chris lying on the floor covered in blood. Hughes took a step back as Cyrus dropped to the floor, tears quickly forming in his eyes as he looked at his wife's lifeless body. He jumped over to Chris's body, then placed his hand on Chris's wound to stop the bleeding.

"No, no, no," Cyrus panted as he moved back over to Sara. "No, what, no," he continued.

He started shaking Sara. "Wake up! Get up!" He shouted.

"What the hell did you do? You killed them!" Cyrus shouted as he looked at Hughes.

"What the fuck did you do?" He asked as he pressed his face up against Sara's limp arm. Suddenly, Cyrus's head jerked up and he bolted at Hughes. "What did you do?!" He shouted as he reached for Hughes.

Cyrus grabbed ahold of Hughes by the shirt, forcing him against the wall. Hughes pushed back, breaking Cyrus's grip on his shirt. Before Hughes could speak, Cyrus lunged at him and punched in square in the face, sending him back against the wall.

Just as Hughes wiped his hand across his face, pulling blood off his nose, another fist came flying in his direction, but he was able to dodge it at the last moment, causing Cyrus to trip forward.

Finally presented with the opportunity to make a move, Hughes dove at Cyrus, tackling him to the ground.

"I didn't kill them! It was someone else!" Hughes exclaimed as he pinned Cyrus's arms.

Hughes's words didn't register as Cyrus pushed back in a fit of rage. Cyrus groaned as he tried to push Hughes off him. He could see Hughes's lips moving, but he couldn't understand a word he was saying, as if Hughes was talking from under water.

Cyrus pushed up with his legs, then threw his body. Hughes fell back as Cyrus sat forward, forcing Hughes off him and onto the floor next to him. Hughes's body crashed to the floor, almost landing on Sara's lifeless body.

As Cyrus rose to his feet, he saw Sara laying there. Her motionless body filled Cyrus with more rage. Pulling out his knife, he charged at Hughes. Hughes stood up quickly, catching Cyrus's hand as he lunged forward with knife in hand.

Reaching down for his gun, Hughes lifted the weapon toward Cyrus, but Cyrus quickly pulled his hand back and smacked the gun out of Hughes's hand, sending it smashing through a window.

Cyrus punched Hughes in the stomach, catching him off guard as his focus was on the broken window, sending him down to the floor. Before Cyrus had the opportunity to pounce on top of him, Hughes shot back up and tried tackling Cyrus, but this time Cyrus stepped back, avoiding Hughes's tackle.

The sound of sirens filled the air as the two men stood in readiness to continue fighting. Cyrus switched his gaze in the direction of the road, listening intently as the sound of the sirens drew ever closer. He looked back at Hughes, who was standing there struggling for air.

"I'm going to tell them it was you that killed them," Hughes said as he regained his composure. "I got here too late and watched you gun down your wife, then all you told me was 'they knew'," Hughes continued.

Cyrus looked at Hughes, then back down at his family.

"You're going to pay for everything you've done," Hughes said as he inched closer to Cyrus. "You will spend the rest of your life in prison just like I said you would."

Bolting into the kitchen, Cyrus started rifling through drawers. Hughes stood there baffled at what Cyrus was doing. Cyrus pulled something out of a drawer, then darted out the front door. Quickly, Hughes followed him out the door.

Upon reaching his car, Cyrus pulled out his keys and popped the trunk. Without wasting a second, he pulled out a bottle of lighter fluid and started squirting it all over the kill kit he had stored in his trunk.

Hughes began circling around the car, keeping a safe distance between himself and Cyrus as he was unsure of what he had in his possession. At the last second, Hughes realized what was going on, but it was far too late. Cyrus had lit a match and dropped it on the bag. It instantaneously burst into flames, forcing Cyrus to take a quick step back.

The flashing red and blue lights reflected off houses as an ambulance turned onto Cyrus's road. Cyrus turned, walking passed his car and around to the side of the house. He shoved the small lighter fluid bottle into the rim of his pants and the lighter into his pocket. Putting on the gloves he was wearing earlier, Cyrus dropped to his knees below the shattered window, feeling around the ground in the dark until he felt the handle of a gun. He picked it up and fled the scene.

He ran and jumped the fence, and continued to run as fast as he could, cutting behind houses and running through yards. Finally, he collapsed near a random house over a mile away from his home and began to tear up. His family was dead. The family he thought would turn him was gone. He wanted to avoid jail at all costs, but never would he have asked for things to turn out like this. *How did it come to this?*

I should have been there, he thought to himself as he dug his hands into the dirt, yanking up grass. "Fucking hell," he sobbed to himself. "How could Hughes do this?" He asked.

"If I was there, I could have stopped this. I could've stopped whoever did this," he continued.

Leaning forward, he punched the ground repeatedly until his fist began to throb. He sat there with his head shoved into the ground.

"Even if he didn't do it, he should've stopped whoever did. He let them kill my family," Cyrus said of Hughes as he lifted his head off the ground.

The feeling was back. The one that made him feel compelled to kill, but this time it was much greater, firmly entrenched within his soul. He didn't kill before. Instead, he went to apologize to Sara, and now all the anger and resentment built up inside of him toward Hughes for the loss of his family only made his urge to kill even stronger.

Sneaking out onto the street, he jogged to the end of the road. It was likely that the police were out looking for him by now, or at the very least they were getting ready, so he had to act fast and stay out of sight.

Making his way into the backyard of a nearby house, he darted between yards, keeping a close eye out for dogs or people. He could hear police sirens in the distance, so he increased his speed.

A bank came into his line of vision. He was unsure of what tomorrow would bring, but he knew money would be a necessity. Sliding his card into the ATM, he entered his pin number and withdrew all the money he had to his name, which amounted to 783 dollars. Sara must have been keeping close tabs on their money, or perhaps she had neglected to pay the bills. Cyrus stuffed the money into his pocket, then took off. He had another stop to make before he could relax.

Since Hughes had taken something from him, he wanted to exact revenge and take something of equal importance away from Hughes. Making his way through yards and down quiet dark roads, he eventually arrived at a blue two-story house.

He recalled the location from when he wrote down addresses at work. There he was, standing in front of Officer Lopez's house. He made his way up to the front steps, then stood there for a brief moment. This was a place he wasn't accustomed to. Taking in his surroundings, he made sure no people or sirens were in the vicinity before knocking on the door.

A light turned on upstairs, pouring out into the night.

"I'll go look," he could hear a man's voice say from the upstairs window.

Cyrus saw a figure move to the window, so he ducked up against the wall to avoid being seen, then knocked again. He could hear footsteps stomping down the stairs.

"Who is it?" A male voice asked from the other side of the door.

"Officer Lopez, there has been an accident," Cyrus said trying his best to sound like a cop.

Finally, the door opened. Before Lopez had the chance to speak a word, Cyrus lifted the gun up and emptied two rounds into Lopez's chest. Immediately, Lopez dropped to the ground dead. Screams emanated from upstairs as his family heard the gunshots. The upstairs hallway lit up as if someone had opened a door.

Cyrus dropped the gun on the steps, then took off running as fast as he could. The police were already on the lookout for him, and it was highly likely they would respond faster than usual now that a police officer had been gunned down. He needed to put as much distance between himself and Lopez's house as quickly as possible.

There was one more destination he had to visit before he could flee the city. He walked for what seemed like forever, avoiding any signs of movement or light until he was miles away.

The parking lot was empty as he walked through it toward the water. There it was. Dave's car. Sitting alone in the dark just where he had left it. Luckily, for him, nobody used this old beat up dock anymore.

As he peeked into the window, he sighted Dave's body, his skin now faded purple, sitting in the driver's seat. This would be his final destination. Looking around at the wind pushing the waves against the old dock, Cyrus's mind drifted to everything that had transpired. This wasn't how things were supposed to turn out. He didn't expect to be standing over his best friend's dead body after having said goodbye to his wife and son.

Taking hold of the lighter fluid, Cyrus squirted some onto Dave's lifeless body. "Sorry, man," he said as he squirted some onto his friend, then onto the car. He walked all the way around, making sure as much of the car as possible was doused in lighter fluid.

Popping open the passenger door, he started drenching the entire inside of the car until the tin bottle was empty. Taking a step back, he had one last look at the car. He lit a match, then flicked it into the car window. Immediately, the inside of the car was ablaze and Dave's body was engulfed in flames.

He knew he couldn't afford to stay there long as the police were hot on his tail, but he stood there for a moment staring into the blinding light of the fire. It was like he was saying goodbye to a chapter in his life. He waved at the car, then walked away. Once again, the time had come for him to put some space between himself and the police. Hughes would know this was Cyrus's work, but there wasn't going to be any proof.

The phone began to ring as Cyrus's call reached Hughes's phone.

"Where are you?" Hughes asked the moment he answered the phone.

"I had to do it," Cyrus replied. "Now, I took away something that was important to you," Cyrus said.

After hanging up the phone, he threw it as far into the water as he could. Then, he looked at the car one last time before taking off.

He jogged down the road for a good hour until he reached the edge of the city. The cops were scanning everywhere looking for him, and there he was at the edge of freedom. Cyrus jogged a little further, then cut away from the road and into the woods. He needed a place to sleep for the night. Stepping over branches and logs, he made his way deeper into the woods.

Cyrus found a spot and sat down. The ground felt moist below him. He didn't want to lay down as he needed to keep an eye out for the police in the unlikely event that they caught on to his whereabouts. Feeling exhausted, he leaned back and rested against the tree, and before he knew it his eyes were closed and he was asleep.

26

CYRUS awoke to his face crammed in a dry pile of leaves. He looked up at the sky, then all around him. Waking up in the woods was not something he was accustomed to. Pulling himself to his feet, he knew it was time to get going. If luck was on his side, the police had already called off their search for the time being.

There really was no way for the police to know exactly what occurred at Cyrus's house. Linking what had taken place at his house with the murders may also prove difficult. It might buy him some time. He started down the small hill and headed toward the road.

Upon reaching the road, he looked in both directions. The road was close to empty. He knew it would be impossible for him to continue on foot for any length of time.

As Cyrus pushed his way forward on the open road, his feet began to get sore. Paranoia filled the corners of his mind as he kept looking up the road for police. He was prepared to jump off the road and take off in whatever direction might lead him to safety.

Eventually, he stumbled upon a small used car dealership with a bunch of old model cars sitting out front. This was exactly what he was looking for. He walked up and down looking at the cars in search of one he could afford with the cash he had in his pocket. There was 783 dollars plus the 50 dollars he already had in his wallet.

He was beginning to lose hope, when he stumbled upon an old 1966 Plymouth Fury for only 750 dollars. He couldn't believe his luck that he had found the sort of car he was looking for. It was dark red and Cyrus couldn't spot any rust.

He talked to the man at the front desk and quickly made the purchase. Cyrus wasted no time. Hopping in his new car, he hit the road stopping only for gas along the way. He wasn't sure where he was headed, but he knew he had to get as far away from this town as quickly as possible.

Cyrus drove down the road heading west. He didn't know much about being a convict, but west seemed as good a direction as any. There might have been more places to hide or maybe there wasn't. Maybe he just wanted to head toward the Mexican border. At least then he would have a place to flee to if needed.

Soon, he entered a new town. He wasn't even sure what the town was called, but he knew it was somewhere in Illinois. As he drove down the road of the small town, thoughts of his family and the police pursuing him, and how he could've saved his family consumed his mind.

He pulled over in the parking lot of a small park and got out. Finding a bench, he took a seat and leaned back. Finally, he had a moment to relax. Cyrus hadn't been able to relax in days. He always had to look around to make sure he wasn't being watched. Always wondering where Hughes was and dealing with his own murderous stalker.

Leaning his head back, he took in a big breath of fresh air, letting it fill his lungs. A lady walked passed in front of him, and he watched as she walked along. Cyrus followed her until she reached a small building. He looked onward as she passed a pay phone hanging on the old brick wall. He stared at it in a moment.

As he pushed himself to his feet, he stretched out his arms and began following the sidewalk toward the brick building. He approached the payphone and stared at it. It hung there on the wall covered in dust and dirt. It looked as though it hadn't been used in months or perhaps even years.

Picking up the phone, he pressed it against his ear. It played the old dead line tone in his ear signaling that it was still functional. Cyrus dug his hand into his pocket in search of some loose change. He pulled out two quarters and slid them into the phone's coin slot, and began dialing a familiar number.

The phone started to ring. It rang for a few

moments and Cyrus thought that maybe nobody would answer.

"Hello," a voice answered on the other end of the line.

"Hey, Hughes," Cyrus said not even trying to cover his voice.

The line went silent for a moment as both men breathed into the phone.

"Why are you calling? Why are you calling me you sick little man?" Hughes asked taunting Cyrus.

"Don't bother recording this. When I hear you click the button, I will hang up," Cyrus explained. There was a moment of silence. "I just wanted to say goodbye," Cyrus continued.

"Goodbye? No, I assure you that you will be seeing me again soon," Hughes muttered angrily into the phone.

"No, sorry," Cyrus replied.

"You little bastard. Where are you?" Hughes demanded.

As Cyrus looked around the empty street, the only signs of life were himself and a young child playing with her mother and a dog down the road.

"You know, I'm not really sure," Cyrus answered

"Do you think you can run from me? You murdered Lopez! There was no need for that! He had nothing to do with this!" Hughes shouted furiously at Cyrus.

"I don't care if you killed my family or not, you could have saved them. You were there. I wasn't, but you were!" Cyrus fired back.

"I don't know where you are, but when I find out

I'm coming to get you," Hughes said.

"I think you might be a little busy with other matters for a while," Cyrus said laughing.

"What the hell are you talking about?" Hughes asked.

"Doesn't it strike you as odd that the killer always contacted you and not anyone else? Or, maybe how you were so obsessed with pinning the blame on someone who clearly didn't have any motive or the police would've investigated further, or what about how you turned up at my house against orders I imagine, and then your partner winds up dead," Cyrus asked laughing loud enough for Hughes to hear.

"Screw you. I'm going to find you," Hughes replied.

"I doubt it. According to the time, I believe you should still be home right about now. There's no way you're tracking me from there plus I'm not even on my phone. By the time you have any idea where I am, I'll be long gone," Cyrus continued.

There was a brief moment of silence before Cyrus spoke again.

"It's weird how all those things happened and then they found your hair on that victim. I wonder how that got there," Cyrus giggled maddeningly.

"That's crap and you know it. You set me up. That won't work," Hughes explained.

"Well, I left you one final surprise. You know the gun they found at the scene of Lopez's murder? It was yours," Cyrus said as a smile emerged across his face.

"This isn't over," Hughes said. "I'm going to keep

looking for you, and when I find you, I'm going to kill you."

"I'll be waiting," Cyrus replied as he hung up the phone.

ABOUT THE AUTHOR

Patrick Reuman is a writer and currently in college to study biotechnology. He has been writing ever since he was 16 when a school assignment pushed his imagination toward creating his own stories. He has one child, a son, named Aidan. He hopes to continue chasing his dreams of writing while pursuing a future in science.

Made in the USA
Middletown, DE
02 April 2016